# THE OLD FAMILIAR

# THE OLD FAMILIAR

## ALIX HAWLEY

*thistledown press*

Thistledown Press Ltd.
633 Main Street, Saskatoon, SK  S7H 0J8
www.thistledownpress.com

**Library and Archives Canada Cataloguing in Publication**
Hawley, Alix, 1975-
The old familiar / Alix Hawley.
Short stories.
ISBN 978-1-897235-49-2
I. Title.

PS8615.A821O43 2008      C813'.6      C2008-904520-3

**Publisher Cataloging-in-Publication Data (U.S)**
(Library of Congress Standards)

Hawley, Alix.
The old familiar / Alix Hawley.
[280] p. :  cm.
Summary:  Dark and witty stories about the crusty undersides of middle-class lives, and the bizarre obsessions that harbor there. Hawley uses controlled tension and psychological scrutiny with diabolically funny and emotionally arresting results.

ISBN: 978-1-897235-49-2 (pbk.)
1. Short stories, Canadian. 2. Canadian fiction – 21st century.
I. Title.
813.6 dc22  PS3608.A8OL  2009

Cover photograph: *Arthur Burtch, Stonehenge, 1969*
Cover and book design by Jackie Forrie
Printed and bound in Canada

10  9  8  7  6  5  4  3  2  1

Thistledown Press gratefully acknowledges the financial assistance of the Canada Council for the Arts, the Saskatchewan Arts Board, and the Government of Canada through the Book Publishing Industry Development Program for its publishing program.

*For Mike*

Contents

# Chemical Wedding

YOU GOT SUCKED INTO THIS, ALMOST LITERALLY. The door is half-open when you get there. A maw, you think. A smell comes from inside. Roasting and cat. You hope these aren't one and the same.

They are ready for you. They have food. And pets. You push the door open fully and see two cats, they of the faint smell, flopped on the carpet. Their hairs shag it, like some kind of luxury knit. In the entry, one stairway runs up, and one down. A voice from the top calls, They're here. So there you are.

She comes to the doorway at the top of the stairs, which must lead to the kitchen. Her apron says, *Because I'm the Mama, That's Why.*

Mawmaw, you think.

She says, Hi there, hi. She pauses, smiling, and says, Well, you look exactly the same. She stares at you, which she did the other day in the grocery store. Now she's above, and larger.

Your husband says hi back, and then you do. She says she'll just be another minute. Come on in, come in. So in you go, into the house, with the feel of being inside a roast chicken, or a cat box. Up the stairs next, obedient pets yourselves. You want to stick out your tongue, it's so warm in here. You would never make a good pet, beneath the obedience layer.

It's warmer inside the kitchen, where you go next, and your nice husband puts down the bottle of white you brought. He says he hopes it will go with dinner.

˙ She smiles at it abstractly, and says, Oh, hors d'oeuvres first. I have cracker squaries, sausage rolls, hot wings, ham pop-ups, beef-jerky toasties, tunafish flips, and olives. The olives were the only things I couldn't make myself, she says. She lists it all with precise slowness, pointing to the evidence. The food is astonishing. It's everywhere, slick and shining, on huge plates on all the countertops. Let's get these into the living room, where we can sit, she says. They're here, she calls, again, in a family voice.

You take a plate. Pop-ups. The ham between the bread looks like tongues, like your tongue. The food is so ugly, but perfect, uniform in its ugliness, its anatomy.

You follow her into the living room, where the carpet is also gently cat-haired. The sound of TV comes up through the lower floor. She is busy arranging the heavy plates on the squat coffee table, just so. Nice place you have, your husband says. It's ugly, amazingly so. Everything in it is part of the solid ugly symmetry. Thick-legged chairs, blocky tables. She smiles at him, planted there in that apron. She knows. The Ma of it all.

Take a look at the pictures, she says, smiling. Our wall of fame.

The pictures are in two rows, kids' school photographs. The two kids in them develop alarmingly from left to right. You wouldn't have been able to predict the buck teeth, the spreading ears, in the first kindergarten photos.

They're great, your husband says, looking at each one, considering.

Diane says, They'll be joining us for dinner. Then she calls out, Bryan, did you hear me? She turns back to you and says, He's downstairs with Curtis. Just the guys, they're bonding.

Her laugh is slow, low, like owl-hooting. You see past her to a painting of cows at the end of the child photo sequence. It looks homemade. She follows your eyes, and tells you, My mum painted that. It's good, isn't it, she says. Everything she says sounds confidential, like something ripped from a women's magazine.

Yes, you say. Yes, it is.

Your husband agrees, and means it. He is nice. You are not so nice. You think rudely about the runny cows. Your mind is often trashy, slightly, a wilting lettuce. This you know. Then her husband comes up the stairs and into the room, with a little boy behind him. Uh, oh, hi, the man says.

It's Bryan. You do remember him, from school. He is bigger, redder of head and neck, but still has his high-school essence. He doesn't look at you, exactly. The boy, in ironed-looking pyjamas, looks like him, but with her ears. The boy, the Curtis, is holding two toys. He stares, then flourishes them at you.

Oh. Wow, you say. What can you say about toys. He's offering them, palms up. He is about to kneel, it seems. You think. Your thinking has slowed down in here.

Your husband is better, and says, Hey, are they those things that turn into something else?

Curtis takes his eyes from you, and blinks at him. His teeth protrude like pillows. They're Inhumanoids, he says. So everyone can laugh, and you are grateful. The boy is not. In his pyjamas, he looks like a hospital escapee. He leaves the room, looking back at you as he goes downstairs, dignified but unable to take you any longer. You know you are the main cause of the suffering, as usual.

Bryan says, Ah, kids, you know. He sits down, and takes a few pickled onions from one of the huge plates. They are shiny, glandular. The TV goes back on downstairs. High voices sing about getting on board the vocabulary ship.

Your husband sits down next to Bryan, saying, So what do you do? Nice place here. Not too far out. Sure smells good. So do you golf?

You hear these kinds of things, beneath the surface of her looking at you, and her talking to you in her low advice-column voice. She is showing you another picture, above the heavy brick fireplace. It's a cereal box front, cut out and framed. *Shakies*. A baby bubbles its lips under the word.

See this one, she says. Guess who.

You say you can't, and she says, It's Curtis, my littlest sweetheart. He won a national contest when he was eighteen months, to be on the Shakies box, she says. Always such a cutie, that one, she says. You feel a drip of gloat from her, just a drip, as you look, you feel it. It seems difficult to believe. He is eyelashed, curled, insanely cute, on the box. Not now. She is still following your eyes. She says, I do a homemade Shakies mix. Try it, it's on the table. Then she looks you over, up and down, and says, No, you never did eat much.

She is still staring at you because you are beautiful, still, too beautiful for this place. You are golden, fair, slender, unlined, unflawed. All those beautiful words. You never exercise, you are just this. She stares on. You have that effect, and have accepted it, mainly: it's like having a huge tattoo. You can adapt, and cover, sometimes. You didn't notice her staring in the grocery store yesterday until she appeared square in front of you. You have an ability to tunnel your vision, because of all the staring.

You and your husband are only back here in town for a few days, to see your parents. You were only in the store for milk, and there she was, as though she lived there, rooted among the produce. Wider than she used to be, even more solid. She knew you right away, and waved and called as though you were far off in the distance, but reachable. She said you had to come for dinner, since you were in town, to catch up, to talk about the old days, high school, have a little reunion. She collects friends, you remember. You had been in the same group in the old days. You had been close. Close-ish. There had been moments of it, now and then. You know she remembers it this way. You are in her collection. She had sweating meat in her trolley then, in the store.

So really, you had no choice. She was looking at you, and she knew you. Your husband was good about it. He has an interest in people, but mostly you. He wants to know everything about your life, before you met, and will often ask about it, as if he were a child asking for a story. He stares at you, too, sometimes, especially if you're falling asleep, but you are used to it. His lucky, lucky face. As though you are the perfect form, some geometrical solid, always the same, with rules, and the solution perfectly visible. *Eureka*.

※ ※ ※

Diane gets up to offer you the platter of ham things. You take one, and look at it. Bryan is still trying not to look at you. His eyes roam over the wallpaper pattern, which has a small, antlike pattern trailing up and down it. Someone designed that, once. Your husband is talking to him about the car, the mileage. Diane concentrates on you again, tilting her head as she sits down. You, the work of art. She's waiting for you to eat, but you still don't. You resist. She says, calmly, Well, how do you like it?

What can you do? It looks good, you say, then you smile, and she does too, with matter-of-fact pride, as if accepting a lifetime achievement award. The same old look. You went over to her house once or twice when you were in school. You think of it, but you can't remember much that happened, or much at all of how you used to be, although you do look exactly the same. Diane says that, again, about how you look, with her tape-measure eyes. Then she says, Well, but I have children. As though you were arguing with her. This is another effect you have. People can have a conversation with you even if you don't say anything. She is looking at your shoes, your ankles. There is a tiny mosquito bite healing, pink on your ankle bone. The only mark on you. Mosquitoes like you too.

She sits up, smiling a little harder. You remember now. Diane in school: the type who felt the need to tell you your faults. There is a type. You have a vague memory of a party at her house, a birthday, or something. Girls rolled in sleeping bags, like hot dogs. It must have been Diane's birthday. She was in a white long-sleeved nightgown, with a bandana around her hair, and her birthday-cake face, lit and waxed. She'd clapped her hands, and made everyone move into a circle, and said, Now, I think we can all help each other. Then everyone had to tell each of you what was wrong with you. It took a little while, but things came out. Talks a lot, or sometimes a bitch, or not very good skin, or too obvious, or doesn't need a bra. It was pretty restrained, at least on the surface. Like girl musical chairs. A slight, pushy undertow.

Well, it could have been a lot worse. Will never hold a job. Entirely undesirable. Completely, completely nothing.

When it was Diane's turn, nobody said anything. Someone eventually said, Sometimes too nice. Everyone nodded, and Diane did too. And she was sometimes too nice. When she set up that game, she really meant to be nice, to help everyone out. A fixer, with a bandanna halo.

No one could think of anything for you, except too perfect. When you went to summer camp once, when you were younger, two of the girls in your cabin put toothpaste all over the sleeping people's faces in the middle of the night. They didn't do you.

You think of it, and wish for toothpaste now. Fuelled with pop-ups and other meats, her talk is off and running, all about the family, the kids. Catching you up, she says. Brandy and Curtis. Curtis the karate pro. Brandy is a musician.

You stall, and try. What does she play? you ask.

Brandy plays electric bass guitar.

Oh. Is the little boy musical, too?

Diane says, He sure is. He can do it all. Right, Bryan? she says.

The men look over. They've been talking away for a while, at a higher rev than you two. Your husband, in his niceness, has a plate of crackerish things and olives.

Uh, what? Bryan says. He has a pop-up in his hand.

He's going to be famous. He'll be famous long after we're gone, Diane says. She is serene.

Who? he says.

Our little guy, she says, laughing. Oh, he's just like his dad, she says to you. You can still hear the TV below. *T-I-O-N, shun shun shun shun*, it sings. The boy is singing along. He's not bad, a birdy warble, a little behind the beat. Diane says to Bryan, You two should do a duet for us later.

Bryan bites his pop-up, so his mouth will be full. You know what he's doing, and you do the same thing. Ham, salt. A membrane of mustard. You take another, bigger bite.

๚ ๚ ๚

There is more food. Dinner. Diane has conjured it all, huge quantities of feeding. Perfect, ugly, again. Big, bald new potatoes with mint patchery, a big chicken in seared skin. Monster peas and carrots. A salad with terrifying croutons. Homemade too. Your husband admires everything, and you do, afterwards. Diane says, Wait until you see what's for dessert.

Then she calls, Curtis. Curtis. He emerges from the depths, and gives you a good stare for a minute. You don't look at him; you spare him. He sits between his parents with his head down. Diane summons the other one. Brandy, she says. The word is like a distress call. It could be, for you. What are you doing here?

*What*, comes from somewhere down the hall. You think of the other child in the pictures, with teeth and ears, but older, a girl.

Diane says, Brandy, get down here for dinner. It's time. We have guests.

The voice says, I have cramps. It is bored, languid, the voice.

Diane laughs. Nothing seems to throw her. Nothing ever did, in school. Not cramps, not tests, not teachers. She didn't like the dirty graffitied washroom, so, camel like, she just never went at school. You remember that. You were in there quite a lot. The carved, scrawled stalls. *For a good time call.*

People had inscribed various names, not yours. In the nurse's office, where you also went sometimes to get away, someone sicker or braver had carved a spiralling fantasy into the wall by the sick bed, about you and your doings in a white lace negligee. *Neglijay.* Someone else had scratched it out. The hard decency of the scratches. You could still read the words, just.

Brandy, Diane calls again. The voice doesn't reply, but Diane laughs still, loading salad onto your plate. Cramps, she says. Well, you know what it's like. She inclines her head in your direction. The lettuce spreads its dressing beneath. You never had cramps.

Bryan is the pale red of tomato innards, now. He says, You, uh, have any kids? Your husband says you don't. Diane nods, certifying. Bryan sits up. He even looks at you for a split second, looking into the sun. He says, Really? No kids?

No kidding, your husband says. This makes them laugh again. Even Curtis laughs, hee-hawing and peeking at you, teeth out.

Diane calls, Brandy, you're missing out. It's chicken, she says. Turning to you, she says, My own seasoning blend, everybody's favourite around here. It was our regular chicken night last night, but we're having it again tonight just for you. She holds out a wing to Bryan with her fingers. Here.

But Bryan is still astonished, rosy. So when are you going to have some? he says. Your husband says he's got enough for now, but he'll leave room for seconds.

You know what Bryan means, though. You say, Mm, which could mean anything. I'll mean whatever you want me to mean, you think, in your trashy mind. Bryan persists, and says, But aren't you going to have any kids?

He is looking straight at you, blinding himself. Curtis lets his eyes flash on you again, too. Your husband, the rescuer, says, We probably will, one of these days.

That's what he thinks.

Diane nods again. She knows all. Bryan ponders for a few minutes, and then starts to talk again, slowly. He says, You know, I was up at the reservoir yesterday, the big one up near Postill, and I was just looking at it all, you know, just thinking about it. All the water, going out to the pipes and then down here into the town, you know. It's for everybody. All the people out there. Your adults, your kids, your new babies.

Your husband chews, nodding with Diane. Sages, both. Confucius says, Eat more chicken. You drive a crouton around your plate. Your husband says, So you must have to test the water a lot, up there.

Bryan settles. Job talk. Yeah, he says. You get your crypto, your beaver fever sometimes. But ninety-nine per cent of the time, the tap water is fine. You could stake your name on it, he says. He gives the table a hard pat.

Diane says, He drinks it all the time, straight from the tap. She shines at you, stainless steel.

Bryan says, You could do a lot of damage up there, if you knew what you were doing. He is warming, licking a finger. He says, You know, there's a lot of drugs in the water, from people who take heart pills, and uh, birth control pills, all that. But we can clean it up. We do, down at the plant.

He's still looking at you, not blinking. His pupils look unfocused.

After a while, and some chewing, your husband tells him a bit about his company. Expansion plans. Successes. Then you say, We buy bottled water.

Your husband says, Sometimes we do. Maybe our tap water isn't as safe as it is around here, eh, Bryan?

Diane puts down her napkin, and looks earnest. You know what Bryan is still thinking about, really. Kids. You say you like Evian, it's your favourite. You think about the wine your husband brought tonight, which is nowhere on the freighted table.

You try some of the lettuce, and parallel-park the croutons. You wonder what Brandy is doing, away from this, in another room. You think you like Brandy. Diane asks you whether you remember so-and-so, and so-and-so, and oh, someone else. You don't know any of them. Even the names sound like exotic herbs you never buy. She remembers everything about school. Every minute. She talks about the History final exam. She still remembers the questions, their unfairness. I don't think you got that one, she says, pausing in her list. You just say no, and she nods, again, surveying your plate. Curtis is humming. *T-I-O-N.*

Bryan has gone quiet. He and your husband have run out of work talk. There is chewing, then your husband asks, So how did you two meet?

You haven't told him anything about them. You don't exactly remember, yourself, anyway. Diane lifts again. She says, We were high-school sweethearts, isn't that right, Bryan sweetheart?

Curtis says, Sweethearts, and makes a lovesick face. He makes it at you, with feeling.

Diane pats Curtis. We had a wonderful wedding. The church was packed. I had six bridesmaids, Jennifer A., Jennifer T., Marlena, Suzanne, Tamara, and Bryan's sister. And two flower girls. All baby-blue satin, she says. She looks at you, seriously. You weren't here then, or I would have asked you, she says.

You know she would have. There's more. She goes on. I had carnations, freesias, and lilies, all white, except for the trailing ivy, didn't I, and my dress was princess-seamed ivory *peau-de-soie*. I made it. Well, my mum had to help with the crinoline, she says. Modesty veils her: a bride again. She says, I had the same flowers for my headpiece, and satin shoes, and we got the bridesmaids' shoes on sale, and they were exactly the right colour to match the dresses, even though the store called it ice blue. It was all meant to be. I always say that, don't I, Bryan, I do, and it's true, she says, bridally.

This is her life. You can practically see the credits rolling past, in her eyes. The bridesmaids' names rattle in your head, knocking up against each other. Jennifer and Jennifer and Jennifer. How many Jennifers? Bryan is smiling, eating, the chicken flesh glistening on the end of his fork. The chicken's better here, you think. Where did you see that? Maybe on a sign, one of the restaurants along the highway on the way out here, where nobody ever stops. There was still hard snow there in places. Hard remains of snowmen and snow forts, a lumpen sculpture garden pointing the way to town. You feel shuttered, back in this place again. Diane says, You would have looked perfect in the bridesmaid dress. Baby blue, she says, again, reminding.

Yes, you say. You picture yourself at Diane's wedding, frilled and satiny.

They are all looking at you, even the little boy, for a second, seeing you in the dress, or another one: low-cut, draped, clinging. Diane says she'll get the wedding album out after dinner, so you can see.

The boy says, Are you married already? Everyone laughs gently. The food gleams. Are you? he says.

What about you two? How did you meet? What was your wedding like? Diane says.

You met through friends, you say. You haven't been married very long. Curtis looks crushed. He splats a pea under his knife. Good, he says to it.

Your husband says, We had a nice wedding. He is looking at you, questioning. He begins gently, It was outside, in an orchard.

Oh, Diane says. That's different. It must have been very special. Her buttery encouragement, lubricated as the potatoes.

Diane is not right about you, she doesn't know you now. You say, We were naked. We're nudists.

You are not making this up. You are, sometimes, when nobody is around, in your house, or the yard, or at the private beaches. You were, at the wedding. The marriage commissioner was fine with it. More than fine, actually.

Really, Diane says. A needle quiver registers. But only for a second. She nods again. That would make sense, she says.

Bryan says, So, uh, tell us about the wedding. He has stopped eating.

Your husband tells them. The orchard, the blossoms, the long grass. Just the two of you, with two friends from the clothes-free recreation society as witnesses. His friends. He'd been a member for a few years before you met. He chuckles a little at his memory, his revelations, stretching out in the chair now, relaxed. He turns to you. It was just so beautiful, he says. Now his eyes swim. His belief in you, his worship. Wonderful you.

You say, We enjoy nudism.

Your husband says, Most people call it clothes-free recreation, or naturism, now. The nudity isn't the point.

Yes it is, you say. This isn't entirely true. You don't even do it that much. You never go to the clothes-free recreation society things. You look at Diane. Curtis has slid over to sit on her lap.

She says, You always liked the beach. You used to undo your bikini top, to tan your back better. You had a cute red and white one, with ties on the sides.

You like this, you like that. Diane is smiling. She is the authority on you. Maybe she is actually right, about every-thing. You know you haven't aged, you probably never will, and you feel younger and younger, with all the inanities and boxcar identity shuntings of adolescence. You say to Diane, You liked the beach, too.

You try to think about the beach. Where did you used to go, then? There was sand, gritty water.

Diane says, I never did. She pets Curtis's head. He is whispering to her, his hand a little cup around her ear. Well, you'll get married one day, sweetie, she says.

You chew some chicken skin hard. Bryan says, Your wedding sounds great. He looks at Diane, carefully, then at you, more carefully.

Your husband says, Yes. It seems a little crazy, I guess, but it was beautiful. Just natural, he says. He even reaches over the glistening peas to touch your shoulder. It was like Adam and Eve, he says. The only people in the world.

Except your witnesses, Diane says. And the commissioner. I don't think there was one of those in Eden. She laughs, her owl laugh. Tu-whoo. You eat more chicken, hoping for a chunk of bone, a gristle parcel. At the wedding, you had stood between two of the apple trees, or cherry trees, or whatever they were, waiting to walk up to your husband. The breeze had been a little cool on the backs of your legs. You had been sure of things, some things. Of your effect, your same old beauty. But nervous, too. Were you the type to get married? Were you allowed to? Were people really going to let you do this, as if you were like other people? Your husband had been in tears, covering his mouth, watching you move forward through the grass. The commissioner too, just about. Now, you feel your clothes on you. The knot at your waist, threads over skin.

Bryan says, You must have, uh, pictures. He looks reflective. His plate is empty. You think of something. Once, in high school, you and Bryan, at a party. Outside, drunk, in somebody's back yard. His mouth on yours, on your neck, his hand slipping up your side, under your shirt, down onto your hip. His hands are big, now, against the tablecloth squares. Wide palms, knuckles. Did that happen? You think so. More than once. You look at him, at what you can see of his face, looking sideways, and it's in there. Even though you never used to drink that much, you feel as though you were drunk all through high school. Maybe you were.

You could ask Diane. You could ask her about you and Bryan; she would remember, if she knew about it. But she's already talking, clearing up the plates. She says she should have made her spiced ham loaf, too, as a chicken alternative. But then, all flesh is not the same flesh, she says, nodding at you, then laughing and standing up. Curtis wraps himself around her leg.

Your husband, passing her the salad bowl, says, Isn't that from the Bible?

First Corinthians 15:39, she says. Bryan, tell them.

What, he says.

About your achievement at church.

Uh, which one?

She tells you, in her confiding voice, Bryan was born-again again recently.

Again again? your husband says.

Yes, a refresher, she says. He went before the church to confirm his salvation in Christ. We have pictures of that, too.

When were you born? you say, to Bryan. Again again, you say.

You look at Bryan in the face, but he can't. All you get is forehead. Diane says she helped him to realize what he needed in life. Oh, here we go. Here it comes. The talk, the promise, the glory glory. Brace position. You look down at the tablecloth, the landscape of checkered squares and grease blossoms. But it doesn't come. Diane is in the kitchen now, and she calls, I didn't tell you I'm starting a newspaper column. My last one was about kids and drugs. I have them all in my file, you can read it. Did you know that kids in elementary school are trying to sniff aspirin? Aspirin, she says. Get your highs on mountains, I tell them, she says. Hey, Curtis, you can do your anti-drugs rap for us.

Curtis peers around the corner at you, and shakes his head. She comes back for more plates, balancing them, a multiple-armed goddess, a beatific Christian one. She says, We'll win this war sooner or later. Her steamroller optimism. You know she is thinking about your high-school ways at parties, but she doesn't say anything. You should tell her you're a crackhead, or a heroin addict, a naked nudist one. You think about it, but she says to Curtis, Go on, sweetie. We all want to see you. His dad is getting him signed up with an agent, she tells you.

Really, your husband says. Good for you, Curtis.

That cereal box must be handy filler in the portfolio, you think. Bryan says, Yeah, they have pictures of all their famous kids all over the walls in the agency office. They say he needs some vocal coaching, maybe, but they might take him on. They have one girl who made the cover of *Triathlon* magazine. The children's edition, he says. He seems to swell unnecessarily. Why is he so happy? Curtis has vanished. Then Bryan says, in Diane tones, Yeah, you know, I'm one of those sperm donors.

Diane says, He has thirty-one donor children. Plus our two, of course. Her voice is caramelly.

Thirty-one, your husband says. What can anyone say?

Bryan can say more. He leans back, and says, Yeah, when I see those pictures at that agency, all those kids, I feel great. Any of them could be from me. See, they could all be geniuses, or uh, actors, or anything.

Yours, you say. You think of ears. Teeth.

Diane says, He's helping others who are less fortunate. It's his personal destiny to make the world a better place.

She goes into the kitchen. You think about taking off your clothes. Maybe just your shirt. She comes back in with a cake, thick stacked slabs of it, mortared with white icing. It's enormous. What did you expect? Now, here's what we've been waiting for, she says, setting it down on the table, which must certainly collapse under the tower of it. You can hardly see over it. Curtis is singing somewhere, or chanting, or rapping, mournfully. One of the lines sounds like, *Cheaters never never prosper*.

❧ ❧ ❧

You eat two bites of the cake. Heavy sponge, thick icing. Diane's family recipe. Afterwards, she wants to show you something, just you. She takes you back into the kitchen, where the computer is. You expect a wreck of food, but somebody has already cleaned. Some of the leftovers sit wrapped on the counter, ready to go, threatening. The good fairy has done it. Or Diane. Take a look, she says, opening a website.

It's the Shrimper Family Fun Page. There are pictures. A cereal box, with a baby. Oh, it's them. Shrimper is their last name. You didn't know.

Here's the My Journal section, Diane says, clicking on an image of a quill pen. You read over a few of the entries. *We sure had fun today! I'm so thankful for my family. We had a picnic: cold-cut sandwich fingers and peanut-butter blimps. Click here for the recipe. My mood: Blessed.*

Oh, so you're going to get it here, instead, the talk. Diane's mood is *Blessed* at the end of just about every daily entry. You look at the leftover packages, waiting for you on the counter. Then she says, I'll give you the web address. It's good to keep up. Here, have a look around, she says. She gets up, so you have to sit at her computer. The chair is warm and slightly hairy. You look down the web page a bit, and see something about *I always knew what my destiny would be.* You don't ask. You already know. But you can't help it, and you ask, half-laughing, So what's my destiny?

Diane is behind you. She says, Well, just look at you. A beautiful wife and mother, of course. Everyone always said you would be a model, but I knew you would be a teacher.

Ha. You don't have children, which she knows. Any children you did have would never be like you, anyway. You think of them, not existing. You are not vain about this. You are a fluke. You did model for a while, after school, which everyone expected. Catalogue, print ads. You could have done more. Until you got tired of the extra staring, the camera eyes.

Then you worked in a pre-school for a while. You liked it, mostly. It was okay. But your husband's company does well, so you don't really have to work now. You don't tell Diane. You click on Guest Book, which unfurls a list of commentary. People have said things like, *You have a great life. Thanks for sharing.* And, *I love your site you should check out mine I have stuff about our city too and dogs dressed as movie stars.* And, *God is awesome. God bless u and ur family. Don't ever stop giving!!!* And, *The Saviour is using you in many ways as anyone can tell.*

Diane is saying, It sure is nice to have so many regular readers. The computer is a miraculous thing.

Now here it comes. Jesus built my computer. He made the internet. You think, God isn't a person. God isn't human. But she starts talking about recipes. You are beyond saving.

Diane talks about herbs. Drugs don't even come up. You don't look around at her. The screen tells you, *It's better than reading a novel.* How did she become this? How has she known what she is all along? Was she born knowing something other people don't? Maybe it's the born-again-again thing, or maybe she can read her own genes. You think about high school again, for a minute. You were pretty good at Biology. You remember a few things. Letters. DNA, RNA. Maybe they do spell things, inside, that mean something. Yours probably spell NAD. Or RAN.

You click back to the main page. Near the bottom, there's a picture of the two cats, then one of the two kids. In it, Curtis has his mouth wide open, and the other kid is playing a guitar, head down. That one must be Brandy, you say. You're trying to be a normal, polite person.

Yes, she says. There's a whole separate page for each of the kids.

You see the links at the top. Curtis Bryan Shrimper. Brandy Destiny Shrimper. We drink a lot of brandy, you say. All the time. Cognac, you say. We enjoy it. Which isn't true.

Yes, she says, nodding. We don't drink. Bryan just liked the name. I chose the middle name, she says. Of course she did. She says, I should get a picture of you for the Friends section. That would be something. The world would love to see that. She laughs, patting your shoulders gently with both hands, a cloak.

You could give her a wedding picture. You, Eve. Wedding porn. Your brain rots and rots. Maybe you don't have a soul. Maybe you are all body.

❧ ❧ ❧

In the living room, the men are still talking. Bryan is asking about kids, again. He is saying, I mean, I could help you out, man, if you need it. He gazes at your husband, tapping his fingers on the arm of the ugly chair. He says, We're making better people all the time.

When he sees you standing there, he says, to your husband, You know, I thought up the test-tube baby in high school. It was my idea. I had no idea how to do it, but I thought it up. I didn't know how to get the eggs out, but now they do, he says. He is looking at you, now, somewhere around your left elbow. You are a good specimen. Maybe that's what he was doing with you, at parties, back then.

Your husband is still nice, listening kindly to Bryan. He says, Well, hey, where are your kids right now? Maybe Curtis could do some of his dancing for us.

Diane appears with a tray of fat-bottomed coffee cups. Oh, he's probably out in the drug-addiction experience box again, she says. You take sugar, she says to you, nodding.

You shake your head, although you would like some right now, a whole handful of it. Your husband says, What's that?

Diane says, Tell them, Bryan. He built a big box that the kids can try out. It's dark when you go in and shut the door, and they feel like they can't get out. They can, of course, for safety, she says.

Bryan says, Yeah. It was a church youth activity for them. Curtis liked it. Do you want to see?

Your husband says maybe you could take a look, so Diane leads you all down past the inert cats, outside and into the garage. You can see your car on the street, waiting and waiting. There is a big box, painted grayish, in the corner of the garage. *Hugs Not Drugs*, it says on the door. You hear crying from inside, real boo-hoo-hoo-ing. Your husband says, Is he all right?

Diane says, He's good at crying. He practises it for his acting career. You're okay, sweetie, you're just fine, she says, patting the box.

But he's really crying, and you know why he's crying. He's addicted. To you.

You start to say that maybe you should leave them in peace now. The car is so close. You could bolt for it. Maybe somebody still sells drugs in the laneway downtown behind the Chinese restaurant, if that's still there.

But someone else is here, coming out of the house, standing in the garage entrance. I'm going, she says. It must be Brandy. Her voice is low, lower than Diane's. Her hair is slicked down hard, and she looks different from any of the wall of fame pictures. Like Diane, somehow, but a reshuffling of Diane's features.

Diane says, Brandy, we have guests.

Brandy says, Yeah, hi. She looks at your husband, and at you, as though you were insects. You love her. I'm going now, she says. She is holding a guitar case.

Diane says, Are you going to practise with your friends? Brandy has a band, she tells you, confiding again. What's it called again, sweetie?

Brandy says, The Weasels. Anyways, I'm going to the open mike night at the coffee shop. She turns. She is going.

Diane starts to say something about cramps, but you say, We could go. Could we? Brandy's back shrugs at you, still walking away. We could give you a ride, you say, after her.

Sure, your husband says.

Diane says, Well then, Brandy will be the after-dinner entertainment. Bryan, you can drive us all. Curtis, that's enough addiction tonight. We're going to see Brandy play. Maybe he can sing, too, she says. Her face glows, satisfied with all she's done for creation.

❧ ❧ ❧

Curtis weeps a little more in the Shrimper minivan, but he's settling down beside you. You feel his small body easing. Brandy is beside him, not looking at any of you. You study her face, Diane's face, but miraculously different. Bryan drives along the old streets. You still remember how to get to places here. On the way, you pass a church that wasn't there before. It has a plastic sign in front that says, *Sunday 10 AM Exfoliating the Soul. Bible Marathon Continues.* Diane says it's not their church. You never exfoliate. You don't have to. But you look at the sign.

The café is small and almost full, mainly teenagers. It used to be a dry cleaner's, you remember. Bryan finds you all a table, herding you to it. The light is warm, like being doused with weak tea. An older man is up at the front, singing a rambling song as he picks at his guitar, resting on his gut. I'm a hummingbird man, he sings.

When he finishes, a teenage boy takes his place. The crowd perks up. He says his name is Joe, and he's not from here. He is missing his right hand, and part of his arm, but he strums his guitar with it anyway. His song is sunny, peaceable, and his voice is good. Bryan pays attention, air-strumming along. Joe could be his offspring. That arm could be all Bryan's fault. You feel like saying that to him, but then he turns right to you, looking at your face, and says, See, there's room for everybody, in this world. Diane nods gently in time to the music, nodding forever.

When Brandy plays, caught under the amber light, it's less musical. The electric bass by itself is a strange sound, with a primeval buzz to it. The undertone of everything. Brandy turns knobs on her amp, which makes the sound stranger, bigger. You can feel it pushing through your chest. But Diane nods still, smiling, and Bryan taps his fingers on the table, and your husband does. You are all packed around the table, almost touching. Your husband puts his arm around you, and Curtis bounces, even letting his pyjamas brush against your leg. They all feel it, the great noise. People in the crowd love it. Some of them buzz along with it. They yell for Brandy when she finishes: they know her. They are young, sealed up, eggs. Recombinations of other people.

Something comes together in you, and you are clapping your hands. You think of yourself being old, one day, with sagging skin, loosened, able to eat anything. Maybe alone, maybe wise. It will happen, even to you, and you'll remember this, the big, equalizing sound. Relief. You think about that self, the future one. You wonder if you'll see Diane.

# They Call Her Lovely Rita

ADULTERY. HE DREAMED OF IT CHRONICALLY, and he wasn't even married. Stroking, slippery embracing, warm palms sliding, damp corners of mouths. Hooks and straps and zippers, all opening. Sinking into the old thickness, then realizing dimly that he was married. And unable to remember the wife's name. A dull surprise. Oh.

Then the dream would stop, and his mind would wander for a while in sleep, as if shuffling through papers in files. What is her name? What is it? The feel of running into a semi-acquaintance, the ensuing foolish conversation, the attempts to wind it around so that no names need to come up. Hey, well, good to see you, see you later, give me a call.

The scenes of adultery often took place in public, in department stores or street corners, sometimes with faint elevatoresque music in the background, and people passing. Even if the scenes were domestic, there were still witnesses of some kind. Once it was just a dog. The faces reminded him of the wife's existence, once he realized they were there. The slightly raised eyebrows, the firm chins. Even the dog's chin: he remembered this detail. The dog was something like a Pekinese: he remembered this, too. The firmness of its chin, beyond the breed's usual shoved-in look.

There was never any shock in the chins and eyebrows. *We knew this was coming.* And once he started thinking about the pattern of these dreams, he, too, knew it was coming, after a while. He thought of quietly asking somebody there what the wife's name was, but he never thought clearly enough, and even in the dream, it seemed a stupid question.

Nothing is more boring than listening to other people's boring dreams. He didn't talk about them to any of his friends, or anyone at all. Even though *Hey, want to hear about my secret-wife adultery dream* might have been a good conversation starter. Think about the word: the *adult* in it. Like adult entertainment. You have to be of legal age. Well, he was getting older. Maybe he'd been secretly married off as a baby, the way the royals used to do, or by proxy: someone had stood in for him at some secret ceremony, somewhere. Maybe in Vegas. Things happen there.

But he'd done Vegas, rationally. He was grown up, which he accepted. Hear the *groan* in that one. And the *own up.* Obvious, of course. But words start to sound more pointed, more personal, even as you start to hear a little less well. The irresistible advance of age, the old cliché. You don't realize a cliché until you're in it. At his age, so many men started to open up a can of King Lear, progressively more mental and angry and blustering at life, at the way it all goes. He'd seen a lot of it lately. Sometimes he worried he was sliding in that direction, when he would start to talk a little loudly, about life, about how life is. And no royal daughters to irritate him or try to knock him off or sacrifice themselves for him. Once, he'd wanted at least one daughter. For a period of time, he's wanted six or seven, interspersed with sons. Visions of proliferation. Go forth and multiply. The sporty tone of it: Coach's orders. Get out there. Just do it. But think about polygamists, for instance. The idea sounds fair enough at first. But pictures of them, the gangs of them, staring blankly in newsprint, made him tired. And he never did get married, and he had no children, as far as he knew, anyway, although he'd had quite a few longish relationships. Not at the same time. Serial monogamy. Some crime to be charged with, maybe. But each was a separate thing, not really related to the others. None of them was terrible, or even bad. None of them ended badly. Most of the girlfriends still kept in touch. Good times, he thought automatically, politely, when he remembered each. He was born grown-up, it seemed.

But real happiness. A real good time. He had found it. Teenage dramas on TV. He couldn't stop watching them. He recorded them when he had to work late. He even watched reruns of reruns; they pulled him in like gravity. He would find himself closer to the TV than he was when the show began. What was it about them? Certainly the gorgeous youth and beauty. Even the parents looked young, but they were peripheral. The teenagers were the centres, the masters of the universe. The plots were disgraceful, but they could make him teary. The girlfriends cheating on boyfriends, and vice-versa. Somebody's best friend was usually involved. *How could you? I thought you were my friend. We can't do this. You're my best friend's girlfriend.*

His friends' wives and girlfriends didn't really interest him, although the idea wouldn't have made a bad romance on the Women's Network: *His Best Friend's Wife*. Once in a while, he watched those, too. But did he even really have a best friend now? He had a lot of friends. That old elementary-school unease surrounding the title. Kids used to compete to be his, in a snappish, almost girly way. Or as if he were the girl, the fair maiden, the prize. The bartering that went on, for best-friendhood, like a team draft. *If you give me that, I'll be your best friend.* Or, *If you come over to my house, I'll be your best friend. I'll give you anything you want.* Those were the sad cases.

But he wanted nothing; he had something that other people wanted. He felt responsible for this, and for them all. At first, he handed out his best-friendship easily, multiply, like cheap valentines, seeing the hurt when he took on one more. Sometimes he would try to hide it: *No, no, I'm just your best friend.* Later, he took more of a politician's tactic: *I'm everybody's friend.* This was true, to a point. But underneath, he didn't care more about any one of them over the others. He liked them all fine. He did want to be their friend. He thought he did.

He used to like to take care of all kinds of things: stranded beetles, birds that slammed into the windows, the class gerbils in kindergarten. A huge joy in it. He loved it, he loved them. But it was tied up with something else, which he started to feel soon enough. He liked dogs, innocently. But then he would get to thinking about all the stray dogs of the world as he lay in bed at night. Some of those were Pekinese. Then the thought of all the loose budgies that had flown from their cages and were lost, just out there. It made him weep as they all stared longingly, invisibly out of the dark. *Help us.*

Their little eyes. There was no question that he would have to be responsible. A boulder slowly, inchingly, began to roll onto him, as in one of those Greek myths. The dogs and budgies seemed to sit on top of the boulder, a wobbling, crushing mass. Soon, his post as Gerbil Boy held a terror. He had minor panic attacks about them, especially during school vacations when he had them at home. He would wake up in the night and flee past the eyes of the invisible strays, the invisible lost, to go and check on the gerbils, to try to see if they were still breathing, under their cedar shavings or inside their toilet-paper tubes.

When he got a little older, girls took on the pets' role. He had friends who were girls, and he had girlfriends. Some of them said he was their best friend, their only real friend. The only person they could talk to in the whole world: the only one. Sometimes this made him a little uneasy. They confided in him about all kinds of things, in breathy voices. Parents, divorce, real feelings about female friends, because you have to tell the truth, possible lumps in their breasts. They would ask him to feel these. *Just feel, right here. Do you feel that?* They looked at him with open eyes and lips, as if he were a doctor. He felt like a doctor. Nobody hinted at pelvic exams, but he thought it might come to that, a couple of times.

There was a lot of crying. Terrible, at the time. It carried on into college. The girls who were his girlfriends seemed to have a lot of personal problems. Maybe this was his type, if he had a type. They seemed to feel that he had answers. He would try to find answers. Sometimes he would just nod, and that would be enough for a while. Sometimes he would put on music, and they'd just sit together and listen. He always said he liked the Beatles when people asked about his musical taste, because it's a neutral answer, almost as if you haven't said anything. And other people always say they like them, too. You have to like the Beatles. The lyrics started to feel like accusations, though, when he listened, again and again. *She Loves You. All the Lonely People. Help.*

Sometimes when he was in bed with a girl, he would leave the Beatles playing. It didn't get in the way, and gave things a kind of ready-made meaning. He would feel himself checking up on the girl, as though she were a patient. *And how are we feeling?* The girls thought he was sensitive, which was a compliment, he supposed. His heart would pump faster, but it was a dutiful faster, now that he thinks about it. It wasn't that he didn't love them. He did. And he did want to get married. He accepted this as a natural process. It is a truth universally acknowledged, and all. They talked about it, all the later serial girlfriends. Some of them mentioned it often, and left magazines open to pictures of blossomy gowns. He liked to see these, but then he would start to feel the panic, the old gerbil panic. It wasn't just the fear of being tied down, tied up, hogtied. Tied, anyhow. He was fine with that. He was used to the boulder by now, even with the girls wobbling on top of it with all the animals. He didn't even think about it. They would talk about weddings, and he would feel happy. But maybe he didn't. Maybe he had no real wishes, no desires at all.

❧ ❧ ❧

A friend of his, maybe his best friend, now, for all he knew, had frequent parties. The day after another one of the dreams turned up, he went to one. This dream had taken place on a beach. The music tinny, tropical. The touching, again, the skin, the heavy pull in the belly. A tongue, he remembers. The crest of a hip. The feeling of fine, wet sand. And of course, then, the old realization: the wife, the no-name wife, the only way to think of her, as if she were some product at a discount store. One per customer. His head still hurt, a little, now, as if he'd pulled an all-nighter studying. No name had occurred to him.

At the party, his friend, Matt, was happy as a dog to see him. Hey, man, get in here. Where you been? The insistent sound. Matt made *been* sound like *bean*, as if the arrival were full of magical potential. Now all could sprout and climb to the heavens.

Hey, sorry I'm late, he said. And Matt beamed back. Forgiveness, friendship, best-friendship. Matt slapped his shoulder, and handed him a beer, and bounded off to the kitchen in search of snacks to offer. Got to talk to you. I'll be right back, don't go away. Looking back once, quickly.

He looked around the room. People huddled and clustered, leaning on things, as if on a ship. He nodded to a few; he knew a lot of the faces. Smiles in his direction. He felt a little sick, maybe seasick. He sat on the couch and lifted the beer. Before he'd swallowed, someone came and sat next to him. A woman. Whenever he has to catch a bus, it's right on time. It has always been like that, for him. He smiled over at the woman, and they chatted, the usual things. The weather, the party, Matt, Matt's house, how they knew Matt.

The woman was happy and lively, with hot, shiny eyes. But he knew how it would go. She would start to reveal something about herself, her past, some strain or problem. He would feel responsible. She would become his girlfriend, part of the serial.

So, he said. What do you do, when you're not at Matt's parties?

She laughed. She was a pharmacy technician, she said. She'd been at the big drugstore for a while now. Matt picked up his prescriptions there. He was so friendly. *Hey, why don't you come to my party?* So here she was. You could see what Matt must have been like in kindergarten, plotting his birthday party lists six months in advance, inviting the whole class, teachers, administrators, the world. Matt was looking at him now, beaming friendship across the room, with a little thumbs-up.

The woman's head moved slightly, a slight dip to the side. A sip of the wine, then the glass held in both hands. She talked a little about work at the pharmacy. Her fingers tapped. Here it came: the easy access, the slip, the fall, the drug problem. Soon enough, after more pleasantry, it all came out. It wasn't like it was an addiction, or anything. Just a problem. Just minor. Just once in a while. Not enough for rehab. No. Maybe just some therapy, somebody to talk to about it, you know. She looked at him sideways. It was a question.

He looked back, therapeutically. Her eyes more shiny now, on him. Sorry. I can't believe how much I'm talking. I'm talking a lot. But what do you do, anyway? she said.

But it didn't matter. She wasn't listening. Just looking, waiting, starving. They talked on, and she told him more, more. The people at work, her boyfriend, well, her ex-boyfriend, the pharmacist, who was sort of like a pusher, since he knew about all the weird drugs that you can't normally get, even on prescription, and he gave them to her, like free samples. Who doesn't like free samples? It's just that there are so many, you know?

I feel like I can really talk to you, she said.

He was very sorry for her. Drugs are too easy, he said. She nodded, slowly, as if all had been revealed.

When she went off to find the bathroom, he stood up, then sat down again. His vision still weaving, sick, when he moved. He was still on his first beer. He hadn't had time to drink it, what with the true confessions. The old feel of being a doctor mixed with something priestly, but still medicinal, this time. Even the beer tasted like medicine.

Then another woman slipped down beside him. It started again. Not a pharmacy technician this time, and not drugs, but a single mother, left pregnant and astonished, going it alone with her child. The wallet photograph of the savage-looking toddler, the shake of the head, the sip of the wine, the lowering of the glass, the resilient, non-man-hating smile.

Men, he said, and she looked back, still smiling, also starving. Waiting for things to get better. He listened. He talked back at appropriate moments. He saw all her likeable qualities, and was sorry for her situation. But he realized his talking was automatic. He knew everything to say.

He said, suddenly, Does the room feel like it's moving, to you?

No surprise came from her. She nodded earnestly. She would have nodded at whatever he said.

He liked them, these party women, both of them, all of them. But his mind was restless under the sympathy and attachment. Why do we do this? Maybe this one was his wife, or the other drug problem one was, or they both were, for all he knew.

At the stereo, Matt had put the Beatles on, the world's safest choice, grinning over at him, then all around the room, as the music traveled it. Oh, God, God. *Don't Let Me Down. I Want to Hold your Hand.*

❧ ❧ ❧

Eventually, he went home, his head banging, the inscribed phone numbers in his pocket already sending out faint siren calls. In the living room, he put on the TV. He'd bought the DVD box sets of several teenage dramas, once he'd found out they were available. Putting them on was like taking aspirin. His head clearing, his hearing bettering. Riches. He'd been rationing them, but now he watched three episodes in a row. What was it about them? He couldn't say. If anyone had seen him now, goggle-eyed and open-mouthed, getting his fix. The drama, the tears, the backstabbings, the romantic impasses. It was dismal, terrible scripting, riddled with holes and shrieking. But the magnification of it all. Life at speed.

He put in another DVD from one of the other sets. This was probably his favourite series, if he had to decide. *Maxwell High*, it was called. The opening credits flashed past; he never skipped through them. The first scene bloomed. Sun through a window. Here, one of the characters in her room, sitting at her dresser, getting herself ready to go to the eponymous school. Close-up on her face, looking into the mirror, touching her cheek as if feeling she were real. The shot went on for a long time. Her glorious complexion, her clear fingernails. The loving self-centredness, the swollen music. But when the camera cut to a car on the street, disappointment. These were the scenes he loved, the introspective close-ups. There were at least two per episode. He waited for the next one.

The show unfurled, with one boyfriend argument revealed at the dark heart. *You don't really want him. Not the way I do. You're no good for him. Oh yeah, well why don't you ask him. He seemed happy enough with it last night.*

He found himself closer to the TV, head moving a little, as if he were watching tennis. The argument carried on, running to histrionic peaks. He loved these scenes, too, the hinting, the secrets, the quasi-adultery. The boyfriend appeared in the doorway, helpless.

A great sympathy rose in him, for that helplessness, that desirability. Yeah. He knew. The girls both turned to stare, to plead. But the boyfriend chose to go back to the dark-haired girl in the end, sensibly. The one for him. At least, for now.

Then, watching the end credits scrolling over the frozen final shot, he felt somehow let down. Partly with the episode, which wasn't one of the best. But partly with himself. That boyfriend had made a choice. He knew something.

Another episode: he switched to it quickly. Decisively, even. But ah, the boyfriend fight continued in this one. More secrecy, more sneaking around. The ongoing betrayal of the dark-haired one. Nothing was really resolved. And he saw: this was what he wanted. The endless repetitiveness, over and over. The characters who attended the school called it Max High. A mundane name, given all the intrigue. But the *high* in it: like a fix. And all ongoing, never over, staying at that level. The max. The great crochet of deceit and liaison was part of this, but the endlessness was something else.

He watched until he was in a kind of trance, mouth-breathing and cramped, only moving his thumb on the remote to get to the next episode, the next, the next, the next, play all. Then it was done. He'd finished the entire box set. Outside, the birds were starting up.

He lay back against the couch. He felt cheated, now, somehow, and hung over. By the end of the series, it was very obvious that the actors weren't teenagers, though they were still playing them. The forehead lines and crows' feet were starting to show, if you looked closely, which he did. He wanted something. *I want.* Not to be a teenager again, but to live it over completely. To be another teenager, like one of these ones. Not a rewind. A revision. He smarted at the unfairness. Unfair. No fair. Do it over. There is so much youth, so many young people, ablaze with their superiority, their do-overs. Their vast, shapeless power. *That's what I want.*

He thought that was it. The King Lear feeling: he got it. The feel of being something bulky, horned and bearded,

42

pathetic. Howling and grunting at his complaint. Wanting. He didn't know exactly what he wanted to do with it, though, what he wanted. Too bad he wasn't one of those women. He would have been able to help himself, then.

He calmed down, and went to bed. But he didn't sleep. He watched the cool green clock numbers flicking forward into other numbers. The birds got louder. What happens to sick birds, or injured birds, if no one finds them? He thought, and then something else came to him, which he hadn't remembered for a long time. Even when he was fifteen or sixteen, long ago, he'd gone to a lot of parties. One was at the lake, way out at one of the beaches that the park police couldn't be bothered to drive out to at night half the time. It wasn't unlike one of Matt's parties, the private talks amidst the drunkenness and jollity, although everything was amplified then. In the summer, the people from school went out to that beach a lot. There was a girlfriend, of course, at the time. Good times, he thought, as usual. What was her problem: a perfect sister, he thinks, and a retarded brother. His therapeutic nod developing, even then. At parties, she would get a little wild, running around, whooping and ending up in her bra, but with one eye on him to make sure he was checking on her. Of course he was. Something would happen to her if he didn't. He remembered the gerbils.

She was shouting, then running back to him to kiss his ear territorially. One of her friends had told her that guys like you to kiss their ears. It's a guy trigger, the friend had said, with authority. The friend had a collection of Cosmo magazines. He liked it, the ear-kissing, in spite of the loudness. The other girls, his friends, smiled and said aw, they were cute, the cutest couple ever. Then he was sorry, because they looked a little sad, the single ones. Again, his responsibility. He got up to go walk around, and one or two tagged along. They headed slowly up the beach towards the point. Confidences ensued. He nodded, but it was getting dark; he hoped they could see his nodding. One of them had a serious problem: a sick mother, cancer, he thinks. He thought about putting his arm around her, which would work, but then the other girl was there. Maybe he could put his arms around both of them. He had two arms. Maybe that wouldn't be so bad.

His girlfriend came running up out of the dark far end of the beach, her bra glowing white on her body. Are you guys cheating on me? she said, gaily. Her breath on his neck, going for the ear, the trigger. They'd all laughed, but he'd felt a jolt. He felt it now, still, lying in his bed. Was he a cheater? He hadn't been, then. He'd gone off into the trees up the beach with his girlfriend, and rid her of her bra and her immediate problems.

Later, he'd been walking right along the shore, just at the edge. That's when he saw it. Out in the lake, within sight of the shore, a shape, slightly paler than the night sky and the ruffled water. It seemed to be bobbing, holding itself steady in place. He faced it, trying to make it out. No detail, no sense of what it was. Just the dim outline. He yelled to his friends, Hey, come and look at this.

Nobody else got there to see it; they came, but it was gone when they arrived. Maybe it was the lake monster, one of them said, and then they were all laughing, all their hands slapping and rubbing his back. It's coming for you, his girlfriend said, around a mouthful of ear.

❧ ❧ ❧

In bed now, he thought, Good times. *Good* times, as if they were pets he was trying to make obey. He finally got to sleep as the sun was coming up. A dream made its way in. It involved that girlfriend, that beach. Her white teenage bra, with its front closure. His teenage self. A grand relief, realizing it. He was young, they were young, yes, this was it, this was all. It was like TV. They even kissed like the people on the shows, on Max High, as if they were the first people to do it, the conquistadors, the only ones who knew what they were doing, who would show all others. Hairs rising along his arms. His mouth open, her neck arching. Her lips closing around the top of his ear.

Here it came. All movement stopped, the dream stopped. The paralysis complete. There it was, the realization, floating in the background, flat as a cutout lake monster, mild and staid. The wife. The no-name wife. Even here, here, in his teenage sex dream.

*What do you want from me?*

&#10086; &#10086; &#10086;

This became a refrain. He even said it to people at work, although he was usually sorry afterwards, and tried to smile, as if he'd been joking. He slept badly, trying not to have any dreams. Sitting up at night, he watched all his DVDs through again, but even in them lurked a kind of suspicion. Any dreams became inherently boring, with the same old, same old realization. Oh yeah. There's a wife here someplace.

He said it when Matt invited him to the next party. But he turned it into a joke about wedding gifts. It was an engagement party. Matt was getting hitched, going to the chapel, getting himself an old ball and chain, and every other cliché in the marital book. The seeking voice on the phone. *So, you're coming, right?*

He did go. He knew what Matt wanted, at least. Just his presence was enough. Matt's puppyish ecstasy knew no bounds. You're next, buddy, Matt kept saying, punching him on the upper arm and quivering. Matt and some of the others bemoaned their coupled states in the face of his singlehood, making sad clown faces and elbowing him. You ain't getting any younger, man. There's one out there just waiting to get you.

I know, he said. He coughed afterwards, to cover the resonant viciousness.

When Matt went for beer, leaving him, he wandered into a corner, and surveyed the room, nerves rising. Unusual, for him, at parties. A stiff shiftiness, as if he were looking for something, or someone. The one out there just waiting. That feeling of suspension, of being strung. He got a beer, and drank it fast, standing under a crimped knot of pink-and-white streamer.

There were a lot of women: engagement parties bring them out. The two women from last time were among them, the drug sampler and the plucky abandoned single mother. He saw them, and he knew they saw him, and that their lives were still disastrous, and in need of his help. And he'd never phoned either of them. Guilt squatting like a toad in his belly. He turned around, and another woman was directly in front of him, looking him in the eyes. Of course she was. She smiled and said, Hey. She said she felt like she knew him. His guts pitching alarmingly. He stared at her. Was it her? Was it?

But it was only the usual. She settled, tilting her head. The chatting. Then, softly, she turned the conversation, and began to tell him about why she limped. Had he noticed? No, no, he said. But he asked her what happened, his face pulling into its serious, listening arrangement. He felt it.

Oh, she said, her voice lowering into detail. Well, I was in a bad car accident, a really bad one. A truck swerved across the line and hit me head-on. The driver said he got stung by a bee, but I don't know, I didn't see any bees that day. Anyway, he hit me, and the car flipped into the ditch, and the firefighters had to cut me out. I nearly died in the ambulance on the way to the hospital. I had to have six blood transfusions, she said.

Immediately, a trickling. Then blood streaming, surging out of his nose. His body giving up, offering it of its own accord. The woman still looking at him the same way, smiling. He knew her. She was Matt's fiancée. Of course he recognized her; she was a regular partygoer. Matt had met her at a store. It was that easy. Oh, it's you — hi, he said, bloodily.

Now she was staring, and worried. She grabbed a wad of cocktail napkins. They said *Matt and Jen 4-Ever*. All eternity, he thought, as his nose bled onto them.

*Is this what you want? My blood? Even out of my nose?*

❧ ❧ ❧

The nosebleed was his excuse to leave the party. It drained on, but slowed by the time he got home, where he sat on the couch with a roll of toilet paper, and put on one of his DVDs. A Hallowe'en party at Max High. Even he had to admit he'd seen this one too many times. The drama felt thin, despite the dancing, and the turmoil over the boyfriend sneaking out on the girlfriend right there at the dance in front of everybody, how could he do this to her right there like that, she thought she knew him, he was supposed to love her, they were supposed to be in love. The girlfriend's shaking lip. The ingenuous whorishness of her angel costume, her thin white arms. The camera gorging on her frozen expression.

Betrayal: one of those introspective moments. His sympathy beat instinctively.

But then he shut it off. He was getting tired of being the human SPCA, taking everything in. The old boulder feeling, the heaped girlfriends and dogs and budgies and gerbils. One of the kindergarten gerbils had eventually gotten lost in the house, and must have died in an air vent somewhere, mummified, never found. He'd suffered the torments of hell. Keeper of Gerbils. He was no good.

His nose was clotted, stiff inside. He didn't try to breathe through it anymore.

❧ ❧ ❧

Wonderful, brainless dreams of brainless sex, in the old way. They were gone. In every dream, now, about anything at all, he was alert to the existence of the silent wife. What do you want? But turn it around. No, what do *you* want: what was it that he wanted himself? He thought about that, therapist like. That didn't work, either.

He still watched his shows, and channel-surfed in search of new offerings, but it wasn't any of that he wanted. It wasn't some fake new youth. He did see that, now. He took some time off work, and sat around the house, and did a few chores, cleaning out the garage. He drove around in the afternoons. Grandmotherishly, he took tissues with him everywhere, in case he ran into anyone he knew, or didn't know, and they got talking. How to trust his nose now?

In one of the boring dreams, in which he'd been lying next to a damp, offered-up body, not touching it, he started bargaining. Look, I'm not against being married. I'm not against wives. I like wives. I wouldn't mind one. Maybe I was just never with the right woman, at the right time, he argued.

It struck him. He argued on: I can't please everyone. So okay. I will get married, and I'll be happy. Just tell me. Just tell me who.

When he woke up, he thought about it, as the daylight hit the side of his face. Maybe he was in want of a wife. Maybe one to cheat on. Maybe that's where happiness comes from. ·

It didn't seem like a bad idea. Vaguely, without really thinking about it, he started looking out for her, for some wife, out there. The Eternal Feminine, that floaty presence. Any woman would do. But not quite. His instinct was to go for something to take care of, what he knew best: a soft, kittenish wife, or even a small-domestic-rodentish one. Not a gerbil, but maybe a guinea pig. And not quite a child bride, but something not far off. Maybe a mail-order catalogue: visions of the desperate, the gorgeous, the displaced and Eastern European, dying to be wives. But the sad histories they would have, the plagues and political turmoil, and boredom and lack of retail opportunities. And his nose. And maybe his internal organs. He sniffed, gingerly, and pressed his abdomen.

He was a fool, but he drove, driven, looking at anybody walking or sitting. He thought of getting out of the car and making an immediate proposal to any woman he saw by herself. He should have had some meddlesome parent to arrange things, to order a ceremony, ostentation, formal wear. *Do as I say*. But his parents were never that way. They were off RVing through the southern US, now, anyway. Well, maybe they could look out for someone for him there; he could send a postcard. His dad had always said, in his sage moods, that a wife and family were a big responsibility for a man, but it was all part of the bigger plan. Maybe that's where the lack of a wife came from, for him: that weight of responsibility. But no, it wasn't that. Now, his parents asked him for help, as everyone did. For advice on cars and computers, in their case. And he was responsible. He was. Consider the gerbils.

Oh, the gerbils. He closed his eyes. Death, death.

Sometimes the sex dreams appeared, with interesting and attractive nudity and situations, but always in the same suspended state, now, the waiting. Look, I'm trying, he would argue. The dream would be silent.

He went to a psychic. The psychic was called Pam. She worked from her apartment, which had kids' toys strewn everywhere, but was very quiet. Maybe the children had been beaten into submission, locked up in some apartment-sized dungeon. Some terrible boyfriend, he thought, his sympathy rolling into automatic action. He smiled, and said, feeling more stupid than he ever had in his life, Um, I guess I need to know who my wife is. Can you tell me her name? But the psychic had only said that it starts with P, like Pam; the wife's name was maybe Pam. Her eyes, the sad half-circles under them. He fled, leaving money and his tissues.

❧ ❧ ❧

Nobody was the wife. Nobody he'd seen. It dragged on him. He went back to work. He went to a party, where he eavesdropped on conversations, and eyed people, thinking up a line: *Hey. I need a wife to cheat on.* The wife started to feel more real than work, the office, the party, anybody. He took more time off work, saying he was sick. The lie: more guilt piling on. But maybe he was sick.

At home, he tried not to sleep; he lay on the couch and watched TV all night and into the morning. The children's shows come on early. They had an appeal. In them, situations were very clear, and quickly resolved. There was dancing. There was spelling. There were puppets. He watched them every morning, and they began to feel revelatory. This is the way it is. Were there DVD box sets of these? He felt a bit better when he fell asleep on the couch and had one of the dreams. The wife must know he was trying.

How would he introduce himself to her, once he figured it out. Maybe under a false name. Madam, I'm Adam. The closed palindromic back-and-forth of it. Nice. But maybe Madam, I'm Madman was more appropriate. What is that backwards? *Namdammi, Madam*. The *dammi* was something. Damn me. Maybe the dreams were just a premonition, a taste of hell, or limbo. This is what's coming to you. First, the forgetting of names, the loss of the mind to age. Then the wait in the stocks, for the hangman, or death by stoning: the eternal boulder on him. But why? What was it he had done? How was he supposed to know who she was? Anyway, wouldn't she know who he was? What about that?

His lower back ached, from its slump on the couch, but he felt a bit lighter, even if he were damned. She would know him, wouldn't she? *Reader, she married me.* He watched more kid shows. The pure happiness, the despair, labeled. Happy face. Sad face. Happy face, again.

The house. The tree. The squirrel. The fire hydrant. Not the wife, but he watched, for a while, half-hoping.

❧ ❧ ❧

He made himself leave the couch. He took the car to the car wash, which seemed sensible. The great soapy storm of it fascinated him. He could have gone through over and over again. The kids' show should do a segment on it: *The Carwash. This is how it works.*

In the clean car, he drove around town, which was quiet, for the middle of the day. He headed south, out through the suburbs. The radio was tutting out an early Beatles song. They were having a Beatles marathon, the announcer cheerfully said, knowing no one would ever call to complain or ask for something else. He turned down the music, and kept going. He drove way out, all the way to the beach, the old beach of his youth. It was still there; he hadn't been out here for a long time. He parked in the lot at the top of the grassy area. Obviously more people had found the place, these days. There were official signs, and meters here, now, which they'd never had before. A great sense of life wheeling along, even speeding. An outrageous hate for the meters arising in his heart. He parked far from the other cars, and slammed the door violently, so it echoed, and didn't put any money in the meter. He stormed through the grass, past the picnic tables and the few families there. Those kids should be home watching TV. They might learn something.

Nobody was down at the water. It was still cold, with a sharp wind. He turned to look around, then he took off his shoes and socks, and rolled up his pants, and waded in. The same old rocks, the same weeds wrapping his feet. The cold pain traveling up his shins. His feet becoming reptilian, cold-blooded, prehistoric, ahistoric. He looked out at the lake, but no boats were out. And no shape, nothing sailing towards him, as it once had. No lifeboat. No dinghy.

The pain was unbelievable. He laughed at it, the insane screeching cold. Then he limped back up the beach. He had to walk around in the grass until his skin dried and the sand crumbled off. His feet had a freezer-burnt look, but he could feel them again. He watched for broken glass, hoarding his blood to himself, now. When he was clean enough, he put his shoes back on, and headed back for the car, away from this empty scene. One of the families had a radio at the picnic table where they huddled. The Beatles, still. Of course it was the Beatles. The endless accusing loop. The family's anodyne happiness, listening and picnicking. He walked past, trudging towards the shiny car.

He saw too late; it was already leaving, deaf to him. The ticket flapping breezily under his wiper. He didn't even try to shout after the little car as it pulled back onto the road. He stood, planted on the asphalt, his feet still shrunken with cold inside his shoes. The radio music reached him with the wind.

He didn't remember the song, at first. His ears stretched automatically for it, though his teeth clenched at it, the Beatles and their blandly sinister messages. *Meter Maid*, the song went. Ha. And someone had been here, checking the meters. Here I am. Snap: time's up. The ticket.

He reached for it, scanning the print on the back. *Please pay within seven days. You have the option of paying at either of our two locations. Office hours are.* He turned it over, fury building from his cold feet: there was no signature, no name: the nameless meter maid. But there it was, coming distantly from the radio. Lovely Rita.

Relief. He sagged and sweated with it in his shirt. He clutched at the ticket. It was she. This was it. The one he'd been trying to deceive, to cheat, somehow. The symbolism was obvious, wasn't it. He nearly laughed out loud. Time running out. She was the wife, she was fate, or fate's uniformed agent. The music continued, distorting in the breeze. *Ubbly Eepa. Lubbly Reepa.* If only the Reaper came in this form. Reaper,

Lovely Reaper. But it was more than just that. Everyone knows that time is running out. Ask not for whom the ticket falls. Own up. Pay up. *I know that.*

His longing was thick. He longed to see her uniform, her nametag. But he had her name. He leaned against the car. Had he been trying to cheat death? No. This wasn't it. He was getting older, but he wasn't old. What might once have been called middle age, even early middle age, but not anymore — not even. He knew it wasn't eternal life he wanted, not the eternal do-overs, the high school in the sky. Not to be a teenager, not to take on all the troubled souls of the world. To be smaller. Free as one of those loose budgies, but budgie-free, too. To keep love and hate pure. No cheating. The longing growing, the ache to go home and watch more kids' shows.

Here it is: what I want. You can be in charge, now. You have the rules, the white chalk on a stick, the tickets. You look after everything.

# YES, THE PEOPLE ARE NICE

THERE WAS HER OWN NAME, her happy name, bringer of happiness, in Melinda's arty lower case. The white little place cards named everyone at the table, but Joy had already forgotten who the man on her right was. She couldn't quite see his card from her position. Melinda had said, You're next to. What was it? Joy couldn't think. She didn't want to lean into the man, his packed bulldog shape. She didn't know his name. It didn't matter. He was happy to talk on, without really looking at her. Now and then, she said, Mm hmm, and surveyed the ruin of the beautiful dinner before them. The candles were low. A bead of gravy next to her plate, a scab of roast potato on it. It had been a good meal. Worth coming.

Melinda was serving hot pie and whipped cream. She put Joy's down, and the man's, and said, Enjoy, you guys.

You had to admire the leafing crust, the swirl of white. The work. Joy took a bite, and nodded as the no-name man said how great it was, just great. The man said, That's what you need.

She said, Yes. The cream was real. It had the taste, the slip.

He said, I don't know why these ladies don't want to cook anymore. I admire women who can cook. That's what I say. You like cooking, he said.

Yes, she said. She did, to a point, although she couldn't do productions, like this.

The man said, Well, that's what I mean. What's wrong with cooking, it's an art, we've all got to eat, he said. He chewed the last of his pie. Mmm mmm. But don't get me wrong, he said. You know what I mean, right? He looked at her then. His eyes were little and bright blue.

Mm, she said. The fork felt heavy in her hand. She took another bite. The pie was an amazing thing, fatiguing to contemplate. She said, Do you want some of mine?

She ended up drinking another two glasses of wine, and two coffees. She'd meant to get away early. The man told her about his three sons. They had two different mothers. The first wife was one sour bitch. But his wife now was just great, just how you'd imagine the perfect wife. The sons were all named Lewis. Well, one of them had it as a middle name, but there it was. And the other two were Lewis up front. Joy watched his mouth from the side of her eye as he talked. His voice went soft as he told her about them, their features, their exploits. He had a picture of the youngest Lewis, which he took out of his wallet to show her. A baby against a department-store-blue background. He gaped toothlessly. Joy said he was cute.

Lewis. Lew. That was the man's name. Of course. It didn't come to Joy until he'd gone. She was the last one to leave. Melinda was saying, I hope Lew was all right. You're an angel, thank you. She was laughing now.

Joy said, Oh, yes. It was fine. It was fun. We should do it again soon. Joy always said that, after a dinner there, although she never felt it for long. She always went back, though. She said it was a good time, and she felt it, until she got home.

Melinda said, Phew, I'm so exhausted. She loved it. She heaped Thanksgiving things on Joy. Leftover dark turkey meat, and the bones, for soup. A wodge of pie. All embalmed in tin foil. Go on, take it, she said. We can't keep all of it, just the two of us. Melinda's husband was washing dishes in the bright kitchen. By the door, Melinda's face shone in the last candlelight. Joy took the food. Her oldest friend. She went home and put it in the fridge. The turkey smell attacked every time she opened the door.

❧ ❧ ❧

Joy usually did evenings at the home. She was a care nurse. She liked the slow work, the usual elderly residents in her part of the ward. Some did die, but most were around for quite a while before that. She had mostly women. Some of them were nice. Some of them liked to talk. They looked similar, with watery bifocal eyes, and scalps showing. Margaret was the different one. She liked having a bath on bath night, for one. Highly ladylike, born in England and never forgot it. She had books about gardens and flowers, and always wanted a dress and stockings on when she wasn't in bed, not the jaunty tracksuit most of the others wore. Joy used to imagine them all running off. Once when Margaret was in the bath lift, Joy had told her that, and Margaret laughed. Oh dear, oh dear, she'd said. Joy had her in the water now, and washed her without thinking about it. The old caesarean scar, vertical, all down the belly. The way they used to do it. She got her clean, and up out of the bath, and dried her off. That's wonderful, Margaret said. Her fluffy duckling skull, her arms around herself.

Joy took her back to her room. Margaret was slow on her arthritic legs. There were three more baths to do tonight. Joy did all Margaret's checks first, and put on a clean incontinence pad for the night. Looks a little irritated, she said. We better put some cream down there. She automatically thickened her gloved finger with it.

Margaret had her eyes closed. She gave a little surprised O, and said, That never goes, dear. Sometimes you just want something in there. Then she said, Well, there you are, and she laughed a little, her thin lady laugh. That was the only time she ever said anything like that.

There weren't many men in the home. A new one arrived in the early winter. He wasn't very old, which was unusual. Middle-aged. Joy saw them processing him at the office. He was in a wheelchair, sitting there with startling dark hair. She asked Hazel about him, out in the dirty parking-lot snow on a break. Hazel's lips were tight around her cigarette. Stroke, she said. Then she said, Or no. I know. Some kind of brain damage, from an ear infection, or a root canal, or something, she said. Crazy.

Joy said, Really? Poor guy.

Hazel said, Yeah. He's going in Fenella's old room. He better not be as crazy as she got, I can't stand another one, she said. She laughed out a puff of smoke.

Joy said, Oh, don't.

Hazel said, What?

I don't know. She might come back and haunt us, or something, Joy said.

They laughed, and Hazel said, You don't come back from that, anyways.

❧ ❧ ❧

The man was in Joy's section of the hall. After she took Margaret to dinner in the dining hall, she went back for him. She bustled in, saying Hello, in her nurse voice. He was sitting in the plasticky chair by the side of the bed. He smiled up at the sound of her, with a young face, incongruous. Hello, Bill, she said. I'm Joy. He seemed to nod. As she reached for his arm, she saw that it was just tremor. His whole upper body was nodding. Well, she said. Are we ready for dinner?

He seemed nice enough, even though he didn't speak. He was still smiling. She looked out the window as the evening sun arrived on the parking lot. Hey, look at that. It's a nice day after all, she said. I saw some kids tobogganing down the hill on my way in today. We used to do that when I was a kid. That's going back some, she said. She laughed, and he grinned at the sound. His teeth looked okay, slightly ivoried. He shook. She sat down on the bed, in the setting light, just for a minute. The ache in her feet came up. Usually she didn't notice it. The room was plain around them. Nothing from home. Margaret's room was snowed in with doilies. Joy said, Well, I bet you like tobogganing, Bill. There was a hill by where we lived, we called it Bosom Hill. Two big bumps. Pretty funny, huh? she said.

He seemed to nod. His springing hair wobbling. It needed a comb. She said, You like your new room, I bet. Then she said, So, let's go to dinner, okay? She got him up. He could walk, if you prompted him. Walk, Bill. We're walking.

❧ ❧ ❧

Bath night was always the worst. Joy's back tugged her at the end. At least Bill was supposed to bathe himself, with supervision. One of the trainees could do that, while Joy did Margaret and the rest. She was splashed and humid by the end of it. But she did like the job, overall. Even feeding the people. Some of them fed themselves, some needed help. The smell of corn pervaded, always. Corn was the vegetable of choice here. Maybe it was cheap. It looked cheerful, anyway. She found a trail of it leading to the big lounge room on the way back from the bath that night. One of the ladies had a huge handful of it, and was eating it piece by piece in front of the gigantic TV. Maybe she thought she was at the movies. Well. She seemed happy, so Joy left her alone. Most of the residents sat there all day, looking at the big smeary screen. *Sesame Street*, or cooking shows, or nature. There was a piano, and a pool table, although you never saw anybody use either. A dog lived in the home, neutered and weary. It, too, seemed to enjoy the TV. Visitors came, and often ended up there in the lounge. There was only so much to say about the residents' little bedrooms. Nerves and brightness on show. People's voices were so loud there, although they had to be. Walking down the hall, you could hear people yelling. Peculiar, because they yelled pleasant things. *How are you. You look nice today, Mum. What did you do this morning.*

Sometimes children came. They liked the automatic lifting chairs in the lounge, pushing the buttons to launch themselves up and out. It was never fast enough. One of the old women, not one of Joy's, was almost blind, and had a talking clock. Her grandchildren, or great-grandchildren, pressed the button over and over when they were there. You could hear it all over the hall. *The time is. One. Fifty. Five. P. M. The time is.*

Some people didn't have visitors. Sad to think of it. One woman didn't seem to mind too much, but who knew? Etta. She was very old, papery, with black blood bulges under the skin, and almost no hair. Joy brought her some flowers once in a while, just cheap ones from the gas station on the way to work. She left them in a vase by the bed. Sometimes she gave her an extra wheel around the halls, if she had time. Just to get her out. She did it that night.

Hazel was waiting in the room when they got back, after Etta's bath. Where have you two lovebirds been? she said. The doctor was supposed to be there, for Etta's checkup. He was late. Hazel said to Etta, Well, your boyfriend isn't here. He stood you up. She lit a cigarette.

Joy said, Oh, come on. The poor old woman, hunched in the wheelchair. Joy's own goodness sank her, a weight.

Hazel said, What? Maybe she likes it. She blew a cloud into the corner, away from the woman's face. She patted her shoulder. Right, Etta. Then she said, Oh, but you better check on that guy, Joy. He might be lost. I saw him walking around a little while ago, but I had to go clean up some puke, she said.

Joy left them. She looked into Bill's room, and he was there, just sitting, as usual. Joy said, Hey, Bill, did you go for a walk?

He smiled at her. Kindly spaniel eyes. She said, Well, next time, let me know where you're going, okay.

She looked around the room. It was still bare. She almost said, No visitors today? But she didn't. The walls felt close. No clock, no souvenirs or photos. Well, it made dusting easier, anyway, for the cleaning staff. Okay, she said. Time for bed, then. He seemed to nod at her. His tremor. Almost jolly. He was still gently smiling. She took him down to the bathroom, and supervised his urination, without really looking. His legs were thin, but ropy with muscle. He held her arm as she took him back to the room. He put on his own pyjamas, but she had to brush his teeth. That was in the notes, because of his previous dental problems. It must have been so painful.

Horrible. The ascending infection, from tooth to sinus to brain. *Be sure to clean very thoroughly.*

She told him to open up, and he popped his mouth open, like a baby bird. How about that, she said. Here it comes. His stubble scratched her wrist as she reached in with the toothbrush. It surprised her, its presence. She dragged the brush back and forth across the surfaces of his teeth. Three of the molars were missing, on one upper side. Only a seamed, puckery hole in the gums. She could just see it. The innocent look. The source of all his loss. When she finished, he grinned at her, foaming.

❧ ❧ ❧

Sometimes there were outings, which were surprisingly peaceful. They went for drives. Joy never minded going along. They had a minibus, and a man to drive it. They did Beach Days, and Autumn Colour. Winter Scenes was coming up next. They put the sign-up sheet in the TV room for the ones who could still read and write, or for their families to do it. Not many of them ever went. They all got a turn, at least once, but some of them hated it. Margaret loved it. She wanted an extra bath the night before Winter Scenes. Not just a sponge, a hair wash and the works. She was so excited. Joy gave in.

Afterwards, she stopped, splattered, at the door of Bill's room. He was already in bed, intensely asleep. Had he brushed his teeth himself? Well. She didn't want to disturb him.

It was just getting dark the next evening when they headed out in the bus. Not many people went. Only five, counting Joy and the driver. Betty, with her fat and her Alzheimer's, looked beached, pushed up close to another dementia patient. Maybe it was some comfort. But Margaret, with her washed hair, was thrilled. Oh, she kept saying. Just look at that.

The Christmas lights on the houses flashed and starred in the purple dark. People started early around here, with the decorations. Many were just plain white lights marching around rooflines, which probably stayed up all year. Some of the lights were red, sinister-looking, or cold blue, or lazily mixed. They drove slowly down a street, then they stopped at the end: the bonanza. It was there every year. A red Santa and reindeer outscaling an illuminated, waving baby Jesus on the roof of the house. Points and spirals flaring all over the building, the whole surface covered. A sign flashing in the middle of the front lawn. *The Reason For The Season.* Mary and another baby Jesus sparkling there, too, with a camel. That must be Joseph standing behind the camel, or maybe one of the wise men, on his own.

Margaret breathed, enchanted. A box for donations to some good cause was hung on the fence. Joy helped Margaret to get out of the bus, on her creaky legs. Margaret put in some change from the little knitted purse. She'd made it in an Arts and Crafts lesson, although she already knew how to knit perfectly well, as she said.

When they got back to the home, Joy put Margaret to bed first. Margaret kept saying, Lovely. Lovely. How could one ever forget that? Her hands were tight together with bliss.

Joy said, Goodnight Margaret, and she switched off the overhead light.

Margaret said, She will, though. Satisfaction in her voice.

Joy said, What's that?

Margaret said, She'll forget. That heavy woman. She will. But I certainly won't.

The next evening, Joy started the checks and bedtimes with Bill. She'd just been outside with Hazel, in the parking lot. It was warm inside, and warmer in the room. Bill was sitting in his chair, as usual. She said, Hey, Bill. He smiled up at her. She said, Didn't you want to come on the drive last night? You should have, she said. She took his arm, to get him to the bathroom.

He put his hand on hers as she pulled him to his feet. His finger pressed into her skin. He said, Cold.

Joy felt like a teacher, a good teacher. That's right, she said. That's good, Bill. They began walking down the hall. She chattered on. He touched her ear, with the finger.

Later, outside with Hazel again in the thick dark, she asked if anybody had visited him that week. He seemed different. Better. Hazel said, Nope. Some of these families. They stick them in here, that's it. I tell you, I hope they shoot me first, you know, she said. Her eyes closed against the rise of cigarette smoke.

Joy said, I'd shoot you.

Hazel said, Thanks. Joy blew out a puff of cold breath, not smoke.

There was another outing, for Christmas shopping. They went to the mall every year. A few signed up to go, more than usual, to get some little things for their families. Margaret was going, of course. Joy heard her talking about it with her daughter on every visit. On the night, they had everyone wrapped up, the wheelchairs loaded, and the others in their seats. But Margaret wasn't there. She was probably packing her purse. She always had a purse with her, even in the dining hall.

Joy went to Margaret's room and found her sitting on the bed, her hair slightly awry. Joy said, Come on, Margaret, time to go.

Margaret said, Oh, dear. Oh, dear. I'm not right today, she said. My arthritis. Her eyes spilling. I'm just not myself, she said.

Joy looked at her, her sad, blown ankles. She said, We could take you in a wheelchair.

But Margaret shook her head. No. Never. She wasn't one of those. She gave Joy her little knitted purse, from inside her bigger purse, and she said, Would you get something for me, dear, please, for Megan?

Joy knew. Megan was her granddaughter, the godlet of the shrine on Margaret's wall. They weren't supposed to take money from residents, ever. But Joy said she would look for something. She put the purse in her coat pocket. She went back out into the hall, and Bill's door caught her eye. It was open; the doors always were. There Bill was, sitting. Joy said, Bye, Bill. See you later.

Bill said, Hi.

Joy stopped. She looked. His smile, his confident sweatshirt. His young face. She said, Would you like to come shopping, Bill? We're going to the mall, she said. It's Christmas.

He said, Hi.

She got his coat, and walked him out to the minibus. Room for one more, she said. She buckled him in. Ribs, and a surprising thickness of belly. She sat next to him for the drive. At the mall, she and two other nurses took charge, herding the residents around in slow little groups. Joy ended up with Bill and Martin, one of the few other men in the home. He was very frail, but still insistently walking, shaking with Parkinson's. They were in the big department store, which was easiest. She had one of them on each arm. They didn't walk fast, or far. Shoppers looked at them, especially when she talked. She had to use the loud nurse voice. It clanged, outside in the world. Look, she kept saying. Look at this.

Hi, Bill said, a few times. He was looking up at the ceiling, with its hanging Christmas decorations, its bright bars of fluorescent light.

They shuffled, and came to the toy department in the centre of the store. That was good; Joy could get something for Margaret's granddaughter. They stood before a rack of stuffed animals with wild beady eyes. Joy said, Which one should I get?

Martin reached with a jittery hand down towards a huge moose. It was wearing a bobbled hat between its antlers. Bill bent forward. Was he going to fall? No. Joy gripped. Bill pulled the moose from the shelf. That's the one, eh? she said.

They went to join the line to pay for it. Bill said, The bear. Joy laughed, and Bill laughed, too. She patted his back. She could feel his shoulder through the winter padding.

Back in the minibus, Bill held the moose all the way home. It sat up proudly on his leg. They were back in time for dinner. She walked Bill and Martin into the steam corn clouds. They left Martin at his usual table, and moved over to Bill's spot across the aisle. She said, Okay, I'll go and give the moose to Margaret now. She'll love it.

But Bill shook. It wasn't his tremor. He meant something. She knew. She said, It's for Margaret's granddaughter, Bill. For Christmas. It's Christmas soon, she said. The clank of plates sounded around them. He looked at her. She said, I can take it to her for you. His fingers tensed on the moose. His soft eyes blinked and blinked. She said, Oh. Okay, she said.

�� �� ��

Joy had to stop at the mall again on the way in the next day, to get something else for Margaret. There was another moose, identical, but she chose a bear instead, a medicinal pink. That would do for Megan. She took it and the purse to Margaret, who thought it was quite lovely. Lovely, she said, approvingly. She was so sorry to have missed the trip. Her knees and ankles were getting so bad. But she didn't like to complain. Would they do another shopping trip at all? Joy said, Maybe.

She checked in on Bill, on her way to get some towels. He was in bed with the moose staring beside him. Bill opened his eyes, and smiled at her. His hair was standing up, and hair was showing in the neck of his pyjamas. He pulled the moose's hat off, and put it back on, again and again, slowly. It was attached by a string. Joy said. Well, that won't get lost. That's good, Bill, she said. He nodded, and trembled, and pulled.

She said she would do Christmas Day when they asked her in the office. She didn't mind; she was alone. She could have gone to Melinda's, of course. She'd often gone there for Christmas dinner, since her parents had died. They'd been friends since high school. But she didn't want to this year. She'd made an excuse.

She did Christmas Eve at work, too. They had a carol sing-along in the TV room, with the TV still on, but the sound off, at least. Some people knew the words. Joy didn't know all of them, but she faked. When they put the sound back on, they all watched a Christmas cartoon for a little while, which involved a battle, and surprising weaponry. Well, she left it on anyway. Then she had to get people to bed. She took her residents back to their rooms.

Bill was already in his. He hadn't been out of bed that day, or for a while. The nurse on days said he seemed tired; Joy read it in her floral pencilled notes. The doctor said to let him be, except to get him to the bathroom and the dining hall. He was supposed to be preserving independence. He seemed happy in bed, anyway. As always.

Joy went in and said, Time for bed. Oh, look, you're all ready without me. She laughed, and he echoed it. *Ha.* She took him to the bathroom. His hand clinging to her arm. His urine splashed over the toilet edge, and she had to mop up. Back in his room, she sat him on the bed, and got out the toothbrush. Here we go. He opened his mouth, and she brushed. His eyes were on her. She looked at his face. His stubble. His beard was growing in. Had he been shaved that day? There wasn't always time, especially with the doctor doing flu shots lately, and everybody with colds. Joy said, Do you want a shave, Bill?

She looked. The individual black and gray bristles stemming, as though under a microscope, still growing. She found the razor and shaving cream in the drawer, and got some hot water. The cream spread across his lower face.

Now you're Santa Claus, she said.

His smile pushed the white foam upwards. He was meek under the razor's draw. She slid it slowly across his cheeks. Over his upper lip, with its notch. Then down over his chin. Slowness. She tipped his head back, so she could reach. His underjaw, his throat whiter. The Adam's apple bobbed at her.

She wiped the cream tufts from his face. His skin warm now. She smiled, and looked out the window at the parking-lot lights. She said, Well, Bill, you don't look half bad. She got up. Merry Christmas, she said.

He was smiling. He shouldn't be here, like this. Not all alone.

Joy said, Do you want to see something? She got him sitting up. She pulled a sweatshirt over his dark head, over his pyjama top. Come on, she said. Come. He held his moose.

Nobody saw them go out the door. The few residents still in the lounge kept their eyes on the TV. She and Bill crossed the parking lot, and she got him buckled into the passenger seat of her car. Then she drove. They went all over the place, seeing the sights, the lights, the fake constellations. She said, I always like to see them at Christmas. You do too, I bet, she said. She was talking quietly. He wasn't old, or deafened with life.

Bill said, You.

The snow was dense, slithery. She drove slowly, in case of black ice beneath. She knew the way. The car was quiet.

They stopped, finally, outside the Jesus house. There you go, she said. They sat. They stared at the flashing. The lit baby Jesus on the roof, the bigger, sparkling one on the lawn, with Mary and the camel and Joseph. See that, she said. It's lovely. Margaret's word. But it was. It was that. Joy could see the spattering colour reflected in Bill's face. He stared, and smiled, and held the stuffed moose, and said, You. You.

❧ ❧ ❧

She didn't see much of him on Christmas Day. There was an emergency with Betty, who fought the nurse getting her out of bed and fell, cracking herself in places. Poor Betty. It took time to sort everyone out, after the paramedics had come. Joy stopped in to see him, late, but he was already in bed, with the light off. The room felt clean and warm. She stood in the doorway for a moment.

She had a week off, then. She stayed home, and didn't phone Melinda. What was there left to say to Melinda, to reveal? She watched things on TV. Old things. Amazing, how easy it is to do nothing. To stare. Hours went by. She wasn't unhappy.

On the Monday she was due back, she picked up some leftover Christmas chocolates at the grocery store for her residents. What was the harm? She would brush their teeth, anyway. She took some to Margaret, who was fretful and lumpy with arthritis but pleased to see her, and full of Megan worship after the holiday visits. She asked for an extra bath, because Joy was the best at it, and when she'd been away, nobody had done it properly.

But there were things to do first. He wasn't in his room. Bill. She left a chocolate Santa on his bed, and got on with her other jobs. She didn't see him in the dining hall, or the TV lounge. Finally Margaret got her bath. When Joy had her in the lift, lowering into the water, she said, Where's your neighbour today, Margaret?

Margaret said, Oh. Do you mean the young fellow? She always spoke that way, as though she'd never taken any notice of anyone before that moment. Joy got her down. Margaret said, I think he's gone.

Joy said, What, gone? Where did he go? She straightened her back.

Margaret said, I don't know. Couldn't you make the water any warmer, dear, she said. She stretched back. The scar splitting up her belly.

Joy checked at the office after Margaret was in bed. The doctor was there, on rounds. She asked about Bill. The doctor looked at his notes. He said, They took him home. It's not going to change. Saves paying the extra fees. He's not getting any better, he said.

Joy said, But he's not going to. He's not going to get better, is he?

The doctor said, Not after an infection like that. Why don't people take better care, he said. He looked interestedly at the chart.

Joy said, He's not going to die, though. He won't get any worse. He's fine, she said.

The doctor was still reading. He said, You don't see this very often.

※ ※ ※

Joy worked. The same work. She washed bodies, and inserted catheters, and doled out pills, and corn. Another week went by. More. Nothing different. A woman was put in Bill's room. She was ancient, twisted with it, but very sharp. She wanted Joy to play cards with her all the time. Joy tried to set her up with Margaret, but they didn't get along. A frozen silence when they were together. Who could understand it?

She switched to days, for a change. One morning, she got in early. She went into the office when nobody was there. She looked at his chart. She was allowed to do that. Then she started the morning meds. She kept working.

※ ※ ※

The address was right. She could see it by the little torch-shaped light by the door. She wasn't supposed to be here. She knew it. But she'd phoned first, she told herself. The person who answered listened to her spiel about being Bill's nurse, and wanting to say hello, and see how he was doing. The person was a young woman, it sounded like. Silent, abrupt.

But in the end, she'd said, Okay. You can come tomorrow night.

So there Joy was, landed. She looked up at the house. Blocky and small. A few lights still strung around the door, but not switched on. She got out of her car, and went up the front walk. Her boot skidded on an ice patch, and she nearly fell onto a concrete squirrel. But she stayed upright and got to the door, where there was another squirrel, and another animal of some kind, caked with snow. Maybe they were Bill's. She thought of the stuffed moose. He liked animals.

She knocked on the door, and waited. A woman came. She was young, almost adolescent-looking. Younger than Joy. Her look felt almost solid.

I guess you better come in, she said, eventually. A chalky voice. She turned, and Joy followed her. It was the living room; it must have been. Everything must have been new in the 1970s. Looped carpet swirling beneath the wood-panelled walls, well-preserved. Almost a museum.

Joy stood. She could see into a small kitchen off this room, and down a short, dark hallway with two doors leading from it. Circles of orange light on her here, from the wall lamps. Framed photographs all over the walls, up to the ceiling, as in Margaret's room. Two armchairs, resolutely fake leather. The woman had sat down in one, with her legs stuck out in front of her. Bill wasn't there.

Joy stood. She said, Well, I'm Joy. I looked after your father. Bill's your father, she said. Was she in the right house?

The woman said, Yeah. Her eyes glared on.

Joy tried to smile. She said, I just wondered how he was.

The woman said, He's fine.

Joy said, It must be hard for you. But nice, too, to have him home. Her calm, inane voice filling the air.

The woman didn't say anything. Then Joy said, Did you grow up here, in this house?

The woman said, Yeah. It's mine now.

Silence. Joy looked around the room, an idiot smile on her lower face. Her eyes found a picture of a young man, with dark hair, and a moustache, and muscled arms. He was standing next to a canoe on a wharf. He was in other pictures, on a motorbike, and standing on a dirt trail in the forest, and in a boat again. Joy said, Is that your dad?

The woman said, Yeah.

Joy said, Oh. She looked at the walls. He was in most of the pictures, this living Bill. She went closer. There was one of him smiling, sitting in the driver's seat of a car, with his fingers flexed on the wheel. He had a beard. Joy scanned across the wall. At the other end was a large photo of two girls, sitting in a patch of dandelions, squinting. Joy said, And that must be you. And your sister, is it? she said.

The woman looked. Yeah, she said.

Does she live here? she said. Her words glittering, crackling.

The woman said, No. Just me. She was staring at Joy.

Joy said, Oh, again. Then she said, I'm a nurse.

After a minute, the woman said, I know.

Joy said, I was just wondering if I could see him.

The woman stared.

Joy laughed, a coughing laugh. She said, I just felt. I just. I was wondering how he was doing. He was always so nice in the home, and I couldn't help wondering. I just wondered, she said.

The woman pushed her hair out of her eyes. She said, Nice, yeah.

Joy said, Yes. He's such a nice man.

The woman got up. She went towards the door. Joy sank. She wasn't going to see him. But it was silly, anyway, her silly wish. She said, Well, I won't bother you anymore. I'm sorry. I hope he's okay. I just wanted to say hello, she said.

The woman said, He's not dead.

Joy said, Oh. Oh. I know, she said.

The woman said, I wish. Her laugh was sandpapery.

Joy nodded. She knew. She said, It can be tough. A connection arose, a sympathy for this woman, looking after someone with such an illness, doing her best. I'm sorry about what happened to him, she said. It's such a shame nobody caught it sooner. The infection.

The woman said, He's a hitter. And one of those.

The air was artificial there. The thick carpet. Joy said, Excuse me?

The woman said, Yeah. Me and my sister got the belt every day until I was twelve. Then he started on the pervert stuff, she said. She bent her head, feeling the top of her skull. See, that's where he cracked it, she said. Frying pan, she said. Her matter-of-fact, smoker's voice.

The woman's puff of hair, the crown of her head. Oh.

Bill, in his bed. The stuffed moose. Joy said, Is he. Are you okay?

The woman said, Yeah. Fine, she said. A challenge. Are you? she said.

❧ ❧ ❧

How did Joy get out of there? She stood in the room for another minute. Then she was back on the slippery walk. Where was Bill, in that little house? She looked back. The living room glowed fluorescent, but every other window was dark. She got in the car and drove. She drove out the highway, for miles, towards where she grew up, out on the farm, out where it used to be. She saw her parents, perfect, in water-colour, with their kind hands, and their usual clothes, and her father's kind scratching face, in their house. The hollow socket-ache.

# Free to Good Home

HOW WOULD YOU KNOW WHAT HE WAS THINKING? How could you, I suppose. They were in the car, then, on their way to the coast, through the hitched-up mountains in the way. The snow was still there in shining spatters, ground into the road in places. The woman looked at the white patches. Why it was still there, even in April, and why were some parts of the road so bare? The contrast: the concrete and the stubborn, dirtied gloss. She imagined it as if from above, as if she were in a plane, at the same time. The car a little metal insect, creeping over bumps and splats. But safe. Very safe. He was driving.

She looked out at the scribbled lines of trees and the clear-cuts high up, here and there. Bald, she thought. She felt the top of her own head then, over the crown. She said, Do you want me to drive for a while?

He smiled a little at the road. She saw it. He said, No, I'm good.

He loved to drive. She knew that about him. Jim. It was one of the things she knew. His hands loved it, the tight wheel, the lack of power steering. She looked at his hands, which were of course the best hands, which were perfect, perfect for doing anything.

She said, You love it.

What? he said.

Driving.

He smiled again, and started humming. It was tuneless, but sounded just like the car. They even harmonized. C and E, was it? She tried to think back to piano lessons and pitch testing. Youth. Then the usual ball hit her in the solar plexus, and she had to reach over and touch his face. It always did this, it always came after her all of a sudden, and then she had to do it, get grabby, touch his face, which felt like a cornfield along the cheek now. She pushed her fingers into his cheek, slightly, and he said, Mm. Smells like shampoo. It was enough to keep the happy winging in her for miles. He steered hard. He had to, in that poor old car, and she watched. C, E, C, E.

They were coming up to the rockslide by then. They were making good time, already getting to the highest part of the pass. Their first time on that road, at least the first time together. She knew he had done it so many times, that drive. Even if you didn't know him, you would still be able to see it in his steering, his ease. She imagined not knowing him: the drop, the thrill. Being able to meet him again. Anyway, she didn't like driving by herself, especially when the roads were so quiet, at this time of year. You could sit there for hours by the side of the road, just sitting, like a plant, if your car broke down. And here there was more snow, less dirt. Which was nice, in a way. Carved white lumps still, in the spring. Oh, that one looks like ice cream, or a polar bear, she said.

What? he said. His eyes slid from the road, slowly.

No, she said, Don't look. You need to drive.

I am driving, he said. He laughed a bit. He flicked the windshield wipers on, and they blinked across the glass once. Insect death and bluish fluid, a stew. He said, See, I can see fine.

Oh. Well, you missed it, she said. Then she felt bad that he'd missed it. She thought of ice cream, the soft kind, in a perfect twist atop a cone. Pretty. But that snow really had been more like a polar bear, a sort of manufactured one.

She said, Do you think we'll see any deer?

We might, he said. His calm, always, unending.

That would be nice, she said. You like deer. He did. Their lightness, their hide. She could picture him seeing them out the window at his place, or here, on the side of the road, shy as a lawn.

Jim said, Yeah. They're, I don't know, pretty.

The word came out in tune with the engine. C. C. She had to fight herself off. She would have grabbed his face in both hands and held it tight. She had never done it yet, though. Sometimes she felt like an infant, an enormous, secret infant, with long legs but an infant stomach and bald brain, grabbing. She looked out the window.

Ahead, the trees were gone. Rocks shouldering each other, the huge slid heap of them. It was always a surprise, although everyone knows it's there. It's a landmark on the long trip now, that rockslide, a *stop of interest*, as the sign puts it. There is even a lookout point, where you can pull over and get out and stare up at the boulders and rocks all over each other, silently frozen all down the slope. *Bang*, is what it makes you think. Had someone started it? The noise from truck brakes, maybe. Or singing. People don't yodel around there, but maybe they once did. Maybe that started the slide. She couldn't remember, although they had studied it in elementary school. *Our Land*: the title of their textbook. That she remembers. But not much else. Rocks, sediment, tectonic plates, things. Things. How do you remember that far back?

There was a field trip to the slide site, though, which she more vaguely remembers. The school bus journey there. The refrigerator smell of the air outside. A parks ranger had lectured them all about it as they'd stood in pairs. Her field trip partner had been that girl who wheezed, and who got to go back to the bus and take her medicine and sit in there. What had the ranger told them? Well, who knows. Geography. At least she still had the word. She wasn't going senile just yet. One thing: the ranger had told them a Greyhound bus nearly got buried under the slide when it happened, but the driver had stopped just in time. One of the boys had asked did anybody die, and the ranger had said yes. This was impressive. She'd been importantly vulnerable on the school bus on the way back. That other girl had sucked on her inhaler the entire time. But the slurp hadn't ruined the feeling. They might all die. Anyone could.

Now, they were passing it, the stiff mountain head with its spilling beard of rocks. She asked Jim if he wanted to stop. He said he didn't mind, so he pulled over, just past the sign. She got out of the car and felt the air, the thin surprise. Fresh air is supposed to be good for you. She said, brightly, Hey, come and get some fresh air.

Jim got out, too, and walked around to stand beside her, next to a heap of dry snow. The car looked coated, roadworthy, cowboy-esque. A movie moment. They stood, as if in a frame, looking at the rocks as though they meant something. He should have had a cigar, or some snuff, or whatever a cowboy might use. There should have been music. Jim never liked the stereo on when he was driving, though. She knew him. She smiled at him, and she said, You like to hear the engine.

He said, Hm. He was looking up. His arm soldiered goosebumps in rows, and she could feel them. He should have had more than a T-shirt on. She grabbed at his arm, and had to stop herself from indenting thumbprints. He was not. Playdough.

Infant. Infant. He smiled back at her, and they looked at the rocks, and she was quiet. It was all right.

Another car pulled up a ways behind them. Other people. She and Jim must have been standing there for a while, getting colder in front of the huge rubble pile. They didn't need to talk to anyone else. She said, Come on, let's go. They got back into the car, which was better, if not warm. She felt happily tinned, a tomato, or a peach. They ground their way out of the gravelly roadside in the safe metal car. In the side mirror, she could see an older couple get out of their car to read the rockslide sign. There was someone with them, maybe a child. Oh, it was a dog, a big dog, dirty yellow. The couple's white hair blended with the snow as they shrunk in her view, taking their dog to the side of the road. The yellow dog would soon be blending with the snow, too. Ha, she thought.

They made their getaway. Thank goodness, she said. Trees and rags of snow on the ground, and the same road. The slide was a ways back now. Jim hummed his hum, the pitch rising when he changed gears now and then. Maybe to an F. She used to have perfect pitch. They did actually test them in school, and at piano lessons, and hers was perfect. She could sing whatever note they threw at her then, no matter how low or high, and name it. She hummed quietly now, too. She checked the mirror for those people, but they never caught up. Good.

She said, I wonder if there were any animals under there.

Jim said, Where?

She said, Under the rockslide. They got the dead bodies out, though, right? The people bodies?

I don't know. They must have. There might have been some animals, I guess.

What kind? she said.

What kind? I don't know, he said. Probably deer.

The wheel of sadness crunched over her. Oh. You like deer, she said.

Yeah, I like deer, he said. Hm hm. Back to C, E. He was looking at the road, with the slow, long hill coming up ahead.

Don't you want to talk about them? she said.

About what? Jim said. His one hand firm on the top of the wheel, the other alone.

She clenched, and said, Oh. He didn't want to talk. Thinking about deer made him sad. It was likely. He was quiet about such things. You might not have thought so, given his job, but the truth was he was full of gentleness. He was.

She had seen it immediately, when he'd come to her mother's to pick up Wizard. The Wizard of Dog. The dog of her youth. The dog had been very old and frosted around his dark face by then, as though an old-lady hairdresser had gotten at him. And he had been dead. Twisted into angles by death, with bent front legs and neck and beany eyes. The most animated he'd looked in years, actually. He was in the middle of the kitchen floor, too early in the morning. Her mother had phoned her, and was crying when she'd arrived, sitting away from the dog, squeezed into the corner of the breakfast nook. Her mother was wailing, But he just died, he just died, why does he have to go and look like that? Wizard was not himself and he was not dead enough yet to be respectable. What do you do? She'd looked up Veterinarians and then Pets in the Yellow Pages, and had seen the ad. *Pet Cremation. We will help you at your time of loss. Quiet peaceful setting. Pick-up service.* It was a little ad, no pictures, not even a box around the text, at the end of a page with listings for Dr. Spung and Dr. Popoff and Hotel Kitty and the Love-a-Pup Animal Care Centre. How, how, could anyone phone any of those? How could places like those exist?

Her mother was still crying, so she had gone and phoned the pet cremation number herself, and Jim had answered, after a few rings. She hadn't even thought about what cremation was. He had come to the door and done everything. He'd even brought a sheet, a nice sheet, to cover Wizard, and he'd lifted the stiff bundle up and taken it to the back of his pickup truck, which wasn't covered, but there was the sheet, and it was all right. One call did it all. He'd left a little card so they could arrange a time for the cremation. *Jim. Pet Cremation.* The phone number. Nothing else. That was all they needed.

People don't attend the actual cremations, but there is a ceremony afterwards if you like. Her mother hadn't wanted to go, by then interested in a Rottweiler-Shihtzu-cross puppy advertised in the paper. She'd said to her mother, What do you call that? A Rotzu? It sounds like a car.

Her mother had said, Well, it's free.

Rotzu. Ignoring her mother, she'd arranged for a ceremony anyway. She had a vague sense that Wizard was looking down on them mournfully from afar. Or vengefully. Oh, Wizard, Wizard. So she'd driven out into the country and found the address, in the middle of the old orchards. Jim was working out of a picker's cabin. Its roof was flaked, like skin. She'd stood in front of it, not knowing what to do. But he'd come out and smiled, and given her Wizard's ashes in a nice blue Tupperware container, and said, Nice old dog.

She said, So.

He said, Yeah. He'd smiled at her.

She said, Could we leave him here? It's so pretty.

He said, Sure. Some people do. You can go over there a little ways.

So she'd gone into the grass and walked in a little circle, distributing Wizard around. He was watching. How do you scatter ashes? Is there a protocol? She'd shaken the container quite hard to get it all out. Goodbye, Wizard, goodbye. Then she said, Well, thanks.

He said, Hey, it's my job. He looked around the orchard, the knuckled trees and long grass. He said, The deer come around in the early morning. So he won't be, you know, alone.

She'd felt the wash of kindness. He was kind. He looked different. He didn't even want the Tupperware container back.

❧ ❧ ❧

Animals loved him. Her mother had taken that Rotzu, a convoluted-looking dog, and called it Wizard because it was easier. But she had told her mother it needed a new name, a fresh start. And it was female, besides. When she was at her mother's, she started calling it Witch, or Witchy, or Wichita, but her mother didn't like that. It ended up as Krystle. Spelled that way. Maybe her mother had always wanted that name for herself. Her mother's name was Jean.

Sometimes she went over to her mother's to take the dog for a walk, if she had nothing else to do after work. She often left work early. Nobody at the municipal recycling office minded. There wasn't that much recycling. One day she'd decided to drive up to Jim's, to see Wizard's resting place, and to show him the new dog. She hadn't thought about Wizard much for a while, and guilt made a fur on her brain. Jim had come out of the cabin when she'd pulled up, and the new dog had tried to climb his legs and launch herself into him in delight, raving, slavering at him. Orbiting, faster and faster. It had never done that to anyone else. She'd said, Down, doggie, and she'd even said, Krystle, Krystle, no. No. But there was no hope.

Jim was still kind. He'd crouched, and the animal had ground its face against his shins, yelping and stopping to gaze and yip into his eyes. He'd smiled at it and said, Hey. Good dog, and it had rolled on its back, offering its light, fish-pink belly, its vulnerability, its life.

She didn't take Krystle when she began to stay up there at the picker's cabin. It was dark and wooden. Cosy, in fact. She didn't help him with the cremations, either, which he did up behind the orchard, on a bare patch. Sometimes she imagined she could smell dead smoke on him when she got in from the recycling office, but she never really could. He smelled like milk, nice milk, and some kind of nice dirt. Earth. Sometimes they went for walks downtown, or to get dinner, and dogs would follow him, yipping or fully crying, and making that face of flattery that dogs can make. People had to yank their dogs' leashes and say Sorry, oh my God, sorry. Cats wound around him sometimes, and once a ferret that some child had on a leash. It tried to burrow up his pant leg. She'd laughed and teased him about it. The ferret man. The ferret's one true love. But he liked them all in the same, even way. It never went to his head. Oblivious, in fact. Even when they actively lunged at him. His smell, or his molecules, or something. Love, love, and love.

Mice, too. There were mice in the cabin, which was hard to take at first, but you can get used to them. She used to think she'd caught them at the edge of her vision some evenings, running over the little stove or table, but they were too fast to see. At night she heard the dash and skitter in the walls, and he would pat her head if she hid under the blanket. They didn't bother Jim, he said. Sometimes they stayed over at her place instead, but that made her more nervous, somehow. He might not like her sheets, or want some food she didn't have. Her taste seemed very fluffy then. Fat pillows, marshmallows, instant mashed potatoes. But it was always all right. He liked everything. But still. Mainly she stayed there alone, or went to his place. His, and the mice's.

He had some old wooden traps, which he eventually set up. She hated their dumb snapping, but they were necessary. They were full the next morning, always. One trap had even caught two mice with one blow, flattening both their heads into one: the brain with two mice. She would look at them, but couldn't empty the traps. Jim didn't mind. He would put the mice in the garbage, though, not cremate them. It wasn't worth it, even though they seemed to keep coming. She'd said, once, looking at the morning's kill, How are there so many of them?

Jim said, I don't know. They must like you.

She'd laughed and hidden her eyes as he wrapped up the dead in a Safeway bag. They were up to thirty-seven. He kept a running count. It was a joke, their joke. If it was a joke.

Was it that night she found the baby mouse? Yes. It was there, right outside the front door of the cabin, lying as if dropped, and she'd heard its faraway peeping when she arrived after work. Finally she spotted it, the source, grey on the concrete path before her foot. It sounded like a squeaky toy. Jim, she'd said. Jim.

He came out, and she was already sogged, weeping and weeping over it, but unable to touch it. We need to do something, she said. We.

He picked it up. It was a speck, a fuzzed pill, in his big hand. Its eyes weren't even open, and its skin showed through its fur. Ah, Jim said. Ah. Just like breathing. The ease of it, the kindness. It made the mouse squeak fiercely, or desperately, in answer. He took it inside.

They kept it in a shoebox, and called it Naturalizer. Its eyes still weren't open, but they fed it with an eyedropper. She got some kitten milk from the pet store. At first she was alarmed that this might actually come from mother cats, with breasts. But it didn't. The mouse drank it, and lived in its paper-towel nest and tottered around its box. It had a smell. Urinous and specific. They kept it going for days. She started staying over all the time, then, even though there was no electricity and she had to wash at the sink and go to work with wet hair. One morning, when she got up, Jim had gone out on some early errand, to get gas, maybe. She shot awake at the old alarm clock and right away, she went for the box on the table. She opened it, calling, Hey, Naturalizer. Hey, Mousie. But the paper towel was dotted with little red blossoms, and the mouse was under a shred of it in a corner, on its back, gulping with its whole body, and then dead. Its pinhole mouth had blood around it. Such a small amount of blood. She'd cried over it for two hours. So.

What had they done?

She hadn't gone to work. She'd cried further when Jim came home, and when he cleared out the daily traps. She wanted him to go and cremate the baby mouse, so he did, but she didn't want to watch. She didn't want to think about it again. She stayed in the cabin and tried not to listen to the scrabbles in the walls. But you have to move, and listen, sometime.

When she got back from the office the next day, he'd been waiting on the front step. He'd said, Hey, look at this. A present, he said. He held a square shape out to her. She lifted the pillowcase from it and saw a cage, a little dented, probably secondhand, with an animal in it. A wheel, and a water bottle, and a toothy, black-eyed little animal. A hamster. It's kind of like a mouse, but it can be a pet, Jim said.

It had its own smell. Urinous, too, but different. Something male about it. It did have strangely large private parts. Fascinating, in fact. She tried not to look. But she watched the hamster, its face-washing and speed chewing and brisk quivering, all the time, and she was proud. She took it to show her mother, in its cage. Krystle the Rotzu sniffed through the bars. Her mother said she should call it Kevin. Eventually, she did, because she couldn't think of anything else. Kevin liked seeds, and kept her awake at night sometimes, running and running on his wheel, or crunching. It isn't right to cry over mice, especially when you are killing them, or hamsters, really, but she had cried, when Kevin died after a few months. They don't live long.

She'd cried more than she had over the baby mouse. She lay on the bed, oozing a damp halo around her face. Jim didn't seem to k

what to do, but he tried. His kindness. He patted her and held her, and said he would cremate Kevin for her. She said, No. There wouldn't be anything left, she said, and stuck her wet, clogged nose into his underarm.

Jim said, Well, I could bury him. And she said no, he couldn't, or the coyotes might dig him up. She felt marooned in that orchard. Cruelty, nature. She said it, Nature, and sniffed. She could hardly stand it. He'd patted her again, and left her to mop herself as he went outside with dead Kevin in the cage. He left in the truck.

When he returned, later in the afternoon, she was dry and sitting outside, a little glazed, thinking about Wizard's ashes over there. He gave her the cage back. It's yours, he said. Kevin was still inside, with new shining eyes and a fat stomach. All his parts. You could see the white seam under his chin. Some kind of cotton stuffing.

She said, Oh. Then she said, How did you do that?

Jim said, A buddy of mine used to do taxidermy, so I took it up there for you. It's still your present, he said. And it was. She'd kept the cage on a shelf at the cabin, hoping it was above where the mice could get to. She had become a little afraid of Kevin. She had before Kevin died, even.

❧ ❧ ❧

There might really be animal bones under the rockslide. She thought more of it, as they were driving, although the slide was a long way back there, now. They were coming up to the little town where you can stop for gas, which is the reason for its existence. Gasville. Gastoria. She thought of it that way, and laughed, and said it. Gastoria. Jim laughed, too. She kept control of her cheek-squeezing hands, a violent maiden aunt. She couldn't think of the real name of the town, and there was no sign. When she'd calmed herself a bit, she said, Anyway, do you want to stop for something to eat?

Jim said sure, and he pulled into the parking lot of the town's little restaurant. That Place, it was called. It really was. Its siding looked splintery. She didn't want to get too close. She'd always seen that place, but had never stopped there before, on her own. It was surprising to find you could actually go inside. They did go in, and a hazy waitress brought them some menus. It was warm, soupy, within. The windows steamed and blank, keeping them in.

Jim said, I think I want the steak sandwich, and she began to beam. She did. She felt herself beaming, really, like a headlight. It was perfect that he would want that, simple and wholesome and protein-filled. She said she would have one, too, and then she changed her mind, and ordered the special. You don't get that every day. You should have a few adventures in life.

She looked around. That Place was full of trailing plants, and a few other customers. A couple was at the table behind Jim, with three small children. They were all testing the remains of their food, and not speaking. But happy. Yes. The children all had their father's flared nose. Beautiful. She said, You know whose kids those are.

Whose? Jim said. But he didn't understand what she meant. One of the children, the youngest one, was staring at Jim's side from his ancient-looking highchair. The child started beaming, too, she could see it, and feel its reflection on her own face. Metallic. She felt that way around the edges, and tried to stop smiling, but how?

The food came. The special was bolstered with mashed potatoes, a circular fort. It was some kind of meat. Maybe it was steak, too. She looked at it. Jim was eating his sandwich, happy. She fed him some of her potatoes, and watched his jaw moving. That baby was still looking at him. She waved at it, but it kept its eyes on Jim's profile.

She said, after a while, Do you remember the mouse?

He said, Which one?

She said, You know, the one. The little one. A fog rose in her, pleasantly. Death at a distance. It was all right now.

He said, They keep on coming.

She said, Yes, and sat back in her fog, thinking of the mouse, and the mice in the cabin, probably dancing all over it now. Then she sat up again. She said, Do you think the children will be happy to see us?

She had been keeping that thought behind the fog, behind the sun, even, on a different planet. On a different planet, Jim had children. Two. She had seen a couple of pictures of them, but never met them. He spoke of them sometimes, but not much. They were going to see them on the coast, in their school concert. She hadn't forgotten. It was there. What play is it, again? she said. Although she did know.

Jim said, I think it has singing in it. A musical.

She said, *Fame*. You told me that time they phoned you, she said. It had been the first time she'd heard much about them.

Jim said, That's it. He smiled around the crust of his bread. He had a seed in his teeth. He was trying to look out the blurred window, at the high, dark mountains, which felt much too close to That Place. He said, Yeah, I can't wait to see them.

She said, Me, too, and he said yeah, again. The pictures she'd seen of them back in the cabin made them look faded, liquid, but that might just have been the developing. A sudden compulsion to run into the mountains, to be up there, cold and raw, meat for bears. But she didn't go. Of course. It was warm in the restaurant, and she belonged there. She frowned at the staring, beaming baby. She twiddled her fork around a few times, and asked Jim what cremations he'd done the day before, and he told her about a couple of old-lady cats. Oh, and an Alsatian, he said.

So business is good, she said. It always seemed to be. Strange, how many pets there are in the world, dying.

Yup. Sad. But good, he said.

It was sad. She wanted to go, she said, so he finished his coffee in a gulp, for her. She felt soothed. He got out his wallet. As he was taking out some money, something fell out of it. A white thing, a solid thing, with a clink to it. She picked it up. Dull white, long. A tooth. She said, What's this?

Jim said, It's a tooth.

She said, I know that. Then she curbed herself. Quiet, you. She said, Where did you get it?

He shrugged. He was looking for the waitress, and grinning back at that grinning baby, who was still there. She said, It's from that Alsatian, isn't it?

He said, What Alsatian? Still grinning.

She said, The one you did that to yesterday. The cremated one, she said. The word always made her sad. Cremated. It had a positive sound, with *mate* in it, but a false positive.

He said, What? Oh. No, not that one.

She said, Then why do you have this? She felt its bone body, its root, in her palm. Someone had once told her about people ripping out dead soldiers' teeth on the battlefield to sell to dentists, to make dentures and bridges with. She said, They don't have to do that anymore. They have other things now.

He said, What's that? He was looking around, trying to see above the wet on the windows. That lumpkin baby was tilting its head, trying to make him look at it.

She tried, but she couldn't stop it. She said, I asked you, where is this from?

I don't know, he said. A dog, I guess. A long time ago. One of the first ones.

Didn't it burn?

I guess not.

Why? she said, and then she coughed instead. She coughed a lot. She felt his wallet on the tooth, his fingerprinting. Can I have it? she said. Covetousness swooped.

He said, Okay, if you want it. He took her hand and pulled her up. Upsy-daisy, he said. She laughed, again. She had it, and they were going. But first she'd better go to the ladies' room, so she left him with her purse and things to take to the car. When she got in, she was happy again for ages.

Then she thought, and looked in the ashtray, and felt around next to the gearshift. Her hand empty. She said, But where is it?

What? he said. He'd been humming again. Hm. Hm.

She had to say it. That tooth. Where did you put it?

He said, What, the dog tooth? I gave it to that kid in the restaurant.

She said, You gave it.

He said, Yeah, there was that little kid in there, and he was crying when we were leaving, so I gave it to him to play with.

Oh. Okay, she said. Her voice tinny in her ears.

It was inappropriate, for a baby, and she knew it. And that baby had been staring and staring and staring. But she was quiet. They drove.

They got closer to the city, where the land flattens out and begins to smell like cow. Barns and silos sprouted out of the fields. She watched. The hay and corn starting up. She thought she saw a black bear, far away across one of the cornfields, but it might only have been a dog, or a cow. It was too late to see bears, anyway, now that they were on the flats, out of the mountains. She said, You know, cremation is wrong.

&ve &ve &ve

She didn't say much else for the rest of the drive into town. Neither did Jim. But he was happy, steering and humming. They found their motel, with all its matching doors in a long row, and went to their new room to change and get ready. Odd, the flat furniture and concrete walls, the reality of them. They were here. She was thinking about the children, and how they would be singing and dancing right in front of them, right up there on the stage. She caught her breath. She grabbed Jim around the waist from behind when he was putting on his tie. You don't wear ties, she said. But he did, for this.

They sat in an auditorium, with a little stage, at the school. She hadn't been expecting that, although she hadn't pictured it very clearly. It was real, too. And then happening. All those children, dancing in rows. Jim pointed out his two. Look at that, he said. Look at that.

The two children, his, were at the front of the dancing. They were very good, and looked very much alike, although not much like Jim. Their faces still, serious, but their bodies dancing astonishingly, as though detached from their serious brains. Their hair didn't move. She couldn't stop watching. When, at the end, the children all stood together and sang the lines about fame, and how they were going to live forever, and learn how to fly, then she quickly excused herself. She followed the handmade signs to the Washeroom, as they said, and went into one of the child-sized stalls. The room was empty. She opened her purse. Her first present. A real present. The real thing. She stroked the fur inside it. Kevin.

She'd almost forgotten she'd brought it, grabbing it from its cage in a last-minute panic of some kind. It had been so light in her hand. The little stuffed Kevin. In her purse, she could feel its glued eyes, its seam, but she didn't want to look. Those children, and Jim, out there, smiling at them in his nice, nice, typical way. She could still hear the singing in the stall, of course, through the vents. You can't get away from it.

# HEARTSTARTER

THIS IS THE STORY OF US. The story. There is love in it, but not that kind.

At first, for a long time, there was a kind of feeling, before it even happened: gentle jabs against the ribs, like finger-pokings, now that you think of it. What was it looking for, the nosing and puffing. A heart, a mouth, under your shirt. You had nothing for it, though, yet. It would have to wait. It did wait.

❧ ❧ ❧

The line had been sitting, inert, forever, since the beginning of time. On the old tractor seat, you broiled, the metal smell stiffening in your nostrils under the sun. The other smell, steam and diesel, stewing evilly all around. You were third in the tractor line, waiting and waiting to move. Something must have gone wrong earlier. You had sat here most of the morning in liquid boredom. Everything slowed and stupefied by heat and age. Even the engine firings seemed slow, like popcorn cooking too long: not enough pops. You wouldn't make it. You wouldn't. You weren't meant to be here. All of the tractors were *genuine antiquities*, as the programme would have it. There was a whole string behind you, with men, either grinning or ceremonial, on them. All antique, the men and the tractors, all happily waiting, as if they were figures in one of those animated museum displays. Push the button to see them move. But you didn't move. You didn't look back anymore. You stared sideways at the wavering heat, your ears crisping, trying to stay utterly still. Why didn't you have a hat?

In front of you, Shemp wore his, the one he'd always had, as far as you could remember. The little baseball cap perched high atop the mound of him. The hat said, blandly, *Wolf*, under a picture of a wolf's face, a propos of nothing. You'd seen it so many times before. The wolf had a simpery look. Under it, Shemp sat, content, the Buddha of tractors. You could see the contentment, even from behind, the contented rolls of him, rolling down towards the seat. O Shemp, lord of farm machinery. He had an expansive collection of tractors. Some of them were just oldish, not really antique, but people liked them all. People do. They like to be amazed about how things still work. The one you were sitting on was one of Shemp's; you'd driven for him in the Exhibition for a few years now. Your dad always said you'd like that, sure you would, when Shemp asked, and Shemp always replied that you'd like that, all right, sure, sure. His content face, his sureness of what people like. Where does that come from? And why do people collect anything? Stamps, coins, hockey cards, thimbles, stickers, figurines, spoons, vases, unicorns, trolls, children, souvenir dish towels, tractors. Faithful people, collecting away, meeting with others to talk about their collectables, building cabinets to contain them, planning to pass them on when they die, if they think of that. Probably they don't. They're faithful, right. They'll get to take their collections with them to heaven.

You were supposed to call Shemp by his first name. He'd told you that a little while ago. *Come on now, you're old enough to call me Bill.* You'd moved on up. He didn't call you Son, or Buddy, or Bud, but you got the feeling he might start, in his mild way, one of these days. When you were little, he'd called you Hey Big Fella. At least he wasn't the back-slapping type. He was calm, and nice enough, and always the same. Maybe he'd leave his tractors to you, in his will. Maybe the whole collection. Bestowing his largesse. Praise be to Shemp, the Great Collector. You could see him inclining his calm head, modestly acknowledging the praise, his due.

In the thin trees along the edge of the Exhibition grounds, the crows were mating. You could tell by their flapping, their noise, when you listened hard above the engines. Gurgling, pleading calls bubbling out of their throats and chests. Unearthly, but maybe with something human about them. You tried to watch, but all you could see was their black raggy wings extending and collapsing out of the trees. Then, after a little while, they started up a happier, repetitive cackle. Not exactly caw, caw. More like ha ha ha. They must have been done. You moved your head, now, trying to get a better look, but the exhaust stung into your eyes, like a punishment: wash your eyes out. Then your tractor burped under you. You wanted to burp back. Not that it could have heard you. You couldn't hear any crows, now, either. The line was still, mired forever in tractor hell. A film of diesel cooking onto your skin. An agonizingly slow march towards something. Extinction, maybe. But you didn't even know yet what you were really waiting for, what was coming to you.

The tractor in front of Shemp lurched forward. Glory, glory hallelujah. The announcer's voice was impossible to hear above the machine noise, but it must finally be time, and you could see him shouting, cowboy-hatted, at the front of the stand. The first old tractor, unpainted rust, ground its way into the show ring, as if it mattered. The man driving it was old, too, probably the oldest there, huddling desperately over the wheel like an old woman driving to the mall. People in the stands clapped, you saw them, although you still couldn't hear anything but the engines. Shemp was alert there in front of you, his flanks spilling over, and when he decisively heaved himself into gear, you followed. Your tractor was different from most of the others, a little slower, with big treads, not wheels. It wasn't as old as some of them, or as big as the red pride of Shemp in front of you. It was lower, serious and tanklike. It turned perfectly when you eased it forward. Shemp usually didn't bring this one out for parades, but he did this year; maybe it was supposed to be some kind of gift to you. Well, whatever. You hated it, you decided. You rocked its nose from side to side, slowly urging it forward through the dirt into the ring, businesslike. But making it move was pleasurable. Some of the people were watching you now, pointing. You saw. You set your lips.

Your treads made deep zipper teeth over the others' wheel marks. You kept your face down, now, but in the corner of your eye you could still see the people in the stand that ran along the far side of the ring opposite you. Still clapping, some of them, or pointing, or poking each other and shouting. Their jerky movement, an anthill seen from far away. The quick, stop-motion film of it, in your peripheral vision. In front of you, Shemp was rounding the first corner, his flesh juddering lightly, mechanically. His calm, flat smile came into your view, and you looked away. Two crows were on the top of the stand, bobbing their black heads, opening their beaks. Maybe they'd been the ones mating, and were making that laughing sound now. When you moved into the corner, the tractor's motion vibrated all through you. It wasn't unpleasant. It made you feel things. But it also had the feel of a takeover, an old takeover.

Tightness everywhere. Your leg muscles stiffening, to hold off the vibration. People were looking. As you moved closer to the crowd, you ran your eyes over the stand quickly, in case anybody you recognized was there, watching. Your parents were probably still off judging 4-H animals and crafts and all of it. You hoped they weren't here, with their own sincere faces, their belief. The sun was blasting now as you ground forward, closing in on the watching people. How was anyone supposed to stand this, all this scrutiny and heat? Like being something microwaveable. *Is it done yet? Is it cooked?* That's what those people were thinking. You kept your legs tight, and kept moving; you still had to follow in Shemp's wake past the front of the stand before you could exit the ring.

But ahead, the old tractor, the front one with the old man, had given up. Steam billowed, then collapsed. The man didn't move from his posture over the wheel. You had to stop, but you kept the engine alive. It hummed, holding itself back. All the engines bubbling and popping. Your skin, too: the crown of your head feeling like paint just before it blisters. You raised your hand to it gingerly. You stopped when some of the people started waving, as if that's what you'd been about to do. Shemp, ahead, under his little Wolf cap, was giving a serene thumbs-up to the crowd. Both thumbs. You ducked your broiling head, staring down at the gauges, keeping yourself to yourself, which is what they'd always told you to do in school during tests, anyway.

The machines were winning. You were stuck, apparently forever. And someone was looking at you. Your face prickled with it. A little kid in the front row, only a few feet away. You could feel his prodding look, through the fumes and the noise. Finally you had to turn and look back. His stare, behind big blue-framed plastic sunglasses. His hair was bleached out to a thin haystack, and he had a stick fluffed with cotton candy in each hand. Staring, he suddenly waggled the sticks like fat tails. Why did he need two? He wasn't even eating them. You gave the engine a little, roaring it. The kid didn't do anything, but continued his looking and waggling, as if signalling you, as if directing traffic. *Look at me. I'm a kid, with sunglasses and cuteness. Look at my sunglasses. Look at my cuteness.*

*You keep yourself to yourself*, you felt like saying. *You keep yourself.* You revved at him twice, but you stopped when he started grinning, showing you his shiny separate little wet kid teeth. There were better things than this. You did already know that, though not entirely, not yet.

Finally, finally, you were moving again. You cursed the ancient tractors liberally, willing the old man not to stall it now. Come on. Come on. It worked: the man inched the machine unsteadily towards the exit. You revved your engine hard, butting up to Shemp's slow rear. And you did get out of the ring, away from the kid, out to the field where the tractors were supposed to be parked for viewings and demonstrations. Once you'd swung the machine around beside Shemp's, you got off, your eyes and skin hurting. Shemp remained enthroned on his tractor, surveying the realm, satisfied. You walked off, squinting, before he could talk to you. Maybe you'd head for the concession and get a drink, if you could stand having to get over there. Everywhere, people were milling around in little gangs, walking slowly and looking at things. The Exhibition was always busier in the afternoons, and people can't walk and look at the same time. You dodged around some of them, and kept going. Your eyes still stinging and squinting.

Something was coming towards you. It was real. A creature. Hot pink, bulging-eyed, thick-limbed. A sketchy look to its giant, raw face, the whites of its eyes, its nostril-pits, its coy hole of a mouth. A huge stuffed pig.

It was carried by a shuffling kid, whose upper body was invisible behind it. The kid must have won it at the amusements, or somebody won it for him. The gigantic pig kept wobbling towards you, its fake size and plush and pink coming on and on. A monster. A criminal object. You stared, even though your eyes hurt more. It would have rammed straight into you, if you hadn't moved out of the way. You stood there, watching it being carried off, the stuffed legs stiff in the air. A hot wave came over you, at the sight of that pig, the thing that it was. You understood it later.

❧ ❧ ❧

Your brother, older, was in 4-H still, one of its shining stars. He practically ran it now. He still bred pigs once in a while, for fun. You didn't see him all that often now, but when you were little kids, you each had a couple of piglets to raise every year after the sows pumped them out in the spring. Your brother always named his Breakfast and Lunch. Sometimes Dinner and Snack, if he had enough piglets. He didn't really mean it to be funny. He was sincere, and matter-of-fact. So were his pigs, which always became solid, their burliness winning him prizes at the Exhibition. He had the pig touch, and other, related touches. He used to write poems about life. They always rhymed.

*Life is like a farm*
*It will do you no harm*

*If you are good*
*And live the way you should*

Why do you remember that? But you do. The solidity, the reason of it: how could you argue? Your brother was always practical, too, painstaking over school math homework, measuring perfectly spaced steps around each room in the house to figure out the house's exact area. You, by contrast, would dash off research reports out of your own brain. You chose what you thought were exotic subjects, so the teacher wouldn't be able to check up on you so easily. *The Zebra. The Platypus. Leprosy.* When you had to do *The Human Body* for a science class, you wrote, *The human foot contains over three hundred bones. Many people do not know this,* you wrote: a challenge. Teachers never said much about it. So maybe you were right. Maybe.

Your brother was finished school, married now already, with a kid on the way, or maybe a litter, which would be more efficient, and more like him.

After a while, when you were younger, you hadn't cared too much about pigs any more, even when they were freshly born and blind. You'd given up on raising them after a couple of years. You tried a few other 4-H things, when your parents nudged. Even Male Baking, one year. Pastry pinwheels, you think you did once, with your mum's little tips on mixing and oven temperature. They ended up looking like swastikas. There were also blown loaves of white bread, hard caverns of air. You weren't a star or even a male starlet of 4-H; you didn't win any of your categories, although you got a third place once, probably out of pity. Some of your brother's blue pig ribbons were in a desk drawer on his side of the room, with other artefacts of his life. Maybe he was collecting them to pass on to his future children, to prove how he had lived. At night, his nose made a very high, soft whistle as he slept the sleep of the right. It had the sound of a faraway pig, as if he were tuned in to one of the sties outside.

He might be over at the Exhibition barns now, where the show animals were kept. You headed over that way, tagging after familiarity, away from shrieky kids and their sunglasses and big fake animals. Maybe you'd go take a look and see what he'd produced this time. Probably your brother had been busy running things here all day, making sure everything was clean and A-okay, as he would say. He had that cleanness, a kind of scrubbed, determined innocence, like 4-H itself, to him. It made you feel sorry for him, but also for yourself, in a way.

Inside, it was cooler. Relief hitting. Quite a few people, but not as many as outside. The cool, known smell. The manure and straw, the wet pathways, hosed down. You wandered down one of the aisles. The cows were big this year, bigger than you remembered, lying in their stalls, close enough for people to touch, chewing languidly. The Holsteins: their pale skins, their still shapes, like warm marble, over life-size. Not unhappy, in their cow life, chewing and giving off heat. No need to be happy or unhappy. You lay your palm on one of them, to show you knew how. The cow didn't flinch or flicker its skin, and you were relieved. You gave it a couple of short pats, thanking it.

That's 3000 pounds of prime beef on the trot. 3000 pounds each.

The voice was near you. Was it talking to you? You turned and saw the man there, staring at the cows. A woman with him said, Oh, but they're so pretty. Just look at those pretty pretty eyelashes, she said, leaning over the stall gate.

Pretty pretty filet mignon, extra rare, the man said, and they laughed, and you moved off, away. You were irritated for the cows' sake. Why? You ate steak, and hamburger, and had seen animals killed and butchered. You'd seen their flesh from the inside.

You headed down another aisle, away from the doors. The pigs were this way, after the goats. Not many people were down here. Good. It smelled cleaner than the cow end, like fresher straw, kind of like your brother. You looked around, but you didn't see him. You walked past all the pens, where the pigs were mainly quiet, some of them making soft sounds. White flesh, pinkish flesh, some with black spottings. Pretty bacon, pretty pork chops, you thought, thinking like the man back there, or like your brother, with his Breakfast and Lunch.

The 4-H prizewinners were here at the end, with stars pinned to their nametags. At the second-place piglet, you stopped. You didn't look at its name; who knew what hideousness had been dreamed up this year. But the pig was pretty cute. It was pink, with heavy, white-lashed eyes and straight little legs. You watched as it snuffled squarely round its pen, then, right in the centre, raised its tail and *eliminated*. Your dad's word, one of his uncharacteristically delicate expressions about the animals. He had a few of these that he aired now and then. Another one was pig *excreta*, which made you smirk and elbow your brother, who would smile politely, but then nod, as if storing up the word for his own uses. Or in the fall, your dad would talk about the pigs *partnering*, as though they were free in the Garden of Eden, seeking out just the right mate for a porcine dance, for true porcine love, for life. The word quite sweet on his lips. As though he and others weren't all standing around watching the partnering in the pig yard, or shoveling up the excreta around them.

The piglet, finished, looked at you. It didn't mind your looking. Then it eliminated again, raising its snout at you as it did. Watching, a happiness came. Happiness: this could be its name, you thought. It should be. But it didn't need a name, a stupid word said stupidly aloud. The piglet was so clean, so upfront about itself. Its contentment nothing like Shemp's, which whiffed of smugness, and nothing like your brother's cultivated wholesomeness, either. You watched the pig in its pen. A wish that you, too, were bare flesh of this kind. Pure pink, with soft white hairs that would shine white out in the sun. You thought of taking off your shirt to look at yourself; it was still hot, even in the shadowy corner of the barns. And it was the Exhibition, after all. The Ex, everybody called it. Down at the Ex. The sharp, final sound of it, even though it was here every year, every year, every year, always the same, the same smells and food and shows and people. But the animals were new each time. The fresh crop of them. It's easy to think they're always exactly the same, too. But they aren't.

*One tipple before lunch keeps the system going.* The phrase whistled into your mind, then. It was Shemp who said this. You'd heard him say it more than once, when you'd been around his place, and he'd offered your dad a quick drink. A tipple. His voice had followed you; you were supposed to meet him soon now to help load the tractors onto his big flat-deck trailer for the trip home again. You left the pig and the barn.

Outside, you felt slowed, as if you did need something to get your system going again. You were thirsty, and your eyes wouldn't readjust to the scorched daylight. Vague thoughts of drinking, real drinking. Shemp didn't seem the type to drink much. He raised dairy cattle. He probably drank milk straight from the cow, healthy white froth on his upper lip.

Maybe that's the tipple he meant. *Milk: make it your tipple,* you thought, in an advertiser's voice. It wasn't bad. The ring of *nipple* about it. What rhymes with udder, you wondered. One of the cows bawled from back in the barn, as if it had heard you thinking.

Following the weedy edge of the grounds, you kept away from most of the other people. At the back lot, where the exhibitors parked, two people were coaxing a horse into a trailer on the far side. The rest was just baked cars, more cars, and trailers. And ahead of you, here was Shemp already, waiting, standing outlined against the afternoon. Short, bandy, the crotch of his pants sinking towards his knees, the pant legs bunching above his ankles. The slant to the back of his head, apelike, sloping straight down into his shoulders. He bent over the trailer hitch behind his truck, loosening something. And he was loosening. He was gently sliding down under it, in the truck's shade, and he was gently landing on the ground, on his face, in the hot, starched grass.

There he was. Your neighbour from down the road, who wanted you to call him Bill, whom you'd known all your life. That's Bill, you thought, with a kind of dumb classification. Not drunk. No. He'd taught you to drive a tractor, to find the gears, to steer, and reverse in a tight arc. Your neighbour from down the road, facedown on the ground in the parking lot, his Wolf cap tipped over.

You stop, then you run, kneeling beside him, turning him onto his back. CPR. ABC: Airway, Breathing, Compressions. Letters to remember, in sequence. And you know them. Your mind works cleanly, this way, for strings of letters, for procedures. You open his collar. The hairs peering from it, the sweat stains creeping around the shirt, the humid, trapped smell rising. You listen for breathing, which isn't there, so you open the mouth, check for obstructions. You pinch the man's nose and seal your lips over his. The poke of stubble, the milky whiff: but you don't think about it, you don't notice, you are only breathing, puffing two long puffs into the slack, soft opening. One, two. Then your hands firmly pressing down and down, above the bottom of the sternum. Thirty pushes, the numbers thumping along as you compress the chest. The soft crackle of ribs beneath the fat. Then two more breaths, thirty more pushes. Thirty to two, thirty to two. The ear to the chest, the fingers searching in the neck. The small gasp, the pulse fluttering and kicking, weakly grateful, the heart soon finding its old rhythm, banging along as if it will never stop again.

❧ ❧ ❧

This is how the story should probably go. But it's not really the story. The real one is the story of us, remember.

That feeling of poking at you, at your own chest, was different. But what did happen then made you recognize its presence. As you stood, rigid, your brain blank, you first thought of tipples. But then a sentence came to you. *Life doesn't owe us a living.* A bit of pride in that, the quiet, ringing tone of it. It was a good one. You thought it again, in the advertiser's voice. You'd heard it before, from your dad, when he was lecturing about blah blah blah, but you understood it differently now. It became clearer. It meant that life shouldn't always go on living just because it's already started. Look at all the litters that die, the coyotes that rip the heads off chickens and leave the rest, the rampant waste. Look: even nature itself was saying so. Shemp would go on driving tractors in the tractor parade for the next few years, until he was the old, old man stalling the old tractor at the front. Or he would be stuck in a hospital, with tubes snaking from him. And men's hearts give out, give up. Easy knockouts.

You went a few steps closer, and tentatively looked at Shemp's face. He had managed to turn himself over, and raise his head, resting it against the wheel of the truck. The face a faded shade of mauve, with loose eyelids and a slick of sweat. A looser sound came from the chest, but Shemp said nothing. Wheezy mouth-breathing only, still coming, getting soft. He didn't lift his eyes to you, though they were open. Accepting. Nobody else could see him. Probably he didn't want to be seen.

&&& &&& &&&

You went on, into the real ending. You went back to the barns, which were very quiet now. The place getting ready to shut down for the day. The cooler dark again. You knew where the piglet was, and you went straight back to it. You looked at its sleeping pink form in the straw. The gigantic stuffed pig you'd seen with that kid was a blaze of mockery, with plastic sewn-on eyes. This was the real thing.

Instinct: we are all supposed to have it. We do. But animals have it better, more clearly. The piglet eating and sleeping and breathing and eliminating. And partnering, of course. You checked the tag on the pen gate, hiding the name with your palm: yes, the piglet was a male. He would have male instincts. It was hard not to think of them as being exactly like human ones, full of twists and corners and a need for flashes of novelty, as well as embarrassment at their own existence. You knew already that this is how it is for us. But you couldn't think of your dad this way, bulging and straining and shooting you into life, having to think of something interesting to make you happen. Splat. Then the inevitable cleanup. Don't think of yourself like this, either, of what you inherited as a member of the species, of that dull dread that is part of it all. Hunching over a little, all the time, in case it announces itself in your pants, and other people see. Igor-like around the shoulders, head down, slouching along squint-eyed. It had nearly happened in the tractor parade today, with the vibrating engine. Immediately, you hunched over, just thinking about it.

But pigs. They'll do it anywhere, and with just about any other pig. The males *going to it* with each other sometimes. This was your mum's expression, which she would say even more delicately than your dad, with his partnering. Even pig relatives going to it. The mother with the sons, or the brother with the sisters. They're all cousins on a farm anyway, of course. And they don't mind it. They don't mind who sees them. They are neutral in expression as they do so, as people look on. The same as when they eliminate. This is what's clean about them, all their instincts. They are intelligent, and they don't mind. They are just there.

You stared at the piglet, bending closer. It was beautiful. Beautiful pig. The most beautiful. You loved it, then. But it wasn't like that. You didn't want to partner or go to it. One of the farm workers was caught that way with the big sows in the sty a couple of times, and that's why he was really fired; you'd heard the rumours. This wasn't what you wanted. Looking at the sleeping piglet, you accepted its separateness. You liked it. You preferred it. The separateness was apparent, a bare fact, different from the way it was with people, which you were supposed to be, though you were not like most of them. You didn't feel too bad about that.

Early on, surgeons tried to perform organ trans-plants — xenotransplants — from pigs. Pigs' hearts into dying people. Not just the valves or tissues, the whole heart. Cows and baboons were other sources. It didn't work, of course, although they got close, with pigs. But what an idea. What a thing to think about. The pure heart, like the flesh of the pig, clean-tasting and pink, no mottling or veining, beating away in a human chest. You'd always liked the taste of ham, bacon. It was part of your liking for pigs. You liked everything. Their deaths are clean, too, like their other instincts. When they die, they just die, and usually they become food, and that is the end.

If you'd had to have a transplant from one, you wouldn't have taken the anti-rejection drugs. You wouldn't have even had to, probably. You would have gotten used to it being there. You would have been all right.

You reached into the pen. The piglet twitched as you touched its back, but it was used to being handled by its 4-H owner. You picked it up, scooping it towards you, stroking its neck and head. Its warm, lightly furred little body, its soft, boneless ears. It made a few sounds, then settled against your inner arm. Slowly, you tucked it under your shirt, next to your skin, and walked out of the building, one arm over your belly, as if you'd eaten too many mini-doughnuts, or you'd snatched and gobbled the cotton candy from that kid in the stand, watching the kid cry. Your body automatically took its hunched position, but now you were happy doing it.

The tractor was still parked in the field; most of the others had gone, except the ones from Shemp's collection. You got on the one you'd driven earlier. It was yours, now, in a way, you supposed. You looked over towards the back lot, where the truck was, with a little mental salute. That was done. You started up the tractor. The piglet's body moving at the engine sounds, its trotters pressing against your ribs as though you were a piano. The snout moving against you, nosing towards your chest. This is what you had been feeling all your life. You turned the tractor towards one of the side exit gates. Hi there, you said, to the pig's small, pulsing movements. You almost said, Hey, buddy. But no, not a buddy. You weren't that. Instead, like two clams sitting, washed up on a beach, just sitting and being, not talking, sealed up, but close.

# ROMANCE

A HOSPITAL, OR A HOME. NO — A HOTEL. A better H. Four stars. More. A flat, sandy beach, then flatter ocean. It will never get rough. There will be hotels along the waterfront, with a promenade, a wooden one, where you can walk. The sunsets will be beautiful from there. People will go out there to walk in the evening, maybe down to the sand, or to the water.

Retired. Old. All women, and their old sloping backs will match the beach. Beautiful. I'll walk there, and they'll all be women, all widows. Then I will be happy.

❧ ❧ ❧

He was there to be a friend. A paid one. *Friendship's Offering*: his mum had an old book with the words frilling down its spine. He'd seen it on the shelf in her room, part of her décor. His mum was the one who set this up. People she knew from somewhere. Golf, maybe. She knew a lot of people.

He stood on the wooden deck and looked down at the yard, the lake. Grass rolling its thick way down to the rocks and water. The kids running around. Watery air, sagging with heat. One of the boys was taking off his shirt, but it got caught around his face. The boy bawled into the material.

Mrs. came out of the cottage. Cottage. It was bigger than most people's houses, with a hot tub and about sixty bedrooms. Not sixty, but a lot of them. He had his own, near the kids' rooms. Behind him, she called, You need to keep your shirt on, Jacob. You'll get a sunburn.

He felt her come up beside him. She was smiling at the little boy, and then at him. How are you doing, Tim, she said.

Ahh, his name was wrong, especially out loud. A storybook name, a tiny name. Fine, he said. He was supposed to call her Ellen, but she was still a Mrs. He didn't usually say her name out loud, either way. He didn't usually call anybody anything. He knew a lot of people, too. People liked him, almost always. Right now he couldn't even remember the kids' names, but it would be all right. The huge lawn, and the baked sky, and the kids under it. The one was still bawling. Tim said, Should I take them inside?

She was warm, too. He could feel her without looking. She said, No, no, they seem happy. Go ahead and play, she said. She touched his arm, as if she would turn him to gold.

Okay, great, he said. That was why he was here. Friendship's offering. Or his mum's. But he was already getting used to it, to being here. Mrs. went back inside, where the other people were talking and laughing in the kitchen. They sounded like birds, maybe quail or gulls. He stepped off the deck into the soft lawn, expanding. His ears were still full of plane and the wrong pressure, but he was in the right place now, and finally he felt it. His skin heightened, aware. A new element. The right one.

On the plane, the kids had watched the movies, and looked at him for a long time. He'd been dreading the trip, in a way. But it wasn't bad. They seemed like good kids. Maybe a little weird. He'd known they were triplets, but his mum hadn't said there was something wrong with one of them. The girl. Her head was oversized, just slightly, and one of her eyes looked as though it were starting to run down her face, like an egg. A whole eye, crying itself out. Tim had looked at her for a while on the plane, but she was sitting the farthest away from him, next to the window, and she seemed to be sleeping. The boys were normal. They looked alike, and they talked a lot, so you could understand, even though they were so little, not even two yet. What was wrong with the girl? Maybe it was because Mrs. was older, probably in her forties. Maybe the babies had been made in a lab, however that worked. He thought about it for a minute: cells, insides.

He was there to help. He was the help, he supposed. Their nanny from home was on her own holiday. Mrs. had told him about her and how good she was, even though she once ate all the Rice Krispie squares Mrs. had made for the children, and she tended to talk on the phone quite a lot. He stretched his neck. The summer paved itself easily ahead, as he walked towards the stuck, yelling boy. He was supposed to be good with kids. He was. No effort. A gift. His neighbours at home had young children, and he played around with them sometimes, and they worshipped him, almost literally. The Church of Tim. When he was over there once, the little boy had wanted to play that he was Tim. The girl had said the same thing, and they'd fought about it, and then both spent the afternoon being Tim. They were serious. The boy had pulled his hair forward, fierce. Go, grow, he'd said to it urgently. That way.

Tim's shadow stood out on the lawn. He was tall already, probably still growing. On the plane, Mrs. had said, It will be so good for the boys to have another guy to play around with. And for Olivia, too, she'd said. And now he was there, with them, alone. That one, Jacob, had finally pulled his shirt up around his forehead, and was running around with it like long, bright hair. The other one said, Me, too, and he came to Tim with his arms up. Tim smiled. You have to like kids. Their little arms and legs, like little working mechanical parts. He said, Okay, and pulled the other boy's shirt up. Then he did his own. His white terrain of chest. The shirt like sweat down his upper back. Were the adults watching? The little boys laughed, and kept laughing. He laughed, too. He would be tanned soon; his skin changed quickly. He lunged after one of the boys, growling and swiping.

Then he saw the little girl off near the border shrubs, tipping downhill. Maybe he should go get her. He looked around, then went over and picked her up, holding her a little away from him, and put her back up on the deck. She felt inanimate, but then she twitched. Hey there, he said, and went back to the boys, and the girl fake-cried for a while above them.

They had a campfire later, down at a specially built bowl carved into the beach. The benches were curving granite, and the fire in the pit matched the sunset, like a paint sample card, which his mum always had all over the place. The little boys sat on Tim's knees, one each. Their easy, roll-over affection. Children that small will love anyone, anyone who is nice enough to them. If their parents died, they would forget soon, if someone kind enough were there to take their place. Tim knew this. One of the boys was leaning against his arm, and he could smell the grassy hair. Mr. and Mrs. and the others, Mr.'s brother and his wife, were still laughing and cocktailing. A catalogue page, the way they were positioned, their clothes. The background of water slipping up the beach, then back. The fire's extra heat, the even lake. This was it. He skewered marshmallows for the boys to toast, and gave them out like awards. The kids were awed. Mrs. said they should be careful, but she was smiling. The little boys held the skewers so carefully, with tight focus. One set his ablaze in the fire, blackening it, and began to cry. Oh no, Tim said. He took it and waved it gently, a wand. I like them this way, he said to the boy. He ate the extinguished marshmallow, the cindered skin, the spilling flesh.

The boy stopped crying. Me, too, he said. Me.

The crackling rose when Tim was threading another marshmallow for him. A distant, staticked wail, an ancient broadcast. Mrs. breathed out. She sounded far away, too, into cocktails. The noise was the baby monitor beside her on the bench. She stood. It's Olivia, she said. Olivia was in bed already, back in the house. She hadn't stopped the miserable fake-crying most of the evening while Tim had played with the boys. But now these sounded like real cries. He listened, for a second. She was something different, something else, something misshapen, misconceived. He hadn't thought of her again until now. Mrs. was dusting herself off, backlit by the sky. The other woman, the sister-in-law, looked at Tim. Her eyes, church windows, high-eyebrowed.

I'll go. I can go, he said, after a second. I'll be right back, he said, to Jacob and the other one. Make me some more marsh-mallows, he said, and they were laughing and waving their skewers, and the women smiled down on everything.

Are you sure? Mrs. asked. She won't stop, she said. Wariness. Relief. Her eyes on him, asking.

Tim said, Sure. And she was already sitting down again, happy in her place, and they were talking again, and it was his job. He started up the beach, and over the lawn. It felt like a long way. The adult voices, then crackling cries dotting the air.

Up inside the darker house, the sound was quieter, muffled, as though something had been turned down. He left the lights off, and went up the huge staircase into the second-floor dark, the boxed heat of it. A cottage can't have air-conditioning, right? No, not a cottage. Ha. He knew the kids' rooms were down the hall from his, and she had her own. The crying didn't change or develop. He found where it was coming from, and stood in the doorway of the dark, warm room. It smelled baby, the high damp smell of diaper and sweat.

After a second, he went in. The feel of walking into honey.

So. What should he say? What do you say, to a baby? One like that. With anyone else, he would have known. He stood over the crib and listened to the unending sounds. She hadn't seen him. Her eyes, the good one and the sad one, were fastened shut, and her wet face shone in the dim. Hey, he said, finally, in his best soft voice. What is it? What is it, hey? he said. She wouldn't be able to see him smiling.

The girl opened her eyes. The sad one drooped away from him, then rolled back into her skull. She heard his voice. Still crying. Little breath catches.

Hey there, he said. He put his hand on her hair. It felt dampened, stuck, like a fur. It's okay, he said. She stopped. Stopped. She turned her face to him, and raised one of her hands, then dropped it.

He looked at her for a little while, and decided to love her.

≈ ≈ ≈

In the cottage, views triumphed from almost every window. Look here. Look. The place was hard to believe. The endless looking. You couldn't escape the lake, spreading itself out, as if for you. There were other so-called cottages up and down the lake, set in little bays and coves as if they'd sprouted themselves, perfectly, like the huge perfect trees. The family had a gardener, and someone who came to clean a couple of times a week. But the house was old, not fake-old. Parts of it, anyway. It had belonged to Mrs.'s family since around the dawn of time. She had told Tim about it on the way from the airport. It was modern inside, with a huge kitchen and private bathrooms for each bedroom, but it had its old log shell around the original part, which was now the main family room, as she called it. They had been going there for years in the summers, even after she got married and they moved out west. Tradition. A line. You could sit down at the shore in one of the old, big chairs and watch the boats in the haze, or listen to mosquitoes. Mosquitoes were everywhere, but they never bit Tim, or any of them, much. The heat shimmered, and the lake was clear broth. It had sharp little mussels living on its rocky bottom. Everyone was careful, and wore water shoes, and made mussel jokes. There were no mountains, which made Tim feel exposed at first, but he started to like it. The little boys loved it all, sunk into it, as though they'd lived there for all time. They could, if they wanted to, one day.

Tim and the boys were mainly outside. He let them run after him, and took them into the water and threw them around if the adults were down on the wharf, or sat under one of the trees and closed his eyes, and sometimes opened them up to watch the kids do tricks for him. They were always laughing, shrieking with it, high on it. He was getting tanned. He watched Olivia, too, but from farther away. He checked on her every so often. She was usually in a playpen on the deck. She was very silent now, after the first day, always playing with two alphabet blocks, C and Q. Mrs. said they were her favourites, who knew why? Mrs. seemed hunched, caught, when she talked about Olivia. Responsible for this. Tim could see it, even though Mrs. was with her a lot, always cuddling and singing at her. When Olivia was in the playpen once, and Mrs. was sitting there with magazines, he said something. He could take over, he said. Mrs. was uncertain, looking at the baby. She's not a people person, she said, laughing again.

But her eyes went to the boats, and Tim said, I can watch her up here. The first two times, she refused, sitting there forlorn and brave with the magazines. But now the others called up from the wharf. They were going to boat over to see some friends down the water, and she clutched. She said, You are a charmer. The kids just love having you around. And she kissed Olivia's big head, and fluttered, and was so obviously free.

Tim watched the boys digging at something in the lawn, happy. After a while, he walked over to Olivia's silent playpen. She had her blocks in her hands, and looked up at him from under her sunhat. Her sad eye, her old-lady face, with it. Hi there you, he said. The appeal. Charm. He felt it coming out. She listened, but stayed quiet. Mrs. said she wasn't speaking yet. He didn't blame her. With those two talking, talking brothers, she probably had no choice. Tim could see them all, jammed in the womb, and she with not enough space, trodden at the bottom. Maybe that was what happened to her. Poor kid. He bent and picked her up carefully. She held onto her blocks. Down in the grass, one of the boys screamed, Lookit. Lookit.

The morning went quickly. He held Olivia, and she didn't cry. She didn't feel heavy now, not even with her wobbling head, although she didn't move much. The other people, the adults, were gone the whole time, but it was fine. Maybe better. Tim made lunch. Happy sandwiches, with ketchup smeared in gory smiles on the bread. The boys were dazzled. He cut one for Olivia into little bites, and she pushed them into her mouth and chewed. It worked. Tim found things in the kitchen, all kinds of things. He was at home. The shining surfaces, the huge grid of stove. The view. He ate six sandwiches and ketchup. Always hungry, despite his thinness. His mum was jealous. *If I had your body*.

He gave Olivia a second half-sandwich, cut up, and she continued to eat. Her head pleased him now. It seemed better than a usual head, thinner of skull, fuller, but secretive. He put his hand on it, very lightly, and she continued chewing.

In the afternoon, the kids had naps. He sat in Olivia's room because she wouldn't sleep. She wasn't crying. She seemed to be listening to something. The air, the speed boats winding up outside. The mosquitoes. When Jacob or the other one eventually woke up and started calling from the next room, Tim picked up Olivia and took her with him. He didn't put her down for the rest of the day. So quiet. You've never seen a kid like it. She was apart. Not uninterested, just separate. Her sad eye and her happier one had balance. She let him look at her, but didn't look back much. Sometimes she seemed to watch the boys running and throwing things, as if she knew the formula for what they were doing: their velocity, their force.

Tim carried her down to the campfire that evening. The boys ran ahead. Mrs. was already there, wind-fluffed from the boat trip, but peaceful. Mr. had his arm around her waist, and the other two were pouring drinks at the granite bar built into the beach. Mrs. said, Oh. Then she said, Well, hi, Olivia. Hello, sweetie pie. She reached out for her, and Tim passed her over. His arms felt loose.

Mr. said, So, what have you guys been up to today? Come on over here, big guys, he said to the boys, but they were sniffing at marshmallows by the fire pit.

Tim said, You know. We've been busy. He could see Mrs. rubbing the baby's toes. The small feet, like little blind underground creatures.

Mr. said, We should get a soccer game going. Would you guys like that? He clapped. Yeah.

The two boys were staring at the fire, hungry for it. Tim said, Yeah, that would be good. He was indifferent to Mr., who was a jock, but old. A golf jock. Tim sat down, skewering a marshmallow for one of the kids' scrabbling hands. He stretched out his legs, and felt the sun sinking west.

Mrs. said, Well, Tim needs time for fun, too. You should go down to the public beach tomorrow for a while, before these little monsters take you over completely. It's nice down there, she said. Queen of her own beach, holding Olivia.

Tim said, Yeah, maybe, Ellen. Her name had come out of him. Easy. Then he said, I actually prefer Timothy, although nobody called him that, not even his mum, or his grandma. Now it was good, in his mind. Its three skipping beats, its harder beginning. It was longer.

❧ ❧ ❧

The boys ignored Olivia most of the time. They didn't seem to recognize her. Tim tried to get them to play with her, house or some other game, but they looked at her for a minute, then turned to dig the yard again. Always digging and rooting. Their land. If they did talk about her, they called her something like Libya, something foreign and untrustworthy. The little girl seemed content enough. She liked Tim, he could feel that from her. Not just general baby like. It wasn't. He was pretty sure now. She was used to him picking her up, and changing her diaper, and carrying her around. He taught the boys to pee standing up, in the yard, or in the lake, when the adults weren't there. It was easier than keeping them in clean diapers, or dragging them all into one of the bathrooms, even though the bathrooms were huge. He let Olivia walk around on the grass, her walk, high-footed and toes pointing, like a wading bird. Or a pixie. How did he know that word? Well, there were things he just knew about, without trying.

He sat in the grass and watched them a lot. He made hordes of sandwiches. He taught the boys to do push-ups, too, when they bugged him. His arms were stronger, maybe from carrying the baby. Ellen made efforts to stay with them, and make meals and snacks, but she moved in and out. She kept telling him to take some time for himself. She told him one afternoon again to go on down to the public beach and see what it was like. She insisted. He could tell them all his stories when he got back, she said. Tim felt her guilt, her nerves on his behalf. He said, Okay. Then he said, I could take Olivia.

Ellen was looking vague. That lake look on her face, flat and smooth. More guilt. Oh, you don't have to, she said. Then she said, Are you sure? Not the boys, just Olivia.

Tim said, Yeah, sure. And he saw the impression in the lake, the drop and ripple of relief. Just for a second. Ellen said he really was amazing, and the boys just loved him, and he was so good with all of them, and blah blah.

❧ ❧ ❧

The turnoff to the public beach was down the way, past some of the other cottage driveways. He went slowly, rolled into warm gear by the sun. In her stroller, the baby looked at things silently. It didn't feel weird to push it along, although he'd never really done it before. He said, So, Olivia, going down to the public beach. He talked to her as he would to anyone else, anyone his own age. *Public* had begun to take on connotations. Like washrooms. Olivia said nothing, and he said, Hard to get. Tease.

In the sand, the stroller had a harder time, like a tank in a desert, maybe. The feel of it, as he shoved the wheels out of a deep, dry pocket. A few feet onto the beach, they stopped. He'd forgotten about other people, besides Ellen and the other ones. Often, he forgot about them, too, because now they were usually out in the boat, or down by the water, or at one of the restaurants, or over at the not quite so rich neighbours'. But this beach was patched with towels and frying skin, and a few sun umbrellas blocked the horizon. Music was wavering from different radios, clinking and booming at once. The hot mass. The huge organism, with so many parts. Some people were playing cramped volleyball in tight squares, or something with a Frisbee, or with racquets. Heads spiked the water. All was moving, everywhere. He stared, and Olivia did, too, he thought, as he crouched down by her stroller, still outside the scene. Look at that, he said. They stayed where they were. The concession stand wasn't far. The smell of grilled things.

A girl came, marching up the sand towards the concession. She stopped, and came towards them, and stopped again. What's wrong with your baby? she demanded.

Her shoulders were crisscrossed with white lines. Another bathing suit showing on her skin, an X-ray. Her bathing suit now was black, shimmering wet. Tim looked up, and said, She's not mine. Then he said, She's fine.

The girl looked at Olivia through sunglasses. She's cute, she said. Hi, baby, she tweeted.

Olivia looked at the girl, who was on her sad-eye side. The full effect. Tim patted the baby's head, through her hat. Showing the girl, keeping her back.

The girl said, So, what is she, then?

Tim said, What?

I mean, is she, like, your sister, or what?

Tim's hand was still on the head, the big head. The word *babysitter* wasn't right. He was something else. He said, You know. Friends. Or whatever.

The girl reached to tickle Olivia's cheek, on the good-eye side. Hi, she said again. Hi. Her arm was wet. Lake. Sweat. She said, So what's your name? She was talking to Tim.

The tendrils, or little tentacles, came slowly. He'd known he had them; he was aware. He'd used them before. Even when he was little. Teachers, girls. They just came out. The girl, Amanda, sat with them on the absurd beach and talked about herself. Her family, school, home, the people she was staying with here. Her torso was lean, a narrow instrument, with the white strap marks on her, and the dark bikini. She did most of the talking, but she felt them, at the same time: the slow twisting caressing strings, making their way out of him. Thin and almost transparent, but living. She was grabbing for them soon. Tim felt the small tugging. The thing. The charm, as his mum or Ellen might say. Amanda gooed to the baby and laughed at Tim's comments, her head back and dripping. She took off her sunglasses and looked at him. He still had his on, but he could see what she was doing, and what had been done.

She talked. She wanted to meet up later, and he said he couldn't. Maybe another day. Amanda tightened, then bounced. She said, I want to see Olivia again. Hey, little cutie baby, she gurgled. Tim said he'd see her. See you. He pushed the baby home.

He didn't go back for a few days, until Ellen made more guilt sounds. Then he pushed Olivia along the road again, very slowly, no hurry. They were fine. He had thought of the girl, Amanda, but not much. Abstractly. Her torso and wet bikini. Various combinations. When they got to the sand again, he wasn't thinking of her. The beach was the same. Public. Swarming, dense with noise. He stood in the same place, in the dented sand, and said to the baby, Hey, remember this?

He stood and looked over the beach. There were shreds of cloud overhead, but the sun broiled. He took off his cap, and looked over everything with stinging eyes, until his vision automatically stopped, recognizing. It skipped over her first, then went back. Amanda's body, slightly apart from the carpet of people to the right. She was looking up. She had seen them. Waiting. He felt her uncertainty, her pause, but it didn't last. After a few minutes of fake ignoring, she came over. He was sitting in the sand beside the listing stroller. Hi, she said, cold. But it was no good, no good. Soon she was sitting beside them, laughing at anything he said, and petting Olivia's cheeks, even on the bad side, and touching her own hair, stroking it back behind her ear. She talked about this guy she knew from school, he was, like, her boyfriend once but not really, not anymore, and he was so annoying, and so immature, you know. There was nothing Tim had to do. He sat there, and looked her over, for a minute. She had a different bikini on, and she was dry this time, with crisped hair. She talked. He looked at the ridiculous beach people. Time passed. Her voice measuring it out, on and on.

When Olivia fidgeted in her seat, he said they should get home, she would be hungry. He was hungry. Amanda smiled. All her teeth. Then she said, She wants us to kiss first.

Look, Tim said. Then he just let her kiss him. Her lips were scaled. The taste of wood. Popsicle stick, maybe. He had kissed others. Many wanted to, he knew. Here, it wouldn't matter. The tip of her tongue came out, then more, further. Then he got up. She still had her mouth slightly open, sitting sideways. She must have been about thirteen. Twelve, maybe, underneath. The things, the strings, or threads, seemed to work faster, with the baby around. He had kept his hand on Olivia's foot.

❧ ❧ ❧

The days had length, and repetition, but in a good way. He watched the boys play, and sat around holding Olivia, and dozed, more and more. His skin darker, spread with gold, standup hairs. He tried to teach the boys to suntan, but they wouldn't lie still. They should keep their hats on, anyway, right? Ellen had wanted them to keep their shirts on all the time, but she wasn't there. The adults had nearly abandoned them, except for some evenings when they stayed around. Tim made dinner for everyone one night. It was barbecued everything, all the meat he found in the fridge. He let the boys hold the tongs for him, taking turns. He kept Olivia's playpen nearby, on the deck, so she could smell it. He poked a bit of steak into her mouth, a tiny bit. And into his own. The boys yelled. He chewed. So good. He was a good chef. When the others came back, they were thrilled. Led up the lawn by the smoke, the promise. Praise and wonder. Perfect. They all feasted. Even the sister-in-law ate, and loved it. Tim had two steaks and a burger. Ellen said, Timothy, is there anything you can't do?

He took Olivia back to the public beach when he felt like it. He was only driven to go there sometimes, usually later in the afternoon. Sometimes that girl would drift across his mind. Or sort of roll across it, onto her back. He would put sunscreen on Olivia's arms and face while the girl, Amanda, watched. A hungry dog. A talking dog. Sometimes he would kiss her. Especially if she was in the black bikini, cold from the lake. She opened her mouth wide. He felt the trying. She took his hands and held them off the sand, waiting for him to do things with them. He knew. He knew everything that came into her crisped head. Once he put his hand on the flat of her small stomach, and slid it up. An inch. An inch. Then he stopped. Her ribcage held up. Waiting. Waiting still.

On the way home, he would push Olivia slowly, feeling the sun going. Feeling himself return, deflate. His blood beating itself back. It would all go. He was waiting, too. He would have to leave, and go back, and school would grind into motion again, with all the school people, and his mum would be there all the time, with her nervous questions and questions and plans. And then what? It didn't really matter. But.

He started feeling it, bending his neck forward. The future. More and more of it. Amanda reminded him. She said things like, So will you be here next year? and, So what's your address at home? She called him Timothy. Sometimes he heard her.

But it was easy, in the house, now. He relaxed completely when they got back to the cottage. Home. The future. The big chairs and stone fireplace. The kitchen.

The others were there. The sister-in-law was in domestic goddess mode for the evening, she said, tossing salad. She'd made a huge dinner, for a change. At the huge table, Tim sat next to the boys in their booster seats, and Olivia in her highchair. The boys rabbited at him, oddly tall. The food was good. Wine in the sauce, he thought. And other things. A complex taste, richness. Delicious, he said, when she asked what he thought, looking at him with her waiting eyebrows.

It was good. It was fantastic. Mr. said, Fantastic grub. He nodded over it, and again when he'd finished. Then he tipped back in his chair. He said, This reminds me of something, you know. He tipped his chair further, his knees angling up, and said, Hmm. Now. What is it, he said. What could it be. He was grinning, coy, distending his words. Then he said, Maybe, oh, just maybe, it's Thanksgiving. This was his punchline.

Oh no, the sister-in-law said, dragging out her vowels. She pretended to hide her upper body under the table.

Her husband laughed. They all laughed. He said, Come on, it wasn't that bad.

It was, it was, she squealed. Don't talk about it. You promised you would never say another word.

They were sputtering, like machinery starting, then roaring into speed. The little boys laughing, too, high and echoing. Ellen laughing into her palm. Olivia looked.

Tim felt his shoulders lift, contract. He laughed, too, but it was just air. Forced. They weren't stopping. It was like a bad sitcom about rich people. They were laughing about it, whatever it was. The hilarious, hilarious, stupid thing. The boys shrieking. The sister-in-law saying, Oh no, oh no, oh no no. They were stupid. Ridiculous. Monstrously sized. And golden, with their matching skin and their hair, and their sunglasses still nesting on their heads. He saw their dad emerging in the two boys, the growth, the golf, the eternal laughing. Gods, in their house. The god house.

When the laughing stopped, finally, they went on talking and talking, more quietly. Thanksgivings, restaurants. Something to do with wine, or corks. Tim thought of a story he knew, a good one, a related one, that would fit the conversation, but he didn't tell it. He was unattached now. The strings tangled, retracted. The baby was looking at their faces, a half-sad owl.

He didn't go down to the campfire after the meal. The kitchen left a disaster, for the cleaning girl to fix. He stayed in it for a while. Ellen had taken Olivia off with the rest of them. He'd said he had a headache. A thin, woman excuse. Too much sun. He stayed by himself, here, in the big, shining, wine-smelling kitchen. Where he should be, and would never be. He exhaled all of it. Fine.

❧ ❧ ❧

He got up late the next morning. He could hear the boys, outside already. Ellen must be with them. She hadn't come to see where he was, so it must be okay. 10:28. He'd woken up on his stomach, free-fallen, arms above his head. Normally he would have gone down early for breakfast, then taken the kids out when he was ready. He closed his eyes again. Downstairs, noise started. The vacuum, its gentle hum. Even their vacuum must be expensive, it was so quiet, like a big American car. Everything here was unobtrusive. Or supposed to be.

Eventually he went downstairs. The cleaner was there. He hadn't really seen her before, or paid attention. Why would he? She was probably about his age, a little older. Summer job. He passed her in the hall, and said, Hey. She smiled, driving the quiet vacuum. Hi.

He went into the kitchen, which was magically clean again. He got juice from the fridge, and drank it from the pitcher. She was looking at him. The noise had stopped.

Want some juice? he said. She was small, but with big eyes. Her T-shirt said *Cabana Club*: one of those fake-retro shirts, not quite covering her stomach. They were cut that way. She was smiling again, and getting a mop out of the pantry, her lower back showing as she reached in. The curve, the dip of spine. He went to the cupboard next to her, for a plate. When she emerged, he looked at her again. Cabana Club, he said.

She said, Yeah, and laughed. The mop starting a slow slide, hushing the floor.

He said, How do you like the job?

It's good. It pays pretty well. It's not hard.

Uh huh, he said. She was definitely older. He tipped his glass upside-down. He said, How do you like the house?

She stopped. I don't know, she said. Well. It's a little bourgeois. You know what I mean.

The word sat in the air for a minute. The *wah* sound, the kiss-off. Tim said, Yeah. He looked at the counters, the tiling. The good taste. It's pretty old, though, he said.

She was mopping again, back and forth. Mm, she said. She had a way of saying it. Weighting it.

He said, You a student?

Yes.

You like university?

She smiled again. Do I like it? I like it, she said. I'm doing nursing. I'm just home for the summer, keeping busy.

Home. He knew it was coming. His own, lurking ahead, moderately sized, dull. He didn't think of it. He went to the freezer and got waffles. Even rich people had frozen foods. They thought of the future, too, obviously. Plans for leaner times. You couldn't get away from it, even here. He started to ask what she was going to be, but he remembered. A nurse. He watched her mopping.

He brushed past her. His sleeve touched her Cabana shirt. It was enough. He felt her stop, for a half-second, then keep on. He watched her as he ate five waffles. She mopped for longer than she needed to. The floor shining as if greased. A skin of syrup on his plate. And his lips. She was asking about him, where he was from. How he liked the place, how he liked it out here. She stood near him, the mop in her hand. She took his plate, and washed it, and tossed the white dish towel at him. A challenge. A plea. The strings had drifted out, light on the air. Sticky. He didn't try, but he felt them cobwebbing. She did, too. He wondered where Olivia was.

He didn't go outside that day. He stayed in the house, in his room, listening to the radio, the unfamiliar stations. Oldies everywhere, it seemed. He listened to the kids outside. He couldn't hear Olivia. She was still quiet, almost always. Ellen still didn't come in to find him. Humidity leached him. He didn't turn on the ceiling fan. He just lay there. *Why must I be a teenager in love*: the radio said it, and he caught it. He rolled his eyes back into his skull.

But a bubble rose there, in the dark. Maybe he was. Too loving. Too quick with it. He didn't have to try. People just came. But maybe he should stop these things from happening.

He was too romantic, that was the problem. His problem. He could still see the girl in the kitchen. The feel of her upper arm: he'd touched it with his own body, not just his sleeve.

And Amanda. Even her. He was too romantic with her. The beach, the backdrop, all of that. He thought of the beach. Amanda there, and all the public people. Some of the women were semi-good-looking. Ahh. There I go again.

He heard the boys shrieking, and Ellen saying something he couldn't make out. He sat up. Seriousness now. He went downstairs. The cleaning girl was still there, dusting the back living room. She was slow today, cutting circles in the nonexistent dust. When they were kissing, and his hands were hard on her waist, and then higher, he felt the strings cutting themselves off from him. Snap. It was all precision now. All him.

❧ ❧ ❧

The girl wasn't back at the house for a few days, and he hadn't said anything about meeting up. He stayed in his room for a while, then came out as usual, and played with the boys, and carried Olivia around. Badly hidden relief on Ellen. He didn't say much to her. He took Olivia to the public beach that evening, before dinner, not saying where they were going. But nobody seemed to mind.

Amanda was there. He knew it before he saw her. The smell: coconut desperation. She came over, and acted aloof again for about ten seconds. Then the collapse: she tried to melt herself and her lotion over him, hugging into his body. He kissed the top of her head, hard. Smack. She sat down in the sand, talking about her friend who'd called her that day, just a little while ago, and how they'd talked about Timothy. And Olivia, she said, pleating her face at the baby. Tim reached into the stroller and got Olivia out, and she looked at him. Happiness in her eye. Some. They were the same, he and the baby, shipwrecked here in the house of the perfect.

Maybe he could marry her one day. But he didn't want to think of her, grown up, at what would become of her. It seemed disastrous.

He looked over the leftover people on the beach. It was emptier now. Large sand patches. A woman was walking slowly along the shoreline. Thin, but with a bump of stomach. A bulb. Beautiful, from here, among the remaining stupid broiled stupid people, with a big hat darkening her face.

He said, Do you think you'll ever have a kid?

He looked at Amanda appraisingly. She was mid-word. She blew out a giggle. Her black bikini. Her puffed chest. The strap marks whiter on her skin now, a negative. Well, yeah, of course, everybody wants to have kids, she'd be such a great mum, she babysits a lot back at home. On and on.

Everybody wants to. Everybody can. Tim thought of it. All the people on the beach. All people everywhere. He clenched. He kissed Amanda, hard, with his hard tongue, and he pushed Olivia home in the stroller. His mouth hurt.

❧ ❧ ❧

He didn't sleep. Images of people, disgusting people with disgusting children. Wrong, wrong. He kept his eyes open and watched the ceiling fan. But he must have slept, eventually. It was late again when he woke up. Day. The boys' sounds outside. Ellen's fatigue growing, thickening her voice. Things like, Don't you do that. I said don't. I said no. Hung over, maybe, or sick. Some dreadful punishment, he thought, for what she was. He didn't get up; he would never move. He watched the fan, its circle. Then his stomach squirmed. He was hungry, always. He went down to the kitchen.

The girl was there, mopping again. The clean shine on the floor. The voices outside were trailing down the lawn, towards the lake. He watched the girl's back moving, her arms. She lived out here, she'd said, hadn't she. Maybe on the lake, somewhere close. It might do.

Hi, he said.

The kitchen was warm. A sheen of sweat on the girl's face. Well, hi.

He was going to say, Do you want some waffles? But then he didn't. Precision. He went over and pressed her arms. He was kissing her, and his mouth tasted like dry sleep when he put it on hers, but hers tasted better. He pushed against her. His brown skin. He could see it. His hard torso. Today her T-shirt said, *Lucky*. He covered it with his skin. She was saying something, but it didn't matter. He pulled her over to the pantry. She still had her mop. Come on.

In the pantry, narrow and long, she dropped the mop. Its clatter and bump. Her arms winding around his neck. Cans on the shelves. So many. Soup. Diced tomatoes. Kidney beans. As though these people would ever run out of food, ever in their lives. They were breathing, and his hands were on her, and up her Lucky shirt, and down the front of her jeans. Her hidden belly, a slight layer of cushion. A surprise. He lay her on the floor, and shut the door. The dark, thank God. He lay down, too. He put his hand back on her stomach, and tugged at her clothes. She was laughing.

Wait, she said. Her breath quick, living. Do you have anything? she said.

What? he said.

She said, through her breath, Come on, you know. Protection.

Her nurseness came into the dark. Her hands were on him now, mechanical, passing time. He closed his eyes. He said, Don't worry. Then they were kissing again, hard teeth, and his hand was right there. Right there. She was the right way now, sighing in his ear, moving below. Their clothes pushed away, somewhere among the cans.

Then she did it again. So, do you have it? We can't do this otherwise, she said.

Come on, it's fine. I'm fine, he said.

She was still, except her hips. Reflex. Above them, she said, nurselike, You might not know that. Have you had a lot of partners?

No, he said. The truth.

Her hips lifted. Oh, she said. Then the next clinic announcement: We don't want to get pregnant, you know.

He said, Don't worry. We don't need anything. His head dove for her mouth, knocking against her jaw. I'll take care of it, he said. He would, he knew, right then. The grand vision began to unroll.

She said, That's not safe. She wasn't moving now at all.

Trust me. Trust me, he said, into her mouth. He squeezed her belly: a grocery fruit. The thought of it, a kernel inside it, his. The answer surging, announcing itself. Part of himself, there, here, a monument in cottage-land, tying him to it. He'd have to come back. He squeezed again, loving. You live here, right? he said.

She gave up, eventually, liquefied. When he was in her, she kept switching into nurse mode. You promise you won't. But she felt it: the strings, still attached to her, and tight. Drifting, at the other end. He pressed his eyes shut again, in the canned dark. She was moving, and dark inside, too. He had just pushed, and was inside. Easy. It didn't take long. They were moving faster, tighter, but she wouldn't let him stay there. No, she said. Come on, you can't.

He stopped. All vanished. It was no good. Forget it, he said, moving up onto his knees. The floor was cool.

What, she said. Are you done? Come back, she said, in her real voice. A little beg hitching it.

I said forget it, he said. Hardening, everywhere but. He would not love. He wouldn't give himself. Not to anyone like this. He felt like spitting.

What are you talking about? she said. He felt her coming closer, her legs shifting.

He said, You're not even going to remember this.

She was silent. Turning in on herself. The mood dropping. Then she said, Whatever. I don't know what you're trying to say.

He said, You should remember this, right now, all your life, right?

She said, Sure. It sounded like *nurse*. Sterility, cleanups.

He stood up. He was standing above her, his head somewhere between the shelves. He said, It's obviously not your first time. This hadn't mattered until now, but he was cooling, clearing.

She said, Why would that matter? She was moving on the floor, trying to find her clothes. She was thinking something like *bourgeois*, he felt it.

He tried. He said, So what, if something happened? So what? Then you would never forget it. Everybody wants kids, he said. Everybody normal.

But she wasn't answering, or listening. She only wanted to get out. He said, Then I'll haunt you. For a second, real fury came. His iris bursting, flooding his eye. Pain in the socket, in his head. The scene: taking up a can, and denting it with her skull, and her body dead, with him still there. The story unfolding. It would be a tomato can, with a red label. The investigation, his escape. And later, his ghost roaming around her cottage, sitting on her beach. But this was wrong. Too lover-like, too romantic. He wouldn't. And she wasn't right. Not now.

She was talking, standing up between the shelves. She said professionally, You should always carry protection. These things happen. You don't want a kid out of it, for the rest of your life, she said. She laughed a little, a different laugh. The zipping of her jeans, the finality. She squeezed past him to the door. The light stinging. He was still naked.

He said, Who would want one with you? He saw her, a charwoman, a servant, rumpled and face-rubbed in the kitchen. Finished. He closed the door on her, her dopey curiosity. He would haunt her, even if she didn't know it, even if she was no use to him.

So. It was his first. He had been in. Not far enough.

He was tired, the wrong kind of tired, and his stomach muttered. The mop started again, after a minute.

*❧ ❧ ❧*

He walked with Olivia for miles along the road. They didn't turn off at the public beach. He tried to get her to talk. He said things like, Bird, and Dog, and Big Dog, or whatever they passed. He said, Tim. It was easy to say. Easy. A little bell pinging. He said it, over and over, in time with the stroller wheels. Tim, Tim. But she didn't copy it. She didn't say anything. He stopped, and crouched in front of the stroller, and looked at her. She fake-cried for a few seconds, then stopped. She was looking out at a tree, or something. Her mixed-up face. The eyes wrong, half-blank. Savagely young.

He touched her head, her big head. The back of her neck. Her hair was growing. The plasticity of the body. He pressed his finger in the skin under her sad eye, its droop. She tilted her head, and flapped her arm at him. All reflex. He knew it now. He had been too romantic with her, too. I need it. A crow on my chest. Its sharp picketty-picking. See me. Love me. Love. Me.

*❧ ❧ ❧*

Back at home, at the house, at the cottage, no one was there. He thought of tomorrow, and the next day, and the days coming up. The vast, blank future to be blankly filled. The dull people. The dull things that had to get done. And then, the way things should be. The terrible difference. He would wake up in the morning here, and things would be wrong, still. His head twinged, his eye socket. He went and sat in the yard in the quiet grass. The baby monitor crackled electronically, and he went back inside, and upstairs, and woke Olivia. She didn't fake-cry, or make any noise, as he picked her up from her crib. He didn't say anything, either.

He took her outside, and she did start up then, her fake, tearless crying. He put her in the grass beside him, under the sky. She pushed herself up with her hands. Then standing. She started to walk, her tipping walk, ahead and away, down the gentle angle towards the water.

# LIVES OF THE SAINTS

## 1

## *Invisibility*

SOME HOLY TYPES HAVE THIS ABILITY, which they can turn off and on at will. The most obvious thing you'd put on a list, if you were given the choice of a few superpowers. And maybe for more than the most obvious reasons, like deception and spying and finding out what people really think of you, and such.

Invisibility is the one most children think they are born with. Hiding their eyes: *I can't see you, so you can't see me.* Satisfying. A level of sophistication does arise later, though: *I pretend I can't see you, even though I know you see me.*

Here's how that starts. For me, it was through checking up on the neighbours, then getting them to look at me through the fence, as if I were entirely unaware of their presence. Sitting in the backyard, thinking up unconscious pensive poses. The slow twirl of an ankle, the languid droop of the head. Soon enough, they heard me coughing or lightly humming, and came to peer through the fence between our yards. Their eyes on me until I nonchalantly turned their way.

What are you doing? I don't know, what are you doing?

Soon mothers became involved. Would the little girl like to come and play? Well, if you're sure it's no trouble.

Two girls, with a semi-cloned look about them. Not a bad backyard. Their dad had built them a playhouse and swing set, surrounded by sand. I'd seen our cat sneaking over there. When we dug in the sand for a while, I knew why.

I said, Let's play something else. What else have you got?

I liked novelty. Even my motives were transparent. A kind of invisibility, I suppose.

One of them said, We could play races.

This sounded good. I agreed. You had to run as fast as you could from the house to the back fence. The smaller one stood there as referee, shouting the start, and calling the winner. Quivering, the older girl and I stood with our hands on the house corner, which was clearly the rule. I didn't need to be told. When the little one yelled, Go, I tore away, barefoot, through their interestingly lush grass. Ours was wispier, less springy. I felt the living thickness on my feet the whole way. Real grass. I nearly slammed into the fence at the finish, my head down.

I won. And I won all the others, against each of the girls, several times. I wanted to keep it going. My heart bouncing with triumph, with my ability. I had a mild confidence in my abilities generally, but not to win like this. Not to win all the time. I could take it, I decided. We kept running, and I kept winning.

After a particularly convincing victory, I was cheering, when I realized someone was standing by the gate to the driveway, watching silently. How long had he been there? See? Invisibility. There it is again.

The man stared, with locked eyebrows. A serious face. A briefcase. He didn't say anything to me at first. One of the girls said, Hi, Dad. He said hello to the girls. He called them Kimberley Jean Elizabeth and Christina Mary Anne.

We're having races, the smaller one said.

Let's do another one, I said, inserting myself into the scene, charging off from the house again towards the fence, winning delightfully, as I imagined. Everyone likes a winner.

She won again, the older girl said.

The man looked at me, then. Her legs are longer, he said, and he turned and went into the house.

Defeat shot through me. The dismissiveness in his voice reached through the clouds of victory. I sat down in the thickness of the grass, examining it.

Why does he call you that? Kimberley Jean Elizabeth, I said to the older girl.

That's what I was christened. That's my full Christian name, my real name, she said.

I thought about it. Possibilities arose, invisibly, but only at first. I'd always coveted a middle name. Maybe a Christian name was what my life was lacking. Visions of myself, long-named and devout, strode before me, projected through the grass.

2

*Immortality*

This, too, is something devoutly to be wished. Something you're supposed to get eventually. Most religions have something to say about it.

I was religionless. Not officially. My mother was a Tibetan Buddhist, which was unusual enough to seem something furtive and faintly smutty, where we lived. Not filthy. Acceptable, but just. Maybe something like a food bank is a good analogy. Why would you go there if you didn't have to?

The Buddhist temple was actually not that. It was a room in the basement of a costume rental place. It had picnic tables and a Buddha statue, and a few shiny travel posters of Tibet on the walls. *Roof of the World*, one of them proclaimed. The few adult members were mild-mannered types, as you might imagine. They had group contemplation meetings, and Sunday School. This was actually on Saturdays, and wasn't called Sunday School. My mother made me go. There were only two others who went; these were both silent, furious boys, older than I was. We were united in being furious, at least, although we hated everything about each other on sight otherwise.

Sometimes the leader was a very young man with fluffy facial growth and a piping tone to his voice. Then we would unite in mocking him, if only silently. It didn't stop us hating each other. Sometimes the leader was an older woman with violently dyed hair. She was very kind, but in the way that made you want to kick her.

We sat at one of the picnic tables, whose presence seemed a cruel parody of a good time. We had little books about the Buddha, but they weren't really books, just photocopies. One of the staples stabbed me in the thumb once. I used the blood to make a clown nose on an illustration of one of Buddha's happy child-followers. We were supposed to be meditating at the time. I was ripping one of my socks on a snag in the table leg and thinking abstractedly upon the large, meaty-looking clown head in the display window of the costume shop upstairs. Maybe that was a kind of meditation. It's probably where my artistic inspiration came from, anyway. The leader woman had brought us ice cream that day, which she made herself from cashew nuts. I didn't see the correlation with ice cream. I imagined the woman grinding up the nuts herself, with her teeth, then squirreling them away in the freezer. I told my mum about it, with squirrel noises, and she thought it was funny, too. She was quite normal, in spite of her Tibetan Buddhism.

After non-Sunday School, sometimes I was allowed to play with the neighbours. Sometimes I would have lunch there, and they would say grace over it. From their everyday talk, I developed a tremendous fondness for Jesus, base and sneaking as I was, and Buddhist. They took me to church with them one Sunday, and I felt like a creep. Creeping along phonily amidst all the cars in the parking lot, the big building, clearly labeled as what it was: *Church of God.* I wanted to be on that team, His team. I liked that capital H, too.

I took to hinting. Saying innocently how we didn't go to church, we being my mother and me. We didn't believe in anything, I said. And the nice Mrs. Lipp, Kimberley and Christina's mum, and their serious dad, Mr. Lipp, both looked at me as if in pain. And they started taking me with them nearly every Sunday. My mum was fine with that; she said it was good for me to understand other faiths. So, being there, at the enormous, happy church, felt like a shot in the arm. I did feel born again. Or maybe I was just undead.

3

*Communion*

I like to eat. Who doesn't, you might say. Saints, for one. Most of them aren't fond of eating. One of the demands of the flesh, which are always holding you down. Saints tend to fast or exist miraculously on air and sunlight. Now there's a diet. Some people have tried it. That didn't go so well. One woman got a book out of it, though, terminal malnutrition set in.

I used to be able to list my favourite foods in order. It was a nuanced list. Red jello, green jello, Hawaiian pizza, orange jello, Black Forest cake from the grocery store, Black Forest cake from the other grocery store, Neapolitan ice cream taken in the following sequence: strawberry, chocolate, vanilla. I liked food with associated locales. This probably says something about me.

It should go without saying that the Hawaiian pizza had to be ham-free. My Buddhist mother and I were vegetarians, even if we weren't fans of cashew ice cream. We didn't eat things with souls. My mother was a pretty good cook, and it's hard to tell that some of those soya products aren't actual meat. Soya beans are soulless, apparently.

The neighbours insisted on family dinner at the same time every night. If I played there long enough after school, I'd usually get myself invited. I'd phone my mother innocently: Can I stay? They asked me.

Mrs. Lipp would make me a special plate of vegetables and the side dishes of their meal, potatoes or noodles, artfully arranged. Usually a large portion of dessert, too, even if Kimberley and Christina weren't allowed to have any, for some infraction, arguing or untidiness. The guest's privileges: I milked them. But it wasn't just the food. It was also the grace, and the way they said it. Mr. Lipp usually began. The bowed head, the outreaching hands, palms up. We would all hold hands. I would try to keep mine from twitching, and to keep my eyes shut, but my heart would thunder, and I'd squint at Mr. Lipp's thick hair, and listen. Things I'd never thought about. We thank you, Lord, for this food today, and for our healthy bodies, and for the plenty you bestow. We thank you for our friends, Lord, and for sending one to be with us at this table.

That's me, I would think, as if recognizing myself on TV.

In the summer, they began having barbecues. Mr. Lipp had a man's apron that said *Number Two Father*. I knew who Number One was, now, obviously. The girls had had the apron printed for his birthday. In it, Mr. Lipp ran the barbecue on the patio. I would have been able to smell it from my house, but it seemed I wasn't there so much, now. I kept telling my mother it was okay, I was invited. They like me there, I would say, with false, starchy humility, as if acknowledging a humanitarian award. And I won't eat, I said, saint like.

But Mrs. Lipp had a plate of veggie sticks and chips ready for me already, as I'd known she would. And then Mr. Lipp handed me a hamburger bun, and laid a burger inside it with his barbecue flipper. He looked down at me gravely, and I said, Um, I can't have this.

He said, You can. It's a special one we chose for you. Vegetarian.

My innards bounded. Special. Chosen. I looked over at Mrs. Lipp, who said, It's all right, dear. Would you like some ketchup?

Yes, I said. Then, trying to control my lust, I said, Yes, please. I poured ketchup all over the bun, and I ate, and it was good. Kimberley and Christina were already working on seconds. Luxuriously, I added more ketchup to my bun. It was also a favourite of mine.

I felt Mr. Lipp's eyes above his apron. He said, You shouldn't put so much of that garbage on your food. You can't taste it properly.

Mrs. Lipp said, Oh, it's all right. She likes it.

I reverted to myself, my real self: something outlandish and quaint, from some foreign tribe with slightly distasteful customs, maybe a cheap souvenir stand. I put down the ketchup bottle. I don't like it that much, I said.

Mr. Lipp said, his head back, But you like that. He nodded at my plate.

I nodded. My hands were ketchup-blobbed. I looked for a napkin. Then he said, Do you know that that is?

I said, Ketchup.

No. Do you know what else you're eating? He looked serious.

I wiped my hands. Guilt, seeing the red smirching the little paper flowers. Mrs. Lipp always chose pretty things, even paper towels.

Mr. Lipp knelt down in front of me. He put his hand on my arm. My lower lip dropped open. Did I have ketchup on it, too? He said, earnestly, It's moose.

What? Um, pardon? I said.

Kimberley and Christina and Mrs. Lipp were smiling. So I did, too. And Mr. Lipp said, It's a moose burger. So how do you like that, eh?

I still had some in my mouth. I was torn. What to do with it? But then Mrs. Lipp said, I'm so glad you like it, dear.

And Mr. Lipp said, I shot it myself last fall. There's some real food for you.

Once, Kimberley had showed me where he kept his gun, which was a secret. And all the meat and bones out in the freezer in the garage. Christina, the younger one, liked going out there to look at it. She wanted to be a hunter, or a butcher.

Now, you eat that all up, he said, and I did. I'd never seen any moose in real life, anyway, so it wasn't as bad as eating a cow. Mr. Lipp kept nodding, and saying, That's good, as if I were a baby.

Thank you, Mr. and Mrs. Lipp, I said, when I'd finished.

He said, How about you call us Uncle Gary and Auntie Lydia. And Kimberley asked if I could stay over, and she told me later that they had to eat meat because the Lord made animals out of meat. It made sense.

I had meat every time I was there for dinner after that. The Buddha says we can't even kill flies, who are our brothers. Yeah, whatever. Flies got on the meat. We had further barbecued moose burgers, and steaks, and regular hamburgers, and tacos, and chicken casseroles. They took me to McDonald's after church, where I ate a whole Big Mac. That's my girl, Mr. Lipp said, and he even smiled.

They didn't have communion at their church. They weren't Catholic. I knew the ceremony and singing and clapping and order of business very quickly. I'd joined in, drinking the punch, knowing exactly what I was doing.

4

*The Wages of Sin*

This is always part of it.

There was a place in town called Death's Bakery. It was probably missing some Celtic accent, or something, some proper vowel pronunciation. But everyone just called it Death's, normally enough, without thinking about implications. I worked there for quite a few years, beginning when I was a teenager. The wages weren't bad, actually. I didn't do much. There's the sloth.

Here is the vanity, one of the more prominent sins. I had beautiful, excellent hair, down to my waist, perfectly straight and shining, as though it had been cut from a bolt of heavy silky fabric. No split ends. That was just the way it was. Sometimes people on the street asked me if I was in commercials, for shampoo or other hair products. Sometimes, people also asked me if they could touch it. Once I said yes, but I felt grubby afterwards, as if I were a prostitute, and I hadn't even gotten anything for it. I washed my hair afterwards. Then I felt some guilt: not everyone had hair as nice as mine, and it was a kind of charity to let them touch it. But then nobody asked for a while.

It was a good bakery, and a pretty good job. I didn't have to do any of the early-morning baking, or any of the baking, in fact. I just served people, standing around behind the counter in the warm air from the ovens in the back, or brushing my hair when it wasn't too busy in there. Sometimes, serving them with bread and buns and such, I would get a feeling as if I were handing it out to the poor, although of course they had to pay, and it wasn't a cheapo bakery. Maybe it was the hair that made me feel noble and pure, like a stained-glass window. Maybe it was the other girl who worked there, who had a hint of moustache.

I sort of made up for the vanity, the sloth, and all the other ones I forgot about. Charity was something I was good at, or thoughts of charity. If someone ordered multigrain buns, thinking they were healthy, and then topped off the order with six sugar cookies, I would sometimes add an extra bun, and only give them five cookies, hoping they would see why when they got home and realized it. I thought of it as semi-holy work, in some dim way, although I'd stopped going to church and Buddhist Sunday School by then. Still. Temptation is everywhere. I knew it. The neighbours never went to that bakery. I still thought about them a lot. I asked myself what they would do, in certain situations.

A man I hadn't seen before once came in for some bread, and when I'd run it through the slicer and given it to him, he looked at it for a second as if it were one of those apparitions of Christ that seem to occur on tortillas in Mexico. Then he read the name off the bag: Death's Bakery. He was incredulous. But he was looking at me. He said, What are you doing working here, baby? You should be a model. You could live forever. He gave me a card with his name on it. *Talent Scouting and Management*, it said. The get-out-of-hell-free card. It was slightly soiled and fingerprinted. But I did keep it in my wallet, and I did look at it, and I can't say I wasn't tempted to call, from time to time, when I was bored. But how are you supposed to really believe in that, in that escape? I didn't think the neighbours would.

Here's another reason: at night, when I cashed out and shut the place and the moustachioed girl left, I would eat all the day-olds. All of them. Buns, loaves, sliced and unsliced. Rye through sourdough. Cookies, gingerbread men, and women, too, and boys and girls, and goggle-eyed bunnies, with their hardened icing. And those meringues that look like mice.

What can I say? I was lucky it was a busy place, so there was never an impossible amount to get through. And it was good stuff. But it was still a fair amount. I'd eat it all. My rack, my screws, my self-flagellation. I guess I could have just shaved my head, like the Buddhist nuns do. I've heard that Catholic nuns do that, too, under their wimples, but nobody seems to know for sure. Instead, maybe I was trying to bring back the fat toddler I'd been; I'd had solid little hips at age three, and large knees, and a roll of belly over my little underpants and clothes. I'd become a tall skinny kid later, and stayed that way, but I was fascinated by that toddler. You have to be like a little child to enter the kingdom, right? That did stay with me. I could hear it in the church pastor's voice. I thought about the burgers and steaks of the past, sometimes, chewing on the heel of a stale pumpernickel loaf. I didn't eat much else in the day.

I kept trying, but I knew instinctively what was coming to me. It was made pretty obvious to me there. The wages of sin is working behind the counter at Death's, possibly forever.

## 5

### X-Ray Vision

Another skill or superpower that would be a useful choice, although you don't see it often in the holy; it's different from foretelling and prophesying. Those neighbours, good as they were, didn't see through me and my desires. Neither did my good mother. But that was their problem. We all have our own paths to tread, saith the Lord, or Buddha, or somebody.

For instance, if I'd had X-ray vision earlier in my life, I'd have been able to catch a few things. Like the fact that Kimberley next door would run away when she was older, not even finish high school, and really escape, disappear utterly. The rumour was that she became a stripper. So that was in her already, when I used to sleep over and beat her at races. Even the faintly stripperesque tone of her name didn't show it then: Kimberley Jean. Maybe I should have seen it. A couple of times, later, I even went into strip clubs in the city when I was down there, partly looking out for her, but I never saw anyone who looked much like her. Maybe I was looking for something too specific. I could see it: a white nightgown, maybe wet. Do they still have wet T-shirt contests, or is that passé?

I still see Mr. and Mrs. Lipp around town sometimes, doing their shopping, looking stunned. They never see me, and I avoid them.

### 6

### *The Problem of Evil, and How to Fix It*

Recently, I got a new dog on a whim. For a little while, its name was Goddamnit, because that's what I kept shouting when it would pee on the floor or rip up furniture out of excitement or boredom or evil. It did seem evil, sometimes, or possessed. The name made me uneasy, though. It wasn't like in those cultures where they name babies something like Ugly or Brat so the evil spirits won't be tempted to take it away. I wanted someone to take the dog away. But I feel bad, saying that. We all have our trials to bear, don't we? I try to think about my life.

Once, I had a plan at Hallowe'en. This was beyond the plan of dressing like a witch, which was my usual costume, because it was traditional, and easy enough. I begged my mother to buy the biggest pumpkin I could find at the grocery store, and then the smallest. Always amenable, she did. I supervised her as she rolled the enormous one to the car, then hauled it into the kitchen at home. I wouldn't let her help me pull out the viscera; I enjoyed being elbow-deep in the swampy, seedy guts. Once it was done, and the face carved out, I placed the tiny, uncarved one in the gaping mouth-hole of the larger. See, it eats its baby, I said. It was an homage to the she-hamster at school, which had done the same thing.

My mother wasn't too sure about this at first, but when I said Buddhist-type things I'd picked up at those lessons, she was okay with it. All life is one. And although it was cannibalism, it was of a vegetarian sort.

How do you fix something like that? The neighbours saw me prancing around the pumpkins on the front steps as they drove by, and Mrs. Lipp promptly stopped and invited me to a party at their church that evening. My mother dropped me off in my witch costume. I used my broom as a walking stick as I strode into the big activity room in the church basement. Thump thump.

It was a Family Fall Fun Fair. Nice. Christian. Singalongs, with hand-holding. Three-legged races. The Hokey-Pokey. No costumes. No references whatsoever to Hallowe'en. That fixed it.

Something similar happened with TV. I was over at their house, again, slightly bored, and I turned on their TV. Kimberley nearly went hysterical. She stood in front of it so I couldn't see. The reason is that is was *The Smurfs*. I'd begun singing along with the la-la-la music. Covering the screen with her body, Kimberley said, You can't watch this.

Why not? I said, trying to see through her.

Smurfs are witchcraft. Don't you know that?

They are? I said. I was surprised. I knew there was a wizard involved in the show, an unpleasant character, and I'd decided not to be a witch at Hallowe'en again, although everybody at the church had been very nice to me, if a little pitying, in their civilian clothes.

Yeah. So you can't. You can never, never watch it, Kimberley said.

Then logic, or something, struck me. I said, If you've never seen it, how do you know it's witchcraft?

Kimberley said, Everybody knows that. And it's communist.

This had a sinister edge, although I wasn't well-versed in political systems. I suppose, now, that it's because the Smurfs lived in a village, with each one responsible for some facet of the system, sharing everything. Even sharing Smurfette, probably, since she was the one female.

Kimberley went on. You don't know it, but you're going to hell, probably, she said. Then she said, Let's go outside.

Okay, I said.

This may not have stopped me from eventually going to hell, but it stopped me watching *The Smurfs*, which isn't even very good, as cartoons go. So that's something.

But here is the big fix. The neighbours' church had a service at the lake in the summer. I was a special guest. There was talk about loving the sinner, hating the sin, and God's great cleansing power, and so forth. The pastor waded out into the water, his robes floating up around his middle. I wondered if he had flippers on. A couple of other people waded out there to him, and he put his hand on their heads and dropped them back into the water. He held their heads under and called their names. When the people emerged, baptized, everyone watching shook their hands and hugged them, despite their sogginess. One man's underwear showed through his soggy white gown.

Kimberley was also in a white gown. The pastor said something about it being an unusual and glorious occasion. Mr. Lipp put his hand on my head, then, standing beside me on the beach at the front of the crowd. Together, we watched Kimberley getting into the water, as if we were watching a movie. His hand directed my head. Standing there with her, the pastor said, I baptize thee, but he didn't say Kimberley's

name. He said my name. He said it as he shoved Kimberley
into the lake and held her there for a second.

She came up grinning, and back on the beach, Mr. and
Mrs. Lipp hugged her. Mr. Lipp said, very seriously, that she
was a good girl. Then they hugged me, too. Kimberley's white
gown stuck to her, then to me. With one hand on each of our
shoulders, Mr. Lipp said, Now you're one of us. This is your
first half-step towards salvation.

Kimberley was saying, I saved her. I saved her. The congre-
gation was cheering. I felt a little foolish, a little defective,
standing there, dressed. I was happier afterwards, when the
Lipps gave cameras to both Kimberley and me in congratula-
tions. You could take underwater pictures with them, which
seemed suitable. So there I was, saved. Safe. And I hadn't even
had to get wet.

The dog. Goddamnit. I've learned to love it, or tolerate it,
as they did with me, and I got it fixed, and that's about all you
can do about evil.

7

## Martyrdom

This happens to most saints. It is, of course, what makes them
saints. It's not usually pleasant while it's going on. Think of
waiting for the arrows to hit, or the flames to reach your
eyes, or the disembowelling party to arrive. But it implies
another super-ability, to sit there and take it, knowing you'll
be something better in the end.

I'm not sure it's ever happened to me. Maybe something
close.

I was watching something on TV, which was one of the
good things about being at home, although I had broad-

154

spectrum TV-guilt, after Kimberley and the Smurfs. My mother also thought too much television was bad for living things, so I had the sound turned down low. Then the neighbours arrived at the door. Not the two girls, just Mr. and Mrs. Lipp, or Uncle Gary and Auntie Lydia, as I kept forgetting to call them, much as I wanted to. I remember this arrival because it was unusual, and because two people were kissing seriously on the TV show; I was torn between the two novel distractions. Eventually, I turned off the television, and went to the living room to see what was going on.

My mum was getting coffee ready. Mrs. Lipp said she was glad I was there, and that it was so nice to see me, as if she hadn't seen me lurking around her own yard about an hour earlier. She gave me a scented hug. Then my mum returned, and said, It's so good of you to have her over so often. I know how much she enjoys visiting you and the girls.

I sat there as if they weren't talking about me. Mrs. Lipp said, Oh, we enjoy having her, dear. She said *dear* just the way she said it to me. She went on: She's a very special girl. So I tried to look even more humble.

Mr. Lipp wasn't drinking his coffee. He looked heavily impatient, full of a coiled energy. He said, We'd like to talk to you about her now. He put his hands together, and I thought I was in trouble, but then he said, We think of her as our own daughter. She's a member of our church family and our own family.

My mother smiled, and said, I think it's wonderful. I appreciate your teaching her about your beliefs. It's so important for her to be exposed to different faiths. She was sitting with her legs crossed up under her on the couch, her feet tucked in.

Mr. Lipp looked at her legs, as if that did it. He said, calmly, We'd like to start plans for adopting her.

My mother said, Pardon me?

He said, We want to adopt her. Legally, of course.

Then my mother didn't say anything, although she was still smiling, as if she were stuck in that gear. Mrs. Lipp started in: She's been blossoming with us. You can just see it, she said. She looked at me, and I felt blossomy, transformable, adoptable.

Mr. Lipp talked about role models, and how there was no real family head for me here. He was gentle, persuasive. He mentioned proper meals, another advantage of their home. He mentioned a good life. I was persuaded.

Then my mother said we had an appointment. So, she said. She was still smiling, but a little strangely, as if something were buzzing in her ear. I asked where we were going, but she didn't say anything. She stood up, and so did they, and the air was tight as an elastic band.

As they left, the house fell, plain, a little frowzy, with that cooked-vegetable smell that you sometimes get in elevators. My mother took me out for a drive. She was kind. All she said was that I wasn't allowed to go over to the neighbours' anymore, and not to church. Not for a while. When we drove past McDonald's, I dropped hints. But then my mother looked as if she were going to start crying.

When we got home, I sneaked over to the fence in the backyard, and watched Kimberley and Christina through it, on their side. They were playing baptism, lying in the grass, moving their limbs around as if they were swimming.

It felt like martyrdom, at the time. A good life: all that I lost. But still, I don't think I'd mind being a saint, if you could get through the suffering. It's like being a superhero. You get a new name, fame, an area of coverage, like travel or childbirth, and icons, and symbols associated with you. And that escape. Maybe that's why Kimberley ran away the way she did, and why she tried to save me by proxy.

I'm still here. So is the bakery. I take shifts there sometimes. I did end up cutting my hair pretty short, just to see how it would look. It wasn't a success. And I'm not sure if Christina ever made it to butcherhood. Maybe that loss happens to everybody. Maybe most of us aren't supposed to get what we want. Maybe that's for our own good.

Maybe Kimberley is the patron saint of strippers, now. I don't know what I would choose.

# Have You Seen the Ghost of John

SHE WASN'T REALLY A CAMP PERSON. WELL. No. There is such a thing, but she wasn't one of that breed. Maybe she should have been. She'd gone every year, as a kid, and now she worked there in the summers. So it was odd. The place was always the same; you'd think she'd have started to feel the love. But she was used to it, anyway. She had already been there two weeks this year, through the younger ones. The Tweens were coming up. Tweens.

The job was okay, most of the time, but a little tiring, repetitive. The next group was arriving in the afternoon. Carla had eight of them on her list, for her cabin. The Tweens are coming, the Tweens are coming. She hadn't looked at the names yet.

It was hot, starkly boring, with boring beautiful scenery all around. The counsellors had to hang around in the parking lot, waiting for the parents to turn up with the new kids. Ten- and eleven-year-olds. Possibly the worst. Or maybe the other counsellors were. A lot of them were Christian. Boring, but in a nice, inoffensive way. She shouldn't say that. She talked to one of them a little now. She thought Jesus might come up. But mostly they just talked about how hot it was again, and how there were no clouds. Maybe there was a secret Christian message in that. Carla didn't know. She felt heathenish. The camp used to be run by a church. Now it was owned by the city recreation department because the church couldn't afford it. It was saved by the regional dental association, who raffled off things like whitening and root canals in a fundraiser. Camp Dentist. It wasn't the official name, but that's what people called it, out of gratitude. When she was little, it used to be called something else: Camp Horned Owl, or Camp Rattlesnake, or something like that. Why couldn't she think of it now? She'd spent enough time here. The same heat and pine needles. The dehydrated blue sky.

Once they'd all arrived, she ended up with an okay group of kids. She checked off the names as they clustered in the parking lot, after the parents had driven away, free. There were two Lisa Maries, weirdly. One was named after Elvis's daughter. Carla asked. One just because, she didn't know why. Wasn't Elvis over yet? No. Elvis was still alive and working in a gas station somewhere, right? Carla said that. Then she said, Thank-you, thank-you very much. The kids looked at her as if she were making animal noises. It wasn't like she listened to Elvis, but come on. One of the Lisa Maries slumped down hard on her duffel bag. She was never going to get up again.

She did, though. Carla eventually managed to get them all up to the cabin, and assigned them each a bunk. Their cabin was Bicuspid, also dentally renamed. She got the kids unpacking, and looked over the name list again. One of the girls was named Ginger. Ginny. She didn't have red hair. It was thick, a brick of deep, solid colour, but not red. What is that colour? At first, Carla kept mixing her up with another girl, in the bunk above hers. Harmony. That one had surprisingly big thighs, and fat flaps as breasts, which weren't breasts yet. The other one, Ginny, was very thin and straight-backed, but they looked the same, somehow, half-formed, but self-sufficient. The Tween age. Carla stood in the middle of the cabin, supervising. They had relaxed now, with proprietorship. Their bed. Their cabin. Their counsellor. They started talking. Harmony had a brother who was coming to the boys' camp next week. His name was Clef. Carla would be gone by then. Thank God. No, not really. She was just tired. She sat back on her bed, the only non-bunk bed in the tight little room. Privilege. When she was a kid, she always read Elvis as *Evils*. She thought about maybe telling them that, but she didn't.

They had to go to the mess hall to be given the introductory talk. Carla could give it herself, by now, practically. The camp family. The life experience. Yeah. And rah. They all clapped at the end. The camp director, Merle, clapped, too, for camp, for herself, for all of them. That's what it's all about. She had her camp T-shirt on, with the wide grinning mouth logo on the front of it. Her own smile was more square, with tea stains around the gums, up close. Carla had seen her up close. Merle had been the director forever, it seemed. She, too, was unchanging. So was the man there next to her. They were supposed to call him Duncle Icky. He lived in a cabin next door to the camp property, somewhere out in the trees. He helped out, fixing things, building maintenance, that sort of stuff. He had a shaved head, which looked as if it had grey seeds sprinkled on it. He was grinning over all the campers. He wasn't slow-minded, or anything. Just old. He also had soft, hairless white legs. When Carla was a kid, some of the girls used to make up stories about him and Merle, the things they would get up to at night. There were lots of bums and I love you so muches in the stories. Ah, youth.

After the happy happy talk, they had dinner. The girls were settling, ordering themselves. Hothouse friendships. Harmony and Ginny were whispering at one end of the table. Already, the other girls were quieter in their presence. The bored Lisa Marie pressed her coleslaw down to her plastic plate, and the boring Lisa Marie ate hers properly. Carla chatted with her for a while, then looked out the window. There was no glass in it, just a screen. Through the wire grid, the lake was dull, passed out in the flat evening light. There was electricity in the mess hall, but not in the cabins. When Merle turned on the lights, it was suddenly like a mall. Mall lighting. Smooth, bland faces. Shopping around.

There was no campfire on the first night. Rules. Carla took her kids to the washroom block to brush their teeth at the long trough sink. The toilets were farther off. The hole-in-the-ground kind, in ripe little outhouses. Last week there had been a bat nesting in the corner of one of them, but Duncle Icky had gotten rid of it, after all the requisite screaming. One of the girls wanted Carla to hold her hand on the way there now. Harmony. No, Ginny. She seemed sweet. Fragile. She must be one of the younger Tweens. Not one of the ones who already looked as if they'd trucked through puberty, now solidified, although there was something grown-up in her manner. Carla waited outside with her flashlight until the kid was done. She could hear shifting and wiping, and then the crickets starting up in the trees. It wasn't completely dark yet. When Ginny came out, she wanted to hold hands again. There was nowhere to wash them in the outhouse. Carla tried not to think of that. The hand was small and crawly. Oh well.

Back in Bicuspid, the girls were lounging. They had set out their things territorially: stuffed animals, hairbrushes, books, flashlights. Retainers. The dentists would be glad of the patronage. Some bottles by one girl's bunk. Vitamins, aspirin, homeopathic stuff. Which one was she? She was bunched up in her bunk already, with her sleeping bag up to the crown of her skull. Some of them are like that.

Carla said it was time for everybody to turn in. *Turn in.* One of those camp expressions. You can't help yourself after a while. She sat on her bed, and let them shine their flashlights around for a minute. The moving light circles showed the rough planked ceiling, the cracks. She watched, too. Her eyes were tired. She could go and sit around with some of the other counsellors, but she didn't. She just lay there.

Some of the girls started talking in the dark. About the cracks, the earth smell in there. Then about families. One said she had three brothers. One said she had a new baby brother. Another one said she did, too. It sounded like Ginny saying that, with her funny smoker's voice. A high little rasp, like a cigar-smoking chipmunk, maybe. She said the baby brother was born at home. Just a little while ago. She got to watch, she said. It was in her mum's bedroom. She watched. He got born, and there was blood all over the place, and the baby was naked, with a plug coming out of his stomach. Then, you know what else, they ate that thing, the placenta. They had a barbecue with it.

It got quieter in the dark, in the cabin. Carla started listening. The word knocked at her brain. She said, You ate the placenta?

How did a kid know a word like placenta? The voice said, pleasantly, Mm hmm. I put ketchup and mustard on mine.

Carla said it was time to stop talking now, okay.

❧ ❧ ❧

In the morning, they started the round of activities. Carla had to supervise them everywhere. Meals, Arts and Crafts, Sports, Canoeing, Swimming, Chapel, Campfire. Following her group around, cheering them on. Yay, and yay again. They were already in evolutionary groups, girl groups. The way it goes. They weren't quite as bad as the Teens, but they were getting there. In the Arts and Crafts lodge, one girl seemed discarded already. She was the one with the vitamins. What was her name? Something like Boone. Or Billy. No, maybe Boone. An old dead cowboy name, meant to be sassy and cute when bestowed on a girl. You could see the parents' hope. But in real life, the girl was like plain dough. She couldn't pull it off. A lump, sitting there at the pitted old table, with her nest of yarn and popsicle sticks. You can always tell.

Carla went and sat down beside her, dutifully. Hey, she said. Girl conversation ran through her mind. She asked her things. Was she one of the ones with a new baby brother? No. Did she have any brothers? No. Sisters? No. What was she making, there? Something.

Something. The Boone girl was polite enough, but what can you do? It was really hot in there. The ancient smell of glue in the air. Carla breathed. Maybe she could get some kind of ancient high. Again, she said, Hey, brightly. She said, Why don't you go and sit with those two? They're making popsicle-stick stuff, too. Ginny and Harmony, over there, she said.

The Boone girl looked up at them, at the other end of the table. So did Carla. The two girls' hair was caught in the shaft of sun from the screened window. They could be an ad for shampoo. An ad for hair. For what hair should be. They were bent together, making something complicated and architectural with their little sticks. All the things you build in Arts and Crafts as a kid, every year at camp. God's-eyes and miniature models of the camp. All that building, still going on. Those two looked as if they had the master plan. Ginny's hair a heavy crinoline, falling around her face. Harmony's lighter, more slippery looking. Carla watched them building and talking. The confidence.

When Carla was about ten, there was a girl at camp for one summer. She was older. She looked a little bit like Ginny: thin, with that high ribcage and neck. Something about her. The calm, expectant expression. She was famous, popular. She didn't come back. Too much for this place. Now, Carla could see Ginny's light, building fingers, her calm lips. A sadness washed in. She would never have those, or that wholly confident ease at the top. She would never be that. She would remember it and think of it when she was sixty or seventy, and still be sad. What can you do?

She looked at the two girls, with their shiny commercial hair, in the light. You couldn't see the fat on Harmony, the way she was sitting. It was clearly her task to be fatter, though, as handmaiden, an acknowledgement of Ginny's superiority. Carla felt the Boone girl beside her, humidly miserable. It was Swimming next. Carla breathed out, and said, Okay.

That girl's name wasn't Boone. Carla couldn't remember the right name, though, and it didn't matter, did it? The girl stood on the wharf, just apart from the rest of the group. The lifeguard was talking to them, and making doggy-paddle arms. The lifeguard had energy. Carla sat with one of the other counsellors, whose cabin was also swimming. Their bodies sucked into the gravelly beach where they sat. Inertia: how rocks stay where they are. Carla ignored the Boone scene, and lifted her face to the sun, her eyeballs sizzling with red shapes. She never burned, at least. The other counsellor, Christine, had a raw, peeled patch on her forehead, as if she were being transformed, or made new. She was one of the Christians, so maybe she liked that. She just loved her kids, the ones in her cabin now, they were such a great little gang. She was going to have a whole bunch of her own one day, as many as she could. Her boyfriend had given her a promise ring. They were allowed to get engaged for real after they were done Grade Twelve. They'd gone up in front of the church to promise, so it was real and everything. Christine had been a counsellor for a long time. Forever. Since the pre-Dentist church days. She probably lived there all year round, hibernating in the winter in Wisdom, her cabin. Carla listened. *Gang*. It tinkled in her head, stripped of violence. Must be nice, in Wisdom.

She made herself open her eyes when there was hard splashing. The lifeguard was making the girls jump into the lake one by one. Cannonballs. One of the kids was standing on the edge of the wharf, looking down. Carla tried to clear the black sunspots from her vision. She squinted. The girl didn't want to jump. It must be that Boone girl. Was it? No. It was Ginny, silhouetted. Now Carla watched, harder. The lifeguard yelled, We're all human cannonballs here, and gave Ginny a little push. Ginny tipped, and flailed, and fell, in slow motion. A crooked splash at the bottom. Ginny's head popping out of the water, a slick cork. Screaming in short whistle bursts, not stopping. So the lifeguard had to jump in, with her sunglasses and shirt on, and drag Ginny to the wharf ladder. It wasn't that deep. Come on, she was saying. Her voice lifeguardy, irritated at the weak, the dissenting.

When Carla got over there, Ginny was gulping and heaving. They took her to the nurse's cabin, where she had to sit and breathe into a paper bag. The lifeguard said, Okay, so we're good, and escaped back to the water.

The nurse was Merle, who was more than a director. She patted Ginny's wet head and said she would be just fine. Then Ginny gasped harder. She rasped, Asthma, leaving her mouth open, like a dying, smoking fish.

Merle's face dropped. Where's your inhaler, she said. But Ginny just shivered and sucked on the bag as if there were a bottle in there. Merle found somebody else's inhaler in the cupboard, and pushed it into Ginny's mouth. Now breathe in, she said. Ginny sputtered and wept, wept, wept. That's better, Merle said. We're all okay here. She smiled with her antique-finish teeth. We're okay.

❧ ❧ ❧

Carla got Christine to take over her group for the rest of the afternoon. She took Ginny and the paper bag back to their cabin, and tried to be nice. Ginny was shaky and silent, but not crying anymore, at least. Carla didn't know what to say at first, but then she tried to get Ginny to talk about her life. She tried to imagine it. The baby brother and all, the placenta. Probably a nice, baggy hippie family. Probably really happy. But Ginny wasn't talking. She lay there on her bunk, bright eyes above her paper bag, looking at Carla every so often. Carla rambled on, then got quiet.

After a while, Duncle Icky came in to ask if everybody was doing okay, there. He had his old-man Bermuda shorts on, with a hammer hanging from one of the belt loops. He said they could go for a motorboat ride, for a treat, just the three of them. He shone at them. Ginny sat up for a second with the paper bag away from her mouth. It was open. She was going to say something. Then she remembered, and let herself back down, saying, Oh. She gasped and wheezed, a huge sucking wheeze. Carla stuck the inhaler between her lips. She'd been holding it hard, the little gun outline of it in her palm.

Duncle Icky's face scrunched. Poor little girl, he said. We'll have to be extra nice to her, he said.

Carla said, Yeah. Ginny had hidden her face in her soggy paper bag again. Her hair still clumpy wet. She exhaled, as if trying herself out.

Then she cried for two days. It was disconcerting. Silent, constant tears running down her face. They looked thick, almost like faux soap-star tears. Otherwise she looked perfectly normal. Her eyes weren't even red. She did wheeze sometimes, sudden squalls of it. Carla could hear her at night. Hee. Hee. Hee. That's how it sounded. You had to feel sorry for her. When the others were doing Sports or Swimming, she sat with Ginny and watched. She braided Ginny's hair into little braids, all of it, and tied the ends with somebody's orthodontic elastics. Absurd happiness in the job, in getting every hair in right. Afterwards, Ginny was silent again. Carla asked if she wanted to go home, but Ginny shook her braided head, and wheezed a little wheeze.

Merle said Ginny was fine. She checked her over again. She gave her the eye, and the talk. Ginny had to learn to tough it out. That's what campers do. Isn't that right, Carla? she said. But she let Ginny keep the inhaler, even though she didn't think she really needed it, she was just fine without that. Merle never changed; she just got slightly more square-shaped. Her duty to keep things exactly the same. She'd been there so long. She should get a real job.

Ginny clutched the inhaler, and her tears kept coming and coming. Carla finally asked if she wanted to phone home, even though that was entirely against the camp rules and ethos. There was a phone, black and rattly, in the back of the nurse's cabin. Feeling like a minor character in a play, Carla took her in there. Come, my lady. Everybody else was at Chapel, which was a few rows of wooden benches in the forest where they'd cut down some trees. It was non-denominational now. They'd stuck pinecones all over the big old wooden cross that was there, so it looked like something else. Maybe non-denominational porcupine worship. When Ginny saw the phone, she seemed happy enough about it, even though she still wasn't talking. She started to dial, then stopped. She gave Carla a look. Such a look.

So Carla stood in the doorway, stung, and watched out for Merle. Disbelief at the heat in her face. She could hear them all singing from Chapel, off there in the forest. *Someone's singing, Lord. Kumbaya.* Was that non-denominational? Merle's happy voice clanged above the rest. *Oh, Lord. Kumbaya.*

Then Ginny was there behind her, and Carla said, Oh, hey. Did you talk to your mum? Did you talk to your baby brother? She tried to sound nice, but not too nice. Casual.

Ginny said, What? Her little rough voice. Then she blinked. She said, No.

❧ ❧ ❧

She seemed to perk up again, anyway. She didn't have to do Swimming anymore. She sat with Carla and Christine on the rocks, and they watched the others getting dive-bombed by barn swallows. There must be a nest under the edge of the wharf. The birds sharp and slicing. Some of the girls looked scared, even the bored Lisa Marie. That Boone girl continually flapped her arm in the air above her head in the water, trying to dog-paddle with the other one.

Ginny seemed fine. She kept calling Carla *Carly*, and leaning on her. The smooth ease. Carla felt herself grinning once, at the proximity, at the contrast of the lifeguard's phony coolness, slouching on the wharf.

Ginny did do sports. Carla worried about her, especially with all the running around. When Carla was supervising, she kept the inhaler in her pocket all the time, the little blue weight of it. She watched Ginny burn past the others in the backwards race, her braids in her face. She came first in the whole camp. Somehow she looked as if she were going the right way. Harmony was ruffled. She'd started out right beside Ginny. I wasn't last, she said to Carla. Arguing.

They had a treasure hunt hike, to find things. There were things in the forest. Birds. Raccoons. Rocks. Pine needles. They were supposed to collect what they found, for the Exploring Our World display in the mess hall. There were a lot of feathers. Ginny had a fistful. Now she and Harmony were picking cushiony moss off a jack pine. Harmony said you could make diapers with it. She laughed a lot, but she stopped when Ginny didn't. The bored Lisa Marie sat on a rock, glazed. So boring, boring, boring, boring. She was already out of there, mentally. Out of the Tweens. Carla didn't make her hunt for anything. The boring Lisa Marie was assiduously collecting different lichens, or whatever they were, with another slightly boring girl. Carla's eyes blurred over, and she closed them. Then that quiet girl, Boone, tripped on something. She was facedown on the trail. Carla said, Oh, are you okay?

The girl looked up. She was right on the edge of crying, but she didn't. It wasn't that bad. You're all right, Carla said. She smiled.

A bright, pure scream came. Not from the Boone girl. Ginny. Oh, God. Carla got up and ran up the path, ahead into the trees, to find her. Where was she? There. There she was. What happened? Carla said.

Ginny's face was indignant, then flat. I got bitten, she said. It bit me. It bit me.

Harmony was with her. She looked at Carla. Her face said, *What are you going to do, you?* Carla said, What bit you?

Ginny said, A rattlesnake. It bit me.

Carla said, Oh, my God. There were rattlesnakes out there, real ones, living their poisonous rattly lives. Everybody knew that; you just never saw them. Your inhaler, she said, stupidly.

Ginny stuttered out a wheeze. Another one. She couldn't talk. Carla scrabbled the inhaler out of Ginny's shorts pocket, feeling like an intruder. Here, she said.

Harmony said, Is she okay?

Carla said, I don't know. Yes. Did you see it?

Harmony said, What? She was staring at Ginny.

Carla said, The snake. But Harmony shook her head, doglike. Carla said, Ginny, where did it bite you? Her heart was skittering. Death. Death. Lawyers. Death.

Ginny gasped, and pulled the neck of her camp T-shirt down below her collarbone. Carla said, Your neck? It bit you on the neck? How did that happen? How did it get that high up on you? She hesitated, then reached her fingers below the hot, thin fabric.

Ginny shrieked. The inhaler: where was it now? All Carla could think of, blinking and blinking, stuck. She said, How did a rattlesnake get your neck?

Ginny said, It was a bee.

Carla said, A bee? She was deaf. Her ears singing. She pulled the shirt down gently, so she could see. Oh. But oh, no. Are you allergic? she said, filling with fear again.

Ginny said, Yes. Her eyes were shining.

Carla said, Oh, God. We have to get you back. Oh, my God, hurry. We have to get you a shot right away. She dragged Ginny up, feeling the heat under her thin arms, her thin T-shirt.

Ginny said, No, no. I don't need one. I'm not that kind of allergic, she said, languidly.

Carla set her back on the ground. She looked at the skin. The little puffed sun of redness, with a white heart, just above the collarbone. It wasn't big. It wasn't swelling, was it? She touched it. Was it okay? It seemed okay. The other girls were all standing around now. Ginny was breathing. The bored Lisa Marie said, Where's the snake?

❦ ❦ ❦

It was okay. It was okay. Merle checked out the sting. It was just your garden-variety sting, she said. A bite, actually. A sweat-bee bite. They aren't so bad, those sweat bees. They just want to taste you. She said that, and gave Ginny a standard-issue hug, and said she hadn't been very lucky lately, poor old thing. But they were getting a treat in Arts and Crafts today, she said. They were having a special extra session. Duncle Icky was going to show them something.

Something. Carla's nerves were still firing. She took Ginny back out into the sun and over to the lodge, where the other kids were already sitting around the table with a couple of the other groups. At least it was shadier in there. More normal. They sat down, and Duncle Icky came in just after them. He held up a bouquet of dead fish, strung together, big and small. Duncle Icky said, Now, look here. We got us some carp and some kokanee. Caught them myself this morning. We're going to do some fish painting, he said.

The fish smell hit the air. Skin, rot. The girls all made puking noises and plugged their noses, Ginny puking loudly and happily. Carla told them to be quiet, but she smiled. This was a new one on her. Duncle Icky was grinning. He said, Here's what we got to do. I saw this on the Frontier Channel, he said. He had a huge satellite dish out at his cabin. He dumped a fish in front of each puking kid. Then he showed them how they had to make a little cone of newspaper, and stick it up into the fish's bladder. Ginny and Harmony were giggling. Bladder. Duncle Icky said, That's so you don't get any of the old urine on your painting.

The bored Lisa Marie surfaced. She said, He means pee.

Then all the kids were a laughing gaggle, even the soft uncooked Boone. She had a bleeding elbow. Did she hurt herself? The laughing didn't stop. Duncle Icky said, Yeah, yeah, funny funny, ha ha. Do you want to do this or not?

The wrong thing to say. Some of the girls sat back in their chairs, distancing themselves from the dead fish. Carla sat forward, automatically. She should do something. It was warm and fishy in there. Fine, she said. I don't care what you do. She didn't. Why should she?

Then Ginny said, I want to do it. And Harmony said she did, too. They were still giggling, but they made the little paper rolls, like Duncle Icky showed them, and shoved them into the spongy holes in the fishes' undersides. Harmony kept saying, Urine, and laughing.

Ginny was calm, concentrating. She twirled the paper roll around in her long fingers, delicate, surgical. Carla watched her. She had a carp, with a fat blown mouth, a glassy eye. The others went quiet, too. Now what? she said. Then Duncle Icky showed her how to coat the fish's side with paint, then press it carefully onto a piece of paper. Oh. Like potato printing, but more sophisticated. It was supposed to be. Harmony splodged hers, so it was a fish smear. But Ginny's was an exact shadow of the carp. Duncle Icky held it in the air, a triumph.

So the other girls started plugging and painting their dead fish. Ginny picked up her paper and smelled it. It smells like him, she said. It smells like the bottom of the lake. She gave a little wheeze again, at the memory. Carla held the inhaler. She smelled the paper, when Ginny held it up to her face.

*✤ ✤ ✤*

Fish. Urine. She thought of the smell all night, until she finally had to go to the outhouse. At least she was alone in there. A strangeness. Just her and the smell, the other smell. She found the toilet with her flashlight. They were real toilets, but with no plumbing underneath, just holes. When she was a kid there, she thought that if you slipped backwards into the toilet hole, you would fall for infinity. The biggest number. Somehow, there would still be an end to infinity. There had to be. Did kids still think that?

She could hear something rustling around outside. There was never any wind there, ever, in the summer. She had her flashlight, so she opened the door for a second. No eyes shone back at her. She went back in and sat down. There was rustling, and movement, and the crawling feel of somebody looking at you when you're naked. She pulled up her underwear and felt for the paper, the roll rattling and tearing. At least they had real toilet paper. One concession to the modern, inauthentic life. The sound of it was real and present, right there with her inside the outhouse. The other was different. When she went outside, she swung her flashlight around, but there was nothing there, nothing at all. She got back to the cabin and got into bed. The exposed feeling remaining. Somebody knocked something over. Somebody was snoring, trucker like. She couldn't tell who.

⁊ ⁊ ⁊

A couple of days slid by. The fish smell dissipated. At breakfast one morning, the girls were livelier again, picking up after the midweek slump. That's how it goes. But Carla was more and more tired. How could she keep this up? She chewed a ball of porridge. Hard work, and slow.

She was next to Ginny, who seemed always to want to sit by her at meals. Carly, Carly: the call, the choice. The ridiculous leap of happiness in the heart, which Carla tried to squelch. Ginny was stroking Carla's arm, now, absently, talking to Harmony about her cat. It died. She found it, dead. And you know what, it was frozen to the road after it got hit by a car. She had to peel it off. Peel it, for real. Her hand went on stroking, as if saying, *Yes, I know you, I know you're here.* Harmony said, My cat got hit by a car, too. My dad hit it.

The Boone girl looked stunned, oozy, down at the end of their table by herself. She was melting. Carla should go talk to her. She really should. But Ginny and Harmony were holding her hands now. Kids think you're great, and want to be with you all the time, just because you're older than they are. The thrill of age, for a while. She reminded herself. But she didn't get up. She just said, Hey there. She smiled around her porridge. The Boone girl looked up. Carla said, Are you okay, down there?

The girl said, Yeah. Then she said, My cat died, too.

That was the first time she'd said much of anything. She was quiet. But she was okay. Maybe a little slow, or something. The other girls were onto a different subject, now. Carla listened. The boring Lisa Marie was saying that sugar on your cereal every day makes you chubby. Chubby: the maternal sound. Then the Boone girl said, in the background, What if when I get home my house is burned down, and everybody's all dead in there?

She was louder. Everybody stopped talking and looked at her. She was looking at Carla. God, she was expecting an answer. She was almost crying now, sniffing back a snotty noseful. Wiping at it with a grotesque, scabby elbow. What was with this kid? Carla had to say something. She said, Um, it's okay. Your mum and dad will be here on Sunday, you know.

She should go and hug her. But the kid wasn't a baby. Something prickled around Carla's heart, a chestnut's green casing. Ginny had a mouthful of toast now. She said, I know somebody who died in a fire. My grandma. And my cat. Her cat. They got burned up.

Later, Carla tried to ask her about that. But Ginny was off and running in sports, or laughing wildly with Harmony, or canoeing with her off ahead of everybody else, swollen and muscular in her life-jacket. She wanted to do canoeing now. She wasn't scared, she said. She was a tough kid. Carla watched, and that night, Carla had a dream about the lake being full of charred logs, or bodies, and having to navigate them like a slalom course. She couldn't get herself to wake up.

There were bodies in there, actually. Everybody knew that. But people still swam in it. It was a big lake, long and narrow, and too deep to get whatever bodies were in there out again. Carla didn't mention that to the kids. She had to supervise the bath in the lake the next night. They were supposed to wash up in there before bed every second night. The camp experience. They did it in their bathing suits. Washing each other's hair, and scrubbing their bathing-suited stomachs with soap slivers humpbacked onto new bars. Everything communal. They were supposed to be learning to make do, and recycle. Ginny didn't have to go in, after she started wheezing tenderly again. She sat on the wharf with her toes just skimming the water, like water bugs. She was undoing all her little braids, flicking the elastics into the lake. Carla didn't make the Boone girl go in that night, either. Boone was hunched up with herself on the beach. A little world of misery. A gumball. A tumour. Carla prickled, again. Fine.

She got them into bed, and let them leave their flashlights on and tell ghost stories. They weren't supposed to, but she didn't care. What did it matter? Nobody was going to find out. Merle was off at Duncle Icky's for sure. Probably talking about wonderful, wonderful things. A sudden, square vision of Merle's bum.

Carla stood up and went outside into the open dark. She sat on the step of the wooden cabin. One of the other counsellors came by, with her flashlight swinging. Christine the Christian. She sat down and talked. About marriage, and how camp is good practice, because you can't get away from people. You just have to deal with it. Christine was aglow. She was full of kindness, even though her cabin had started a food fight in the mess hall and hadn't stopped when she'd asked them nicely, and even when she'd had to get mad. Well, that's life. That's what Carla said.

When Christine wandered off to dispense more forgiveness, or whatever, Carla went back inside, feeling relieved. There was low, sandy whispering. It was Ginny. Carla listened. It sounded like a story, the end of one. Ginny whispered, and then she said, in her normal voice, I am the ghost of my grandma. That didn't sound too terrifying. But the way she said it, her rasping voice, made her sound like she could be somebody else. Anybody she wanted. Some old smoking woman, just dead. Carla pressed her arms to her sides, to feel them. Ginny switched on her flashlight and held it under her chin. Her head a lantern. A couple of the girls screamed. Carla told them to settle down. That's enough. Flashlights out. She didn't say Ginny's name.

They eventually got quiet. Later, when she was floating into sleep, she could hear somebody snuffling, and a round of puffs. She sat up. Was it another asthma attack? She grabbed for her flashlight. There was someone moving along the bed, with feet slippering the concrete floor.

Can I get in with you? That's what the person said. It was Ginny again, her skinny little body, still hot, as if she'd just come in from suntanning. Carla said, Did you have a bad dream? Are you scared?

Ginny said, No. She pushed herself into the mattress, and breathed, satisfied. Sleep breathing. She had a peculiar, pungent smell. Like a can of tobacco, or the inside of a drawer, maybe. Carla couldn't tell what it was, and now she couldn't sleep with it. The smell got into her. The snuffling went on, from one of the other beds. Baby sounds, helplessness. But really, what was she supposed to do?

❧ ❧ ❧

On the Friday, the whole camp was supposed to be doing the canoe trip partway up the lake, to have pancakes cooked over a campfire up there. A highlight of the week; they always put it in the Camp Dentist brochure. The cabins went in shifts. Carla's group was first up, at 6:30 AM. She was coated with sleep, fuzzy as a tongue. She never liked pancakes. But the kids were excited. Even Lisa Marie looked awake. Maybe the canoeing would get rid of some of their energy. Carla's seemed to be leaking all the time. Where? Was she old? She was getting there.

She walked on her new old legs down towards the beach. Ginny was beside her, and Harmony trailing. She checked her pocket. The inhaler was there. Good.

Somebody was shouting up ahead of them, then one of the girls came running back towards them. She was yelling, There's a dead body on the beach, Carla, and it's dead. She was trilling with excitement. Ginny shot herself off like an arrow, and Harmony reeled behind her. When Carla got there, a circle had already knitted around it.

Carla said, Let me see. What happened? Everyone looked at her. She looked, and it wasn't a body. It was. But a deer's body. Its mouth clamped shut. Holes in its smooth muzzle. Its ears still pricked and startled. Sticky blood puddinged on the rocks under its face, its dead eye.

The bored Lisa Marie said, Look, there's a hole in its ass. She was interested, for once. Carla looked. Was it shot? The holes in it were small and even, as if on purpose. Piercings. A pierced deer. Punk, Carla thought. Punks.

Ginny said, Wow. Her eyes glittering. The deer was stiffly dead, with stick legs. A secret white bone shining through a rip in its hip. Was that what it was, a bone? The lake was level and bland behind them.

Carla said, Oh no. All she could think was, Doe. A deer. A female dead deer.

But the Boone girl burst: this was it. She was crying for real now, for the whole week, for all the world's suffering, for all infinity, that's how she was crying. She kept saying, Uh. Uh. Uh. Her voice engorged with slimy bubbles of snot, spit. Baby sobs flying out of her dough face.

Carla felt the hardness of her own ribs, her own hands. Her own distaste, the round solidity of it. It's fine, she said. It's just a deer. She tried to sound kind, to pat the girl's face, but there was so much wetness coming from it.

I, the Boone girl said. Uh. Uh.

A wheeze crept up into Carla's ear, a sailboat wind. Heee. Oh no, are you okay? somebody said. Yeah, are you okay? somebody else said. They were talking to Ginny, who was on the rocks now, reclining, flat as the deer.

I need, Ginny said. Carla closed on the inhaler, kneeling in front of her.

Oh. Uh. Uh, the Boone girl said. She was a mess. She should never have been given that name.

❧ ❧ ❧

It turned out that Duncle Icky's dogs got the deer. That's nature's way, he said. But he was sorry about it. He looked sad. The dogs were supposed to guard the place, but they got bored sometimes. Dogs are like people. He wouldn't let them out at night anymore, he said. Carla could imagine them chasing the deer, running it down, until it got to the lake and gave up. It wasn't worth it. The deer was nothing special, it seemed to have decided for itself. It wasn't going to swim out into all that water, even though it could have. Survival of the fittest. That's where they must have gotten it, the dogs, right on the beach, making neat punctures with their teeth.

They didn't have the pancake trip. They did have a special campfire that night, though. The last night. Every cabin was doing a play or skit. The show must go on. It really must. Merle gave a little talk about the dead deer, and how it was sad, but it was okay: the great circle of life. She said it mystically, musingly. Christine wanted to say a prayer for the deer, but

Merle said that wasn't appropriate. Carla didn't want to think about the deer anymore.

They started the show. Christine's cabin did a skit about people in love. There was no point to it. Another group did a dance, but there was no music. No electricity out there on the beach rocks. Mysterious, watching them bobbing up and down, spinning occasionally. They obviously had a song in mind, but you couldn't tell what it was.

Carla didn't know what her cabin was going to do. It was a secret. Or else they hadn't prepared anything. She was a bad counsellor. She shouldn't be doing this job, should she? What did she know? What did anyone? Age is just a number of repetitions, scratches on the wall. She stared at the wavering fire, cross-eyed.

Ginny walked out, high with certainty. She spoke for the cabin. She introduced them. She nodded at everyone, one at a time. *Do it.* They were all in a string, trailing beside her. Except the crying girl, the Boone girl. Maybe she was still in the nurse's cabin, or something. She'd been stung by a bee right near the eyelid, after the deer, when they'd all been sent to sit in the mess hall. A wasp, from a nest someone had brought into the Exploring Our World collection in there. The nest wasn't empty. The wasps weren't dead, just pretending. They were vicious this year. They went in cycles.

But it didn't matter. The kids were singing now, wasp-free. A song about a ghost. The ghost of John. Long white bones. Merle's face was set in jollity. It was fun. It was supposed to be. They sang it again. It only had one verse. *Have you seen the ghost of John. Long white bones with no skin on. Ooh-ooooh. Wouldn't it be chilly with no skin on.*

Ginny sang it twice, at the end, by herself, loudly. Her voice scratched and strong. No wheezing. She said, We made it up. I did. Her triumph. She held her flashlight under her chin again, like in the cabin, but it wasn't really dark enough outside. It gave only a faint circle, as if weak in the face of her. The heat of the leftover daylight, the smoky waves of campfire. Everybody clapped, a slow, hard rhythm. Ginny looked out, hands on hips, utterly fearless.

≈≈ ≈≈ ≈≈

It was late when Carla got back to the cabin. The counsellors stayed around the campfire after the kids went off to brush their teeth. The last night for this bunch. No drinking, or anything. Just sitting. Merle and Duncle Icky had gone off, probably to discuss what to tell the parents about the dogs and the deer, to make it part of the learning experience. Carla kept thinking of the cabin. When she did get up from the campfire, she stopped at one of the outhouses, but she couldn't make herself go in. She didn't have her flashlight. She stood outside it for a long time. Hours. Hours. *Wouldn't it be chilly with no skin on.*

It was dark back in the cabin, and very quiet. The smell of a cellar. The girls must be asleep by now. She hoped. But the feeling, again, of being seen, all the time. She fumbled in the thickness of the dark, trying to find her nightshirt. She could smell campfire all over herself, too. This place, with its same smells, and Tweens, and pit toilets, and killer animals, and cabins named for teeth. Some big experiment. Some great trap. She sat down on her bed and took off her shoes.

Try it. No. Do it. She heard a puffing noise, then a suck. Do it, the voice said. It's drugs. It makes you feel weird.

There was a little moan, short and cut off. Did she hear it? Carla stopped moving. She stopped listening to herself. But there was nothing else. Then it came out again. There was no joke in it. A high, animal sound. Carla looked for eyes, for movement, in the dark. A scratching, and a clicking. A catch. She saw a low little flame in one corner of the cabin. She spoke. She said, You guys. You can't have candles in here.

No. She didn't say it. She should be saying it. But her hands pricked and pricked, and her hairs felt alive all over her, as if her skin were lifting off, as if she weren't there. *You should be in bed*, she should be saying.

She couldn't see any faces. Just the small round of light. A birthday candle, maybe. A cigarette lighter. She heard someone whisper. Say it. Say it. The spitting, emphatic spit. There was a gulp. Oh. That girl. Boone the Weak. I am the deer, the first voice said, conversationally.

Carla did speak. Hey, she said. This was her brilliance.

The voice said, I am the ghost of John the deer. It's me. Now do it, it said. Puff it. That's what it's for.

The other dissolved. It was wet, piteous. No, no, no, no.

It was a female deer, Carla thought. Then she walked towards the flame. She said, Ginny, I know that's you. She could hear the adult in her voice, the wheedling effort audible. What was the other damned kid's damned name? Then she was close enough to see. Ginny's face, her little face, grinning in the dark, all teeth, on her lower bunk. The other girl hunched in her sleeping bag on the floor, halfway under the bed. Ginny had the inhaler in one hand, and a cigarette lighter in the other. She held the light high. It was near her fish print, stuck on the cabin wall. Her triumph still glowing. She said, Hey, we could do a deer print. We could go get it. What did they do with the deer? she said.

The other girl was gagging on herself, her sobs. Uh. Uh. Uh. Carla stood. She felt her shoulders drop. She was nothing.

She couldn't do this. She said, You guys, stop fooling around. Get into bed.

She stood there. Trying to impress them with her older, bigger self. Just because. That's how it's supposed to work.

Nobody listened. Ginny turned. The lighter made a hot circle on the fish paper. The fish's eye. Ginny said, I seen a dead deer before, you know. Then the light grew. It grew up along her hair. It crackled like cereal, and popped into life. It was surprising, how fast it went. Her hair bright, with her face in the middle, looking straight through her, which Carla would always see, clear as a clock.

# Everyday Living

THERE IS A WOMAN WITH TWO CHILDREN on an airplane. One of them, the children, laments. The uncanniness, here in the air. He won't have it. He comforts himself by wailing, then inhaling, in time with his kicks on the back of the seat in front. Huh-wah, huh-wah. Then, aaaaahhhh. His lungs feel pleasantly tight. So do his fingers inside his fists. The seatbelt is the worst. The worst thing in the world. There is nothing, nothing to do. Only his voice breaks up the flowering boredom in his head. The kicking is an accompaniment. Huh-wah, huh-wah.

The woman is heedless. She is his mother, although she might as well be anyone. She isn't listening. She loves being sealed in the plane, its soiled tundra air and burgundy blankets with their colonies of lint. She has the free headphones on, listening to something. It's the movie; it's a good one. Last time she was on a flight they showed something about a snowman who came to life. Or a man who turned into a snowman, or Santa, and then came to life. He came into the house and kissed his wife and kid. They pulled him around on a red wagon. There were puddles and tears at the end. It wasn't very good. But this one is. It's got that girl who looks

184

like a young Meg Ryan in it, and the male star is convincingly in love. Not that that would be hard if your girlfriend looked like Meg Ryan. Or your wife. Whatever.

The other son is drawing a picture with some crayons the red-headed flight attendant gave him. He is drawing a picture of the flight attendant. Tentacles of orange shoot out from the round head. Fire comes out of her fingertips and toenails. Now they're very red, burning. Her blue uniform surrounded by wings of flame. He has no green, and can't remember how to make it. He hates her now. He sees fire eating out her heart, burning it all to black inside. He colours a black spot onto the blue. It's nice. Satisfying. He passes it into his mother's hand.

Look. Look. Mum.

Mmm, nice, Felix.

No, look.

Yes, I said nice colouring.

She sees the orange on green. Pretty. Felix is so arty. Someone across the aisle wonders why on earth the woman named the poor child that. And why she won't shut her other boy up.

Mum, you said. You said.

Quentin has stopped wailing. Again he says, You said, Mum.

The woman looks at him sidelong, pulling off one earphone. What, she says.

You said.

I said what?

He is silent. He gives the back of the seat in front of him another exploratory kick, digging for the best resonance. The man in the seat suffers.

I said, she repeats, in a murmur, her eyes on the white-washed little airplane movie screen. Everything on it is pale, watercolour. The bright sky radiating in from the plane's cell windows. She loves this. The Meg Ryan girl and the man are going to kiss in a minute.

Quentin goes back to his kick pattern. He tells the seat back, You said.

Felix takes a fresh sheet of paper and thinks of drawing a picture of Quentin. The paper is scrap from the computer at home, with things printed all over the back of it. One of the biggest words is Dog. It's from when Holly was lost. Dad was making Lost posters on the computer to put up on poles and walls around the neighbourhood. But then they found her down the street in somebody else's backyard. She didn't want to come home. She ran away when she saw them coming.

He takes up a purple crayon. He starts with Quentin's shoes, which are black. Close enough. Then it changes into a picture of Holly, wearing four purple boots. Mum says Holly's not really a girl anymore, she's an *it*. Mum thinks that's funny. He brings it up. Holly's an it, right, Mum? he says.

Meg Ryan Girl is now about to take off her shirt. Will they show this on the plane? The woman is interested. She clicks the little volume button on her armrest to turn up the towering soundtrack.

Mum. Mum.

Yes.

She's an it, right?

What.

Holly. She is.

Mm hmm.

She is. He knew it, but Mum didn't laugh. She's watching the movie. He colours Holly's fur, and gives her a black staring eye.

The movie is badly edited for airplane audiences, and the screen jumps and splits for a second before the girl would have slipped her light blouse from her frail shoulders. Now it's an innocuous street scene, with anonymous people sliding by.

Stop. One of them is looking at her. For the tiniest moment, a film extra seems to see her, his eyes straight on her. He's gone, but he turned his head to look at her as he passed onscreen. What. She blinks. Oh my God. Could it?

She wishes they could rewind the film. She even looks around for the flight attendant, for a second. But already the camera has turned itself on the girl, now in a cosy winter coat, walking, downcast, through a shopping mall. But that was him, before. It really was. How on earth. How bizarre.

Felix shades in the ground under Holly's feet, making it orange, a hot sidewalk. Quentin, grunting, seizes the orange crayon and swirls a fireball with it, above the dog. Felix gets mad. Automatic. It's his crayon, his picture. Then interested. What is it? He likes the orange. He points to it and looks at his brother. He asks, A fire?

Quentin shakes his head. He says, Dad. He licks the waxy paper, then pushes it into his unseeing mother's acquiescent hand with a big grin.

❧ ❧ ❧

How old are the lettuces? Clarissa fingers romaine heads. Out of habit her mind has been counting the lettuces in the pile. There are twenty-two. She is forty-four. Is there something in this? Probably not, but she feels a little spike of thrill at the pattern beneath everything. Then a wash of heat. This keeps happening. Isn't it too early for this? Her mother was fifty at least. Well, it's not that, then, is it. Suddenly, she's wearing a vest of sweat, and it's melting down the small of her back onto her legs. She feels like gasping, only she's too embarrassed. She is nuclear. She leans slightly into the produce shelf, wishing that the periodic spray of water would burst over the lettuces, and her, right now. It doesn't. The pattern must have curled back on itself, stopped. Oh well. She would have looked silly if she'd gotten really wet. The heat subsides into the furnace in her, and the sweat is still hidden under her jacket. It's happened four times since she went to bed last night. Twice as many as yesterday. She stands up straight and looks at her list. Lettuce. She still hasn't chosen one. She guiltily prefers iceberg, its crisp tastelessness, but romaine is better for you, so a fattish dark one goes into her basket. She should get some multi-vitamins, too.

The trek across the megastore to the pharmaceutical aisle seems vast. A wasteland, she thinks, then finds the thought witty, sort of. She begins the walk, feeling fatigued, noble. He enjoys all this good-for-you food. She'll remind him to take the vitamins. She heads past Snacks and Cookies in Picket Way. The aisle is named after a neighbourhood street that was half-razed to make way for the parking lot. Picket. Pick. Signs. Scabs. Ah, her wit. She feels the sneaking breath of a laugh in her throat, the kind you can't keep down. It escapes out of her nose. She is stupidly obvious. She suddenly turns down the next aisle to look more self-propelled, self-controlled. It's Arbutus Street, an avenue of frozen things. She pauses to look at frosty microwave pizzas. Somehow they make her want to laugh again. They're ridiculous, moonlike, with cheesy craters and dried sausage lakes. Again the laughing air escapes from her nose. A little, whinnying horse. She feels happier in the frozen avenue. Nobody else is there. Maybe she'll buy one of the pizzas, for luck of some kind. There are at least thirty of them. Forty. Forty-four, when she quickly, unthinkingly counts. This is surely amazing. Cold and happiness itch her fingertips as she reaches into the freezer cabinet for one. Yes.

She realizes she has said this out loud when someone leans over her shoulder, close to her face. Someone huge. She turns a little, looking over her raised shoulder, waking up. It's an enormous puffed-up snowman. He is three balls of fluffy synthetic cloth, with inert eyes and mouth stitched on in black felt. An orange foam carrot nose, combative. He is very close to Clarissa, the fluff of his body approaching the nap of her jacket, seeking her stockinged knees. He is wearing a green woolly hat and scarf, nothing else, except three black felt buttons that button nothing down his body.

Would you like to try Frosty.

She can see the grimy tips of sneakers nosing from the bottom of the snowy costume.

Pardon? She says this cheerfully.

Would you like to try Frosty.

The voice is ancient, muffled. Lost. A fluffy limb holds something out to her. Oh. It looks beseeching, the arm, holding a tray. She looks at it closely.

It's Frosty.

Sorry?

It's Frosty. Mini-quiches. Frosty Frozen Fresh.

She thinks this is what he has said. Maybe it was *flesh*. She's beginning to feel quite cold. This is a pleasant change, but she wants to escape. She focuses on the particles on the tray. They look amusing, but this time she doesn't feel the laughing push in her nostrils. What are they? Cubes of quiche, with something pale green caught in them.

Oh, thank-you, no. No thanks, she says.

It's Frosty. When freshness counts.

Pardon? No thanks.

Frosty.

He keeps holding out the tray as she smiles hard and turns to walk away. She doesn't want to eat. She can't erase the giant figure from her mind. She needs vitamins. Then she realizes it, or half-realizes it. Without thinking, she turns back. She doesn't go too close, but she can see. There is a semi-circular mesh insert under the snowman's neck. She looks at it, still smiling pleasantly, and she can see two real eyes behind it, under the snowman's dead head. They're looking back at her. They're his. They're him. They're smiling. One is about to wink. She thinks of fortune. He turns around to shuffle off, with a little wave. Then she starts to feel the drench of heat again, starting at the back of her neck. So. What should she do, because this can't be.

❧ ❧ ❧

Meg Ryan girl is doing something else, but she still looks damned good. The woman can't keep her eyes off the screen. The actress's hair is such a halo in the winter movie sunlight, and her coat is so stylishly cut. She is also a bit like a curly blonde Audrey Hepburn, if that's possible. The same sure deer legs and boy ribcage. She's alone, alone, and the camera is upon her. A tear is born from the corner of one eye, missing the lashes as it falls in close-up perfection. Its path is fascinating. The soundtrack music is like a heart beating in three-four time. A sick heart. Ba, bump, bump.

Quentin boots the seat back, out of sync. He isn't wearing headphones. The movie is madness, boring. He can't feel his bum. His lips taste crayony. He whips out a hand, snatches another of Felix's crayons. It's a nice one. He nibbles the paper around the point. He is a rabbit with long teeth, biting. He is a rat. Chewing off the tip of the point, he tastes the blue.

I want that one, Felix says. Felix is looking at his brother. He has taken back the drawing from his silent mother and is working on it. Quentin's front teeth have a coat of wax. He bares them, widening his nostrils. Felix says, I want the blue.

Quentin snuffles, a rodent wheeze. He opens his mouth wide, then stage-whispers, Nooo, as if someone has just fallen off a cliff with him watching. Onscreen, the girl is talking to somebody.

Felix sinks. He says, I need the blue. I'm not finished my Holly.

Quentin chews off a curl of blue paper, experimenting. He doesn't have to look at Felix. The crayon cigarlike between his besmirched teeth. He casually unbuckles his seatbelt. He keeps looking at the movie, his eyes narrowing, critical.

Quentin. Quent.

No answer. Felix tries again. Quent, he yells. Despair. He needs the blue for the sky around Quentin's orange cloud of Dad. Felix likes it, objectively, even though he is mad at the takeover. His picture. He remembers. He says, Your drawing is stupid.

Quentin ignores. He is turning into his mother, his eyes matching hers in their focus and line. He slips the headphones over his ears.

It sucks. You can't even draw. You can't draw anything, Felix says. He turns to his mother, displaying the picture like a wound. Mum.

She is deep within the movie. Her eyes intent on the screen. No outside motion.

Mum. Mum.

He brandishes the drawing near her head. Quentin, beside him, takes the crayon out of his mouth. He says, Linda.

Snap. She says, Quentin, what did you say?

He grins, and Felix sits back into the upholstery.

What did you just say to me? she says.

Linda.

He tests the word out on his tongue, rolling it out from behind his waxed teeth. He utters it to himself again a few times.

You know you don't call me that. I'm your mother. That means you call me Mummy, you don't call me Linda.

Linda.

This time he calls it. An angel's high, clear purity. The capital L is cold and sweet in his mouth when he breathes it in.

Quentin. What do you want? she says.

He only says it again, as if he'll never stop saying it. Linda. Linda.

She says, What does he want, Felix? So Felix takes his chance. He thrusts the picture close to her ear, sliding it up between the headphone and her head, and she has no choice. Oh. Did you do this, sweetie? she says.

It's not finished. Quentin is eating the blue, he says.

Oh, Quentin.

The boy looks at her. I did it, too, he says.

No you didn't, you just wrecked it. He scribbled, Mum, Felix says.

It's nice to work together. And share like good boys.

Look at it, Mum. Look what he did.

She glances at the screen, where subplot people are still talking unimportantly, and then looks down at the bright paper in her hand.

Nice colouring, you two.

Know what it is? Felix asks, with hope. Challenge.

Mm.

Her mind drifts back to the movie, as the romantic theme begins to pump in her earphones again. Then she remembers what she was thinking about before. Him. Of course it wasn't. But it looked like him on the screen, and it certainly felt like him looking at her. The way he does. He used to do that more.

What, Mum, Felix says.

Mm.

What is it, then, Mum?

She sighs and closes her eyes. The two-second scene from the film plays across her eyelids. The man in his dark suit and tie, striding across the road behind Meg Ryan girl's figure, turning his head for an instant to the camera. He knew what was going on. That she would see. How absolutely weird.

Tell me. Mum.

She feels the picture with her thumb, eyes still closed. Oh, she says, Is it our house at home?

Nooo. You're not looking.

Yes, I am.

Her mind flickers. Her husband in the dark suit, looking at her. Is it? Is it your school? she says.

The plane bumps into a bubble of nothing, and a lead egg in her belly drops.

No. Why don't you get it? You're so stupid, Mum.

She opens her eyes and looks at Felix. What did he say?

Felix, she says.

You are, he says.

Don't you talk to me that way. I'm your mother.

Well, you didn't look.

Felix says this to himself. His eyebrows are heavy. You don't get it, he says to her. Quentin clambers onto his brother's lap as the plane gives another tentative lurch. He lifts the headphone from his mother's ear. Lindaaa.

Quentin, she says. She snatches it back from the child. She wants to see the man again, giving her a private blue-eyed look from the screen. She wants to be sealed in the plane with only him. She wants to be the Meg Ryan girl, with him at her back. Crossly, she slaps Quentin's hand. He splays his fingers in front of her face.

Linda. Linda.

Stop that. You're not behaving, she says.

Felix says, You're not behaving, Mum.

Quentin says, Linda.

Yeah, Linda. You don't even know what it is.

The plane sinks into a tube of weightlessness, then heaves itself back upwards. The boys grin and bounce, their arms around each other, locked like monkeys. The captain announces that the flight attendants should return to their seats and that the in-flight entertainment will be turned off for the hopefully brief duration of this unexpected turbulence. She isn't behaving. The screen goes a soft, planet blue. Everything has vanished into space. Where is he? Supposed to be waiting for them at the airport, and he turns up in this movie. Well, whatever.

She crumples the picture in her fist. I'm your mother for life, she says, arguing. She thinks of him, standing in the airport, waiting for them and their airplane smell. Or not.

❧ ❧ ❧

Melting, so hot she can hardly stand it. This time Clarissa knows her jacket is soaking through under the arms and in the hot small of the back. Its dark grey will have darker blooms. She hopes the snowman can no longer see her, as she fans the neck of her white blouse in and out. She wishes she were back with the pizzas, but not with him. Not with Frosty, but *him*. Too strange. Is she being silly? No, that was her husband, with his eyes, in there, all right. But she couldn't let on that she thought so. She suddenly wants to go back to the frozen aisle, munch on a quichelet sample, ask him what he's doing in there, talk with him quietly, but there's no way to do it without looking foolish. What if she's wrong? And his little wave had been one of finality. Farewell.

She swings her basket around casually, hoping to cool her heated bits with the motion of her arm. She decides to head for Pharmacy and Health to keep quiet. Maybe they'll have something for her besides vitamins. What is it that you're supposed to take? Evening Primrose Oil, or one of those herbal things. Anyway, she's too young for this. It must be something else. The heat rises up her body in waves. She wants to drink air. The hair around her temples is starting to dampen. And stick. She walks a little faster, for the breeze.

He's supposed to be at work. She doesn't quite know what his job is exactly. He works in IT, has a lot of meetings, is always ready for dinner when he gets home. If he gets home. He's often so late. He works so hard at all he does. Anyway. A healthy dinner. That's why she got the romaine, for tonight's salad. Maybe they'll go for a run together first, unless he's too hungry to wait. Maybe some exercise would help knock off the heat inside her. Some bug, maybe.

She walks past Dairy and picks up a litre of skim milk. It looks bluish, sad in its plastic jug. She holds its coolness in her hands, feeling wonderful. He likes this kind. It's from a local dairy, too. Organic. Good. The best way. She takes out her list again while she's stopped, since the heat is beginning to die and she's calmer. She feels healthful. Tofu, the firm kind, and rice noodles next. She can do Crying Tiger stir-fry tonight for the main course. Tofu is in the refrigerated section, not far from the milk, so she aims for it. She takes the seventh package on the shelf. There are twelve this time: nothing. She puts it on top of the things in her basket. The bloated, pale pizza asserts itself when she looks down. Heavens. How can she have picked that? What was she thinking? There's no way he would eat it. She knows him. And neither would she.

Backtracking, she heads towards the frozen Arbutus Street aisle. When she reaches it, Frosty, his huge fluff bulk, looms in her mind. She peers around the corner before she turns down the aisle, as if she were just standing there inspecting the cheap buckets of synthetic ice cream in the corner fridge. As if. But he isn't there. Her heart accelerates. She counts forty-five, forty-six, forty-seven beats in quick-time. But he isn't there anymore. She was half-hoping to see him again, to look knowingly into the face, to not give him away. To show him that she knows, that she is on his side, whatever he is doing. But the only figure in the aisle is an elderly person looking cautiously at bags of frozen vegetables. Clarissa walks back towards the pizza section, just as if she'd chosen the wrong thing, not as if she couldn't pay for it if she so chose. She hopes she looks this way. She puts the pizza back on the shelf. It has no more luck. She passes the person on the way back, peering at packages of spinach with a snowman logo. *Frosty Frozen Fresh.* The senior looks up at Clarissa going by, and remarks, This one again.

Clarissa keeps going, without even a smile of response. She is sorry to be impolite, but she's got things to do. She's got to get to the vitamin aisle and get home, so she can start cooking. He wasn't there in the store. He'll be home soon. He will. Something is about to attack, and she knows it. She holds her head up and tries to look like a pleasant, normal person doing her shopping. The list says vitamins. Hurry up.

She's nearly there, just passing Baking Needs. Glacé cherries jump around her head. She used to love them, as a child. But the dyes. Hyperactivity. Cancer. Glacé. Cancer on ice. She wants to laugh again, but then something cracks hard into her. It's not the heat, almost expected now. It's a person, solid, and Clarissa's basket arcs into the air, hurling its contents as it goes. Her purse bounces onto the floor, and her cards scatter themselves. Her driver's license lands near the person's feet, face-up and grinning.

It's a young woman, maybe twenty-three or twenty-four. She's wearing a pharmacist's labcoat and has tied-back hair, beautiful hair, the colour of an Irish setter. She picks up the cards while Clarissa stands, dignified, stupid.

I'm so sorry. That was all my fault, the girl says. She glances at the license while handing it back. She says, Clarissa. What a pretty name. It's so different. Old-fashioned. She laughs a little peal.

Clarissa feels her bedraggledness. Heat rising. Pearls burst out upon her chest and forehead. She inhales sharply.

Stupid.

Sorry?

Stupid. The name.

Oh, says the girl, I don't think so. She looks closely, kindly, youthfully, at Clarissa.

Ma'am. Ma'am, she says. Clarissa. Are you all right?

Clarissa thinks of the frozen aisle, the lost paradise. Maybe they have flash-frozen eggs, something nobody would have thought of, years ago, instead of the fresh ones, with the dates on the packaging, the stamped little numbers, stamping along. She closes her eyes and imagines looking at this pharmacist girl with glittering dark ones. It isn't over.

I want something for. For. Pregnancy.

This comes from nowhere as the fire chafes up and down her spine. It's interesting. An interesting condition, as the old novels say. Life should be more interesting. But instead, people accept things, all kinds of things, she thinks. Odd, the things people can accept about it, to keep things the same. Odd, that we aren't surprised more. She accepts that she is covered in sweat. She isn't old at all.

For pregnancy? the girl says. She has a slight scent, a breakfast odour, a morning greeting. Toast and eggs. Wake up, wake up. I'm awake. Why aren't you? She is probably bursting with eggs. Clomid, Clarissa thinks suddenly, naming her. One of those fertility drugs. The sound of clouds, of clones, of humidity, of middles. The promise.

Oh, you know, Clarissa laughs. She opens her eyelids. A Madonna smile amidst the sweat. Maybe you can help me, she says.

# Things Happen

THESE ARE SOME OF THE THINGS THEY DID. They made up songs and recorded them onto blank tapes. One of the songs was called Shattered to be Living, and it was really good. Carrie wrote most of the words. It went like this: *Shattered to be living. All alone again. Shattered to be living. Really need a friend.* And they sang it in rock star voices, so again sounded like *agin* and living sounded like *liven.* They played it for their mum, and at first she thought the words were Shattered to be Liver. She was perplexed, but civil about it. When they told her what the real title was, she said it seemed like a sad song and was everything all right. They just thought it was funny, because it was. But also it was really good. They recorded themselves telling stories onto tapes, too. One was about some little humanoid animals or fruits, and nothing really happened in it, but they kept it anyway because Essie accidentally did a fart in the middle of it, and that was so funny. Carrie found the spot on the tape, and she laughed, and then they couldn't stop laughing, because they knew exactly when it was coming. So they recorded themselves laughing too, and listening to that made them laugh even more, until they nearly choked. Then they recorded themselves farting.

Once their parents got a video camera, another thing they did was make videos. It was a big, heavy box, and you had to balance it on your shoulder. Their dad let them use it though, because he didn't mind what they did most of the time, as long as they piped down at dinnertime during the business part of the news. He ordered it, *Pipe down*, as if they were old-man smokers who needed to quit. Lay down your pipes. They sneaked and recorded him saying it once, and that was hilarious. They did some music videos with the camera. Essie did *Cherish* really well, that Madonna one, where in the real video she's rolling around on the beach with the fake mermaid people. In their video, it was only the backyard, but the pool was kind of like the beach. Essie, as Madonna, had her bathing suit on for that one. It was the first two-piece she'd ever had. Carrie was filming it, but she forgot and started talking, and said that Essie needed to get some boobs. You could hear her say it in the middle of the video, so that wrecked it, and they had to do it again. That time they put some water balloons in Essie's bikini top, though, so they looked better. Their mum got this look on her face when they played it for her. She said Essie could only wear the bikini in the yard, and not to the beach. She told them that that was what their dad had said, but they knew it was her. She just made up things the dad had said when she didn't feel like a big confrontation, and he didn't care.

So anyway, they did some more videos too, of Essie modelling. She wore her bikini for one part. They didn't show that one to their mum. They also didn't show her the horror movie they made, which was like *Jaws*, with Essie getting eaten by a shark in the pool. The shark was actually an inflatable killer whale pool toy they had, but it looked impressive, especially with ketchup all over the place for blood. Then they did show it to their mum, and she even liked it, after she'd seen it once. Essie was good at drowning. Carrie filmed it, and directed it, and also did the *da da da da* music, breathing it out quietly, faster and faster.

Also, when they were really little, they made forts, which Carrie designed, and played weddings, where Carrie was the groom. She didn't mind. They played McDonald's Drive Thru after the weddings. Essie rode around the car on her bike, and opened the gas tank cover to place her order, and then she would pick up her Happy Meal or whatever from the front window, where Carrie was the server, handing out fake food. That was a good game. Carrie still remembers it now if she goes to McDonald's. May I take your order. Here you go.

One time they were riding their bikes down the hill towards school, and Essie swerved and knocked Carrie over, sprinkling sparks from the bike frames as they both spun into the road. It was like a car crash in a movie, all in slow motion and everything, the big tangle of it. Carrie's knees were pulpy, and Essie's elbow and arm, but Essie was so upset, and made her promise not to tell their mum how it happened, so Carrie said okay. She didn't know why Essie did it, why she just knocked them over. Essie didn't know either, she really didn't. Sometimes she just did things. Sometimes things just happen, was the way she put it, with a holy expression. She'd heard that somewhere, probably on TV.

2

It doesn't seem that long ago. More as if it were part of a different time, or an unreal time, not quite black-and-white, but in that violent brightness of older colour movies, where everything moves a little faster, at a jittery speed. Them, those people. But not everything ends up different, in the present.

Them. They used to look more alike, with the same clothes in different colours, and the same haircut. At school, later, sometimes people were surprised when they found out that Carrie was Essie's sister. Essie was a year older, and famous. She didn't do anything, really, but everybody just knew who she was. Carrie was not famous, but she was in drama; she did the lighting design and things like that for plays, and hung out in the lighting booth at lunch by herself, or with a couple of the other drama people who lurked there. She seemed to have a good eye for it, anyway. Maybe the old home movies had helped. Sometimes she went to parties with Essie, when Essie asked her, at the last minute. *Come on. You're coming, aren't you?* As if it had all been arranged for months. Usually Carrie had to drive home, since she was less drunk. Sometimes she thought she was actually more drunk, but just quieter.

She was writing things. A play, for one. She was trying to come up with a good pseudonym. A real name. She would think vaguely about it during the parties, watching other people talking and flirting, watching what their hands did. Essie would laugh and swing her head back, her hair bright with campfire. Then she would look over, calling out, *Carrie*, in a singsong. That's all she would say.

One time, at a bush party, they ended up together by themselves at the fire pit, near where everybody had parked, the cars scattered all over the place in the trees, the headlights like wild animal eyes. In Carrie's mild drunkenness, the eyes looked friendly. Essie was smoking; being drunk made her do it, she said. That's what you do when you're drunk. She flipped her ash into the fire professionally, and said, Hey, you know what.

So of course Carrie said, What?

You know that play?

. Yeah. Carrie knew what Essie meant. The one she was writing right now. She hadn't told anybody much about it, but Essie had a weird knowledge of some things.

Essie said, I should be in it.

Carrie said, You're a drunk. Which she said to piss Essie off. Usually it worked. It did now.

Essie said, I so am not drunk. I am so not drunk. And she took a huge drag, and blew the smoke into Carrie's ear. She was quiet for a bit. Then she said, softly, Hey baby. She inched closer to her, on the log where they were sitting.

What, Carrie said, again. She could feel something light coming from Essie's skin. She knew it, like a smell. Her own skin twitched.

I could be in that play, Essie said, again, in her soft voice.

It's not finished yet.

Why not?

Because it's not. Carrie punched Essie's bare arm. She was strong. Ha ha, she said.

Bitch, Essie said. You're such a man.

I'm your man, baby, Carrie said.

Then they started giggling, and they couldn't stop. This guy came wobbling up to them, out of the trees. Seeing them laughing, he was ready to laugh, too. He said, So what's so funny? But they couldn't answer. He just stared, his drunk face still eager, still waiting for the joke.

Then Essie said, Shattered to be liven. And Carrie was laughing so hard that it turned completely silent, breathless, as if her life were squeezing out of her. They both said, All alone agin. They were going to choke.

The guy laughed a little, and said, casually, Essie. Hey, Ess. Want another cooler? But they didn't listen. Nobody listened to him. They were a fort, the two of them, built to keep anyone out. So after standing there for a while, the guy put his hands in his pockets, and went away into the trees.

They sang, Shattered to be liven. Really need a fren. Then they sang it more seriously. It went kind of sad, by the campfire, in the dark. Carrie said, Where the hell did that come from. I should put that in my play.

Essie said, You should put me in your play.

❧ ❧ ❧

Essie didn't have friends, exactly, in the usual sense, but she knew everybody, and did things, breezing in and out. You always knew when she was home. You felt her. Carrie kept to her own bubble. She wouldn't have minded being one of those diseased kids in a bubble, maybe without the disease. She was working on her play a lot, anyway, when she was home. It was going to be good, she thought. Surreal, but also kind of gritty, or something. The way life is, when you're in a car, and everything is flashing by, and you catch sight of something, like a sign for a laundromat or vacuum repair shop, and suddenly all becomes clear: this is it. This is what it is. That's what the play would be like.

She still hadn't thought of a good enough pseudonym for herself. She did like the word, though. Pseudonym. Maybe that could be her name.

She was on her bed writing in her notebook when Essie came in without knocking. She always said that she didn't knock because it was her trademark. Carrie was always just in her room, anyway, Essie would say. She stood in the middle of the carpet now, silent and looking.

Carrie tried to keep writing. Then Essie said, Mum says you should be doing your homework.

Obviously their mum hadn't really said that. Essie's nerves were up, like a cat wanting to be stroked, but not too much. Carrie said, I did it already. This is important. Could you please piss off. She said piss off with an English accent. But she did say please. She knew to.

You sound like Dad, Essie said. She sat down on the carpet, stretching her leg out. Or Mary Poppins, she said then, in an English accent. She could imitate any voice, any movie voice. She stretched her neck, now, exposing her throat. Hey, remember that time we made that video?

Carrie was still writing. No. Which one?

That one where I get killed. Essie was looking at her toenails. They were a hard, candy shade of orange.

Yeah. Which one? Carrie said, staring at her page, thinking about something that she couldn't get hold of. Then she had to think about Essie's toenails.

You know which one, Essie said.

I'm trying to write, here. Carrie tapped her pen. She was. Trying.

Do you think we still have them?

What?

Those videos, like I said. They must be somewhere around.

I don't know. I'm busy, Carrie said.

Well, I want them. Help me find them, come on. You're always just writing, Essie said, as though the writing were not only extremely boring, but a personal wounding.

Ha, Carrie said. She felt boring. She knew she was. But she also felt slightly mysterious, which was better.

Essie said, again, Come on. She lay back on the floor. I want to see myself, she said.

Why? Carrie said. An idea about the play blew across her brain, about how to fit everything together. Yeah. If she could get it to work. She started to write something down, but Essie wouldn't shut up. Be quiet for a second, Carrie said.

Essie sat up, sharp. No, she said. Don't be such a bitch. I need them, she said.

Fine, Carrie said. But the bitchery is all thine, she said. A Shakespearian feeling. Good. Is bitchery a real word? Probably not in Shakespeare. She wrote it in her notebook. Maybe she could use it somewhere.

Essie's voice rose from the floor, softly now. Carrie. Care. Eee. Only she could say it that way, like a hungry baby, sincerely hungry.

Yes, what?

You don't listen to me. Ever. Essie rolled down onto her front, flatly. And Carrie's stomach dropped. She knew the whole series of Essie moods, as though she'd been collecting them into an album. Exactly the way it would go from here, the descent and speed.

After a minute, she moved to the edge of the bed. Essie's profile sharply outlined against the tired carpet. Her eyes closed. She was beautiful, of course, which everybody knew, but she had something of the crone about her. Her young profile, tight and clear, but you could see it: one day her nose and chin would collapse towards each other and nearly meet. Memento mori, Carrie thought, then. She'd read about it. Those old death's heads, the skull carved into the cradle, or placed like a jewel on a beautiful young lady in a painting. The sudden image of Essie's sad ghost, melted, wandering the grey earth in grey, flying rags, open-mouthed and helpless. Carrie had had this before.

I am listening, Carrie said, then. I'll help you look later, okay? Why do you want them so much, anyway?

I don't need to tell you. If you really knew me, you would know, Essie said, into the carpet.

Carrie stayed still at the edge of the bed. Ess, she said, a few times. Ess. A good name for her: just the smooth, sibilant letter. I'll help you, she said, again. Maybe Carrie's name should have been Emily. Em. Ess and Em.

But Essie stayed viciously silent. Carrie stupidly watching. The feel of being a bumbling 1950s husband, the hubby, like on those old TV shows: trying to please, blinking behind thick glasses, stunned by the swing and swoop of moods, the hormonal mysteries, the furious dependence. Carrie even said, Lady, I'm your man, trying to make her laugh.

Eventually Essie sat up, calm-faced. Again, the flash of the crone as she turned: the sinking profile, the teeth vanishing. But as she looked at Carrie, the message came from her. She was the source. The memento mori was for others, when she looked at them. *Remember that you too must die.*

≈ ≈ ≈

Carrie did finish the play. She was going to direct and produce it too, in the theatre at school. Quiet happiness shooting through her nerves. When they were having dinner at home, she told them about it, casually, trying not to sound fake-humble. So I finished my play, she said, after a bite of salad. It was spaghetti night.

Their mum said, You did? That's good news, isn't it? She said this to their dad. She said his name.

He said, What is? The news was on. Then he said, when she told him again, Oh, yes, it certainly is. Well done. When will we see the production?

Then Essie said, You finished it?

Yeah, Carrie said. She took a drink of water, as if she didn't feel Essie's eyes lasering her.

But I haven't read it yet, Essie said.

So, Carrie said. Then she laughed, a little. Yeah, it's finished, she said.

Their mum looked at Essie, and said, Can't we all just get along? She tried to make it sound funny, like a little tune, as usual, but it was so old.

Essie said, You promised.

Carrie took a mouthful of spaghetti. She didn't listen. She imagined she was deaf. Only the sounds of herself chewing. Spaghetti, sliding down into her stomach. Down down down, down the esophagus. La la la. The world of the deaf, just themselves and their chewing.

Then she couldn't stand it anymore; she fled from deafness, and said, Okay, what. I never promised anything about it, Ess.

You did. You said I could read it first.

I did not, Carrie said. She could not believe this. Yes, she could, looking at where Essie's face was going. The wild cat-on-catnip look rising in the eyes. Carrie knew it. It was like drugs, but it wasn't drugs. It was her. Essie would give catnip to Farley the cat sometimes, watching his own pupils dilating hugely, his claws scrabbling at the air. She would say the cat was nipping out: the sound making it seem colloquial, British, as if the cat were off on a quick errand. But Essie's nipping out: a fuller absence, a void. She was doing it now.

You said I could be in it, Essie said. You did say it. Her pupils vast, gorged with suffering.

I never did, Carrie said. God. What the hell.

But you did, Essie said. And then she started crying, truly crying, with her elbows on the table, her hands to her mouth. She was looking at Carrie the whole time, crying and crying and crying.

Their dad said, Quit arguing, you two. That's enough.

Their mum said, Oh, Carrie. She patted Essie's shoulder, as though she were some lost dog, homeless, out in the rain. Pat pat pat. Couldn't she do something to help with your play, maybe? she said.

Carrie was staring now too. She was the younger one. Wasn't she supposed to be the one to have fits? The light sobbing went on and on, almost musically. Real suffering. That was the worst thing.

Then Carrie sagged, the old sag. Fine. If it means that much to you. You can be the psycho, she said. There wasn't any psycho in the play, but she said it anyway, in spite of the guilt that she knew would come right after. A prehistoric thing, the guilt, the sag; she'd always had it. She looked down at her salad. The dressing, the tomato seeds, the remains.

The sobbing slowed. Essie breathed out. Then she said, Okay. I will, as though bestowing a favour. She was calmer, but still not calm.

See, there. That's great, their mum said, still uneasy. She looked at Carrie mutely; they knew how this went.

Essie was taking a bite of spaghetti, chewing it. Mum, she said.

Mm hmm, their mum said.

Why didn't you get the real kind of sauce, the one I like? Essie said. She still looked terribly sad, stricken, at her thought. This Ragu sucks, she said.

### 3

Carrie did end up putting a psychotic character into the play, a minor one. It wasn't actually a bad idea, and it made it grittier, and more like real life, but still surreal. Then she let Essie see the script; she read it closely, hard. But she told Carrie it was really good and awesome, and she couldn't wait to be in it. She'd never been in a play before, and Carrie had worries. But what could she do?

Essie said, So I'm really excited about it.

Carrie said, Yeah.

Aren't you? Essie said. You're the writer, and everything. You're so going to be so famous, my child, she said. A huge smile. Sometimes Essie would say things like that, like *my child*, as if bestowing absolution, with her saintly look. Two guys at another table were looking at her as she smiled. Blessings upon them, upon all.

She and Carrie were out having a celebration. That was what Essie called it. Let's go for a celebration, she'd said, when she came into Carrie's room. Don't be boring, she'd said. So they were here, at the Chinese place, the real one, at the end of that little alley downtown, not the fake one in that plaza out by the mall. Their dad liked the fake one. It had an obscenely wide TV, and you got chips with everything. But they were by themselves, and Essie wanted to check this one out. They'd never been before. The menus were mostly in Chinese. But not being able to understand it seemed kind of cool.

So, how do you think it should end? Essie said. Still with the huge smile.

What, Carrie said. The play?

Yeah. Yeah, Essie said. I think maybe I should die onstage at the end, she said. It would be a great ending, so real, don't you think?

Um, maybe, Carrie said.

Come on, Essie said, you're the writer. You can rewrite it. Don't you think it's kind of boring the way it is now? Her earnest, appraising look, as if interviewing someone for a job.

Well, it isn't you, it's a character, Carrie said. It's kind of a minor character, and she's not there at the end. And it's supposed to be surrealistic. It's fiction.

Essie slid the chopsticks up and down between her fingers. She said, Well, whatever. If I die, you know, in real life, you'd better keep me. There's no way I'm being an organ donor. Nobody is going to chop me up and take parts of me. She was still smiling as she said it. Again, the image of her ghost howling in a void, knocking at windows, looking for its lost parts.

Carrie laughed to force the picture away. She said, Did you even read the ending?

She saw it coming: the bristling. Of course I did, Essie said. Didn't you see me? I read it. She shoved her hand into her bag. I want a smoke, she said.

Well, it is my play, Carrie said. You can't smoke in here.

I'm helping you with it. I'm in it, aren't I? Essie looked into the depths of her bag. Goddamnit, she said. Then she looked at Carrie, and said, You should smoke. It would calm you down. That's what it's for. She looked coolly over at those guys, their blatant stares. She slid her hair over one shoulder, pulling it down with her hand. She always did that, just like hair product ads. Another of her trademarks.

Smoking actually looks pretty cool, when cool people do it, in movies. Carrie thought of herself in a cigarette ad. She couldn't see it. Then she said, Excuse me, but it's still my play, Boss Hogg.

Boss Hogg. Whatever, Essie said. You know I'm Daisy Duke. The only hot one on the show. She struck a perfect Daisy pose, one shoulder hotly curving up.

No way, Carrie said. They started to laugh. The safe subject: old TV. What a great show that was, she said. Classic. I loved it. The pick of Friday nights.

No, Essie said. It was my favourite. But she was laughing, still, so then Carrie laughed, too, again.

Well, Boss Hogg, we need us some food, Carrie said. She looked at the menu, with the Chinese characters running up and down the pages. Luckily there was some English too. Some of it was peculiar, though. Carrie started to read it out loud. Shredded duckling soup, she said. Duckling. Shredded. It sounds evil.

Ew, Essie said. She looked at her menu. Or how about, noodles with three delicacies. Whatever those are, she said.

It says *noddles*, Carrie said. It did. She smirked. Or how about, eight delights.

Like me. I'm full of delights, Essie said, calmly.

What, more than eight? Carrie said. They started giggling again. They were getting pretty loud: the fort building itself up again around them. It was just them, it was always them. They ignored the men at the other table.

Carrie, still laughing, said, Hey. You know what we need?

What? Besides a smoke, Essie said.

Some Happy Families. Look. Carrie pointed. It was under Seafood.

Oh yeah. What the hell. We should get some.

Okay, Carrie said. Then she said, Oh. But it's minimum two people. Actually, minimun. *Minimun.*

Now they were really laughing, again, as if they would puke. The waitress came, and thumped down two glasses of hot tea on the table; they tried to smarten up, to *pipe down.* But the vast relief of it, for Carrie, the double laughing, the old laughing, not being the one locked out of it. No sympathy for the angry waitress. They said they would share Happy Families, which turned out to be a herd of different-sized shrimplike things in reddish sauce. They were still laughing a little by the time the waitress brought it angrily to them.

Essie looked at it. Oh. It looks like babies. What do you call them. Fetuses.

Carrie said, Yeah. Or feti, she said. She picked up a clump with her chopsticks. Mmm, she said. Happy happy, she said. She gave a toothpaste-ad smile, teeth and shrimp.

More like dead fetus thing families, Essie said. I'm not going to eat that, she said. She sat back, and went quiet.

I am, Carrie said. It didn't taste too bad. She ate some more, keeping her smile on, trying to halt the slight fading.

You are Boss Hogg, actually, Essie said, watching her.

Yep. So come on, little lady. It's our celebration, Carrie said. She tried to make her voice sound exactly like Essie's. Celebration: what an Essie word. The reckless, musical joy around it.

Essie didn't notice. Yeah, for the play, she said. Then she looked happier again. It's going to be so good, she said. Especially the end, you know. Now she was perking up.

Um, yeah, whatever, Ess, Carrie said.

Essie stared, for a long time, as if down a tunnel. Then she said, You know, you used to be a lot nicer. You've totally changed, she said. Her voice saddening.

Say, now wouldn't you like to try some Happy Families, my dear, Carrie said, the 1950s husband. She chewed animatedly.

❧ ❧ ❧

When they got back home, Carrie went to her room to read. Boring, of course, as Essie announced: surprise. She did read for a little while, skimmingly, but her skin was aware. When the house seemed very quiet, almost uninhabited, she thought she'd check on things. Which meant on Essie. Always the need to know she was really there.

She went up to the living room. It was pretty late, but Essie was there, watching something on TV. Carrie stood behind her and looked. It was one of those videos, those old family ones. Essie being attacked by the shark, which was the blow-up killer whale, and ketchup gore splattered everywhere. She was flailing in the pool, which was supposed to be the ocean off some tropical island. She was saying something, but the TV sound was turned off. Essie raised the remote to rewind it, so that the little her jumped in the water and got attacked and flailed around again, and then went underwater. You could see the bubbles coming up, the ketchup dissolving thinly. Then she rewound it again.

Behind her, Carrie said, Hey, you found it. I remember that one. Oh my God, all that ketchup. Look at it. I remember, I almost dropped the camera in the pool when I was filming you. I kept telling you to splash more. God, she said.

Essie didn't say anything. Her eyes on the TV. She was rewinding again. That's me, she said. That's me, she said. On the TV, the little her was under the water, blurry and faint. Isn't it, Essie said.

4

The play was real, out in the open. All the time, Carrie thought about Chinese food. Lists of words and smells. Shrimps. Ducklings. Sickness. Chopsticks tapping her head. The night before the performance, Essie came into Carrie's room. She was wearing her costume for the play, which was a raggedy black dress, supposedly like something a psycho person would wear. Also it was kind of sexy. She'd modeled it for Carrie at rehearsals.

We should go out, she said, now, standing in front of Carrie. I should wear this.

Carrie groaned. She turned over, facedown on the bed. She said, into the pillow, You're making my stomach hurt.

What? Essie said. I can't hear you. Don't be a bitch.

It's not you, Carrie said, with her face in the blanket. It's the costume. Oh my God, I can't believe the opening is tomorrow. Thanks for reminding me, she said. Why are you wearing that right now, anyway?

I know it's tomorrow, Essie said. Why wouldn't I know that?

Carrie didn't say anything. Her vision spotted, her eyes pressed against the bed. Interesting shapes rising and falling. Then Essie said, Come on. Let's go out, come on. I look good in this. It'll be good advertising.

Carrie didn't say anything. If she was quiet, maybe Essie would just go quietly. Ha. As if. She was present, even though she was dead silent. The feel of her, an electrical field. So then Carrie had to say something, and she said, flatly, No. I have a stomachache.

Not enough. It wasn't enough. It was weak. And Essie stood. She stood. Time went on around her. She kept on standing.

Carrie fought the pull to turn and look, to go out with her. After a while, she must have fallen asleep, but even then, she knew Essie was still there. Essie turning and running, leaping off a cliff, into water, into a black hole, vanishing. But not entirely. Coming up again and again, doomed, but not going.

Probably that was a dream. When Carrie did wake up, she felt stiff, doomed. It was already early morning, and she was still in her clothes. Essie was gone from the room. At breakfast, the only thing Essie said was, You look ugly.

Fine. Fine. Carrie stayed at school all day, and into the evening, getting everything ready. In the lighting booth, she watched the final run-throughs, feeling seasick. One of the crew guys told her she looked kind of sick. She said, You do too, but it wasn't true. The thought of what Essie had said, and how Essie was right. Where was she now? Carrie hadn't seen her yet. She couldn't feel her. A nervousness at this, but also the continual floating speculation. Essie's whereabouts, her existence. What it was like to be her. This never shut down, her Essie antenna. The inhabiting of Essie's mind, as if renting it, knowing the place already, ready to move out, but still paying.

She checked her face in the little mirror in the booth. She did look pretty ugly. Essie, again. All their lives. Essie knew her, too, push push pushing with that knowledge. Spitting out pips of it now and then. And they were real, the things Essie saw, that Carrie thought nobody would see. She thought nobody saw her — the honest belief that she was invisible, not quite a real thing walking around. Happy enough, in this. But Essie showed that this wasn't true. She chewed on the core, seeing the softened spots, as on a baby's head, pushing a finger in.

She still hadn't turned up. Carrie sat at the lighting board, running her eyes over the little buttons, so tidy in their little rows. The stage looked far below, with little people appearing on it as the house lights and the hush fell, and the show started. All the world's a stage, she thought, brightly, hysterically. Yeah. Intellectuality. A slightly better feeling, now. It was her play. She had written it. The people were saying the things she had made up. She had organized it. They believed her.

The audience seemed interested, quiet. They weren't laughing, at least. Her mum and dad were there somewhere. Her mum had bought her a corsage before: old-school, misplaced ceremony. She wasn't wearing it. She was wearing her black turtleneck. She felt turtly, too hot. She thought she wanted a cigarette, or something, even though she'd never smoked yet. Weird. But she did. There was something she wanted.

The lighting cues went off right. The play was rolling. Essie did turn up in her scenes, when she was mostly just wandering in the background with a few other characters dressed in black. The relief of it. It was working. Then Mike was centre stage, doing the big final soliloquy. About life, about revelation, about seeing it. The good part. The answer. The guy, Mike, looked right as the main character, half-blind and sort of haunted. He was lost in Dizzyland. That was the name of the play, which was meant to be like Disneyland, of course. They'd been to Disney in California when they were kids. Essie had been crazed with joy at it, but Carrie hated it. When Minnie Mouse bent down to hug her, she saw a person's face darkly through the mesh in the Minnie Mouse costume's neck, and she'd started freaking out. She'd had bad dreams about it for years. She never told Essie, though; Essie would have had even worse dreams. The ruin of Disneyland, the sacking and scorching. But now, Carrie watched the stage through the little window, and her throat dried, to know that she had done this. This. It was working. Almost the end.

She knew how it worked. The surge of feeling, knowing what was next. Something lifted from her skull. When she looked up from the board, down to the stage again, Essie was there, behind Mike. The psycho. She wasn't supposed to be there now. Carrie could tell that Mike could feel her there. She could feel her, even in the booth: the snap of clarity, the old sight. But Mike was marching on with the monologue. His character was supposed to be blind, legally blind, so he wouldn't be able to see her, anyway. Essie just stood there, a ways behind him, looking out at the audience, quite calm. The look on her face familiar, just like a movie character's, although Carrie couldn't think of exactly which one. Then Essie just knelt, and lay down on the stage behind him. She closed her eyes, and didn't move anymore.

Mike could obviously still feel her. He hurried to finish his speech. He said, Is this the end? which was the last line, and then the curtain dropped. Essie didn't move throughout the curtain call. She just kept on lying there, serene, eyes closed. Snow White. There was lots of clapping, though. Someone in the audience was calling, Author author, which was probably their dad. But Carrie didn't go down to the stage, because of Essie there, and also because she had the pseudonym, like a real writer, which was in the programme and on the posters. It was C. E. Duke, which was good because the first two ones were her real initials, but you couldn't tell if it was a man's name or a woman's, and Duke sounded regal, and vaguely smart. There were the Dukes of Hazzard from the TV show, of course, which she hadn't thought of until Essie called her a

Daisy Duke wannabe when she saw the first poster. Essie had said that it was stupid and fake, to change your name. And that she herself was the real Daisy, of course.

Carrie stayed where she was, now, hidden, a half-happiness surging, but still watching Essie's form down on the stage, lying there. The anchor dropping and dropping. Was she all right? Carrie watched, unblinking. Then yes, a real happiness did come, after all the other actors went off after their bows, when Essie got up, alive, and stood, and gave a wave, and then there was some more clapping, and she waved again.

❧ ❧ ❧

The cast and crew party was back at the real Chinese restaurant. It was Essie's idea to have it there. She said it was a cool place, and that they'd been there, so they knew. Her thrilled, bright face. It was still all right. She had one of the photocopied play programmes against her chest, as if it were a baby or a winning lottery ticket. She'd been getting the cast to sign it. They'd written things like, *You are a great actress. You are a wonderful person.*

Carrie, Essie was saying. But Carrie didn't answer. She was trying to drink the Chinese tea, but the glass was too hot for her fingers. Carrie, Essie said again. Care. Eee. Her soft, hungry voice. The signal, and Carrie knew it.

So she said, What? But she said it into the glass.

Essie wasn't looking at her. She was smiling out over the room. I was good, she said. Wasn't I? In the play. She asked it appealingly, still in the sexy psycho costume, which slid perfectly down one shoulder.

Carrie looked at the menu. Lots of people were already ordering. One of the crew guys patted her on the back as he went past to the bathroom. Nice work, he said. Then he looked at Essie, and said, Nice.

Carrie had to say it. Yeah, but that was kind of a surprise ending, she said.

Essie's smile. That's what we said I was going to do. That's what you wanted, right? she said, still appealing.

Carrie shook her head over the tea, but Essie was still talking. I'm going to get into more acting. I've always been good at it. So you can help me.

It was noisy at the table, so Carrie could have pretended not to hear. But she didn't. What do you want me to do? she said.

I'm going to be an actress, Essie said. I'm going to. Don't you think that would be great? she said. Her face so happy.

Fatigue, Carrie's own happiness weak now with the strain of waiting. Uh huh, she said. The menu said, Free bottle of house wine with main course and free gift special Chinese. She said, You could get a free gift, you know. Special Chinese, she said.

You're not listening, Essie said. She leaned forward, blocking out the guy beside her.

I heard you, Carrie said. You're going to be an actress now. See, I'm listening, she said. She read, Chicken with Chinese sauce, special.

Yes, I am, Essie said. And I need you to help me. You're the writer, she said. She'd said this before.

Carrie said, Aren't you hungry? Her sickness had become voraciousness. The play was over, and it hadn't been a disaster. Not a complete one. Most people seemed to think that the ending was on purpose. They said it was really good and also really surreal, and also like a real movie. She needed to think about it more. I'm going to order something, she said. Everything on the menu was special, it seemed.

No, Essie said. Come on. She looked at Carrie, her eyes hot. Let's go, she said. I want to go somewhere else and talk.

Ess, I'm hungry, she said. Look, eight delights with chili sauce. Someone at the table had just gotten a big dish of something that smelled good, and also special.

No, Essie said. She pushed the programme into Carrie's hand. Come on, she said. You're the writer, you wrote it. Her voice accusing. You need to help me, now. Let's go, she said.

Essie, Carrie said. You are on crack. It's the cast party. We can't leave. It's my play. Essie looked at her. The hard-pupilled look. The nipping-out look. The need for rescue, for dry land. Then Carrie said, Fine, it's our play. So we can't leave. Come on, not yet. She looked around the table, at all the people talking and laughing and stuff. This is fun, she said. It's fun.

It is, Essie said. Now her pupils melted. Her mouth opening, empty. The void, the ghost: Carrie saw it.

Oh, don't, she said. Even more tired. Happy Families, she said. She pointed to it on the menu. She laughed their laugh, to make Essie do it too. But Essie didn't. Don't you want some? Carrie said. Her stomach gnawing at her. Happy Families sounded like the best thing ever.

Essie grabbed at her arm. Come on, she said. We need to go now. Her strong fingers.

Carrie rolled her head back, and said. Fine. Fine. If that's what you want, woman.

The husband. Husband like, she let Essie out first. They went towards the door, without saying goodbye. Everybody was talking anyway. When they were getting their coats from the hangers in the lobby, Essie suddenly said, Oh. Look. She was pointing to something in the corner. A video game.

What now? Carrie said. Her stomach squeaking at the smell of food. Oh, so now you're all happy, she said.

It's a game, Essie said. She went over to it. She picked up the mallet hanging from it. Look, she said. It's like Whack-a-Mole.

Carrie went to look, grudgingly. But she did remember. The game really was like Whack-a-Mole, only it had Chinese writing on it, and little white heads in the holes instead of moles.

I used to play it at the fair. Essie's face softened into happiness.

I did, too, Carrie said. You have to hit them when they pop up, right? she said. I used to play it all the time at the arcade. I got the top score. Twice, even.

No, you didn't, Essie said. Hey, do you have any change? I want to play. She tapped the game thing with the mallet. I'm the best, she said, bright again, her teeth bright with joy.

I thought you wanted to go now, Carrie said. You never used to go to the arcade with us.

Essie gently lay the mallet down. The guy at the front desk was looking at them. She said, Since you always get what you want. Since you always know everything. Since you always have. She tapped all the white heads with her fingertips, a rattly echo, and stalked out the main door, her rags fluttering, an orphan, a waif.

Carrie stood there, but only for a moment, and then she followed, as she knew she would. The man kept looking as she passed. Under the Chinese writing, the machine said, *Show Your Ability to Hunt Ghosts.*

The ground was nude, all the trees pulled up and chipped or turned into logs. It was different; the developers had been at it. It used to be just trees and rough ground, good for hide and seek or forts. They'd played out here a few times. Essie's eyes raked over it, furious. Why does it look like this? she said. She said it twice. Carrie knew she drove around at night sometimes, checking up on the town, on what it's doing. How dare it change itself.

So they didn't go home after leaving the restaurant. Essie was driving. She said she didn't feel like going home. So Carrie said, Fine, do whatever you want, which was supposed to make her think about what she'd said before, but she clearly didn't think about it. Or at least she didn't say anything. Neither of them said anything. They sat there, driving around in the dark.

After a while, Essie took a deep breath, and said, as if having rewound the conversation, So the play was really good.

Carrie said, Yeah. Okay, she would talk to her. This was the way it went. She said, Yeah, it was good. So now you want to be an actress?

Essie said, Mm. So listen, she said, conversational. You need to help me, right?

What am I supposed to do? Carrie said. Since she was the passenger, she had to be the DJ, so she was looking for a good station on the radio, but there was nothing on. Just country-style whining.

Well, I'm going to L.A., Essie said.

Oh, uh huh, Carrie said. Somebody trying to sound like Johnny Cash, only with a weak, birdy voice, was singing something lugubrious and trembly. She didn't know country singers' names.

Essie said, I am. I'm going. So I need probably a thousand dollars, she said.

Whatever, Carrie said. Like I have any money.

But you're the writer, Essie said. You can write something and sell it to a TV studio. She said it as if it were mapped.

Oh sure, Carrie said. Like that's going to happen. But she thought about it. What if? She switched stations. The radio shrieked static.

Essie said, You must have lots of cash in the bank. You're always saving it, since you never do anything fun. So come on, she said, brightly.

Oh sure, Carrie said again. I'll just slip you some of my millions. What do you need a thousand bucks for, anyway, she said.

Essie turned left. The light was already red, but there was nobody around. For my pictures. I need a portfolio, she said. For when I get to L.A. I have to get an agent, too, she said.

Oh, Carrie said. What to say to that. The radio was bad tonight. There was really nothing on. They were quiet, listening to the static.

Carrie's jaws tightening. They went off the main road, down a street with lots of new pink houses. More development. The subdivision hadn't been there for long. Carrie looked, but she couldn't see the name of it on the street sign.

Essie said, then, You should come with me.

Carrie said, Oh yeah, whatever.

No, seriously, you should, Essie said. Don't be boring, she said. You could write screenplays there. You could. And I could be in them, and you could direct them. Or you could be my agent, she said.

Carrie could see her smiling into the side-view mirror at her refined plan, the smooth path. Carrie said, Yeah, sure. But

Essie didn't get it. She thought Carrie really meant it, yeah sure, so she looked satisfied. She said, And that can be my name, my stage name. Somebody Duke.

Carrie said, You know I can't go. I have one more year of school than you do, remember, she said. Essie looked over at her, then. Carrie said, Watch it. They almost hit the kerb.

But Essie wasn't looking at the road. She said, What am I supposed to do? Nothing ever happens for me.

The car engine pushed faster. Essie went on. She said, What happens? What happened to us? The question hanging in the car. That terrible, bottomless sadness again: her belief in them, in the mythical land of childhood, safe and permanent as the Smurfs' village, there every morning at the same time on the same channel on TV.

Carrie tried to rewind the conversation: Essie's trick. She said, Oh yeah, like nothing ever happens for you, Ess. The road curved, and the car lunged at the corner, just making it, without brakes. Finally Essie looked back at the road, but it was as if she was doing it to show Carrie that she'd never look at her again, that this steering was for Carrie's sake only, though Carrie meant nothing to her now.

The car careened. But Carrie felt oddly calm, or calm enough. If this was it, the finish, they were both here, at least, instead of only Essie. Carrie would know how it happened. She pushed in the tape that was sticking out of the machine and pressed the play button. Maybe this would be something better. Music to crash cars by.

*Shattered to be liven. All alone agin. Shattered to be liven. Really need a fren.*

That was the tape. It was them singing, their own voices as little kids. Carrie said, Oh my God. When did you find this? She started to laugh. She listened. She couldn't pick out which of the voices was hers. I can't believe you found this, she said. I totally remember it.

Essie hit the brakes hard. The seatbelts nearly decapitated them. They stopped, in the middle of the road. There was nobody around. But still.

Whoa, there, Carrie said.

That's my tape. That's me, Essie said.

It's me too, listen, Carrie said. I remember when we made this, she said. I wrote the words. I can't believe it. She was still laughing, even though her neck hurt from the seatbelt burn.

No, Essie said. That's me. I did it. You don't know, she said.

Carrie thought about it. She listened to the tape, blasting out the song with a crackly sound. It was old. She remembered when they had made it, didn't she? She did, and she said, No, it's me too. Listen to it. Remember, I wrote down the words, and we recorded it, and we went to play it and I pushed too hard and got it stuck in the tape player, and Dad had to use a knife to get it out.

That was me, Essie said. She was driving again, but quite calmly now. Under the speed limit, as if she were on her driver's test. She said, calmly, I got it stuck in the tape player. I got a spanking.

I got the spanking. It was the third time I jammed the machine, Carrie said. She did. She knew she did. She remembered being a little kid. She remembered. That was me, she said.

That was me, Essie said, in Carrie's exact voice. They were heading out past where the new houses ended, over the bridge. The street lights ended.

The tape was over, and the radio was rippling static again. Carrie thought about being a kid, about singing it. She couldn't hear her own voice, her kid's voice inside her head. She couldn't remember it. You should turn your lights on, she said.

Essie didn't turn on the headlights. They sat in the car, stopped. The fort walls lifting around them again. Built to keep others away. No way in, and no way out. The hard knot of love bunched in Carrie.

I'm your man, she said, to Essie.

I know, Essie said, quietly. It made her happier. Carrie felt it on her bare arms.

I think that was you on the tape, you know. You were good, Carrie said.

Yes.

Carrie handed over the past to her, packaged up like a wedding gift. What she wanted. Essie's profile, where Carrie had seen the crone, looking out at the dark. Memento mori, memento mori. Not a threat, a reproach.

## 5

Another thing they did when they were little kids was shows for their mum and dad. Sometimes they invited the neighbours to watch, too. Once they did a fashion show, and Essie couldn't wear her bikini in that one, but she wore it underneath her mum's satin dress, which she was modelling, so she was happy about that. Carrie was the emcee, and the one filming it, and she described everything that Essie was wearing. Well, not the bikini.

In one show, which was a play, Essie was Snow White, and she had to be poisoned by the apple. She did this brilliant slow poisoning death scene. You could hardly even see her breathing after, when she was lying there on the floor in front of the fireplace. Carrie had to be some of the other parts, including the Wicked Witch, and when she died at the end, she tried to do it like Essie. She held her breath until she was going to explode. Then she was bursting, panting, and Essie was angry, at first. She said Carrie was supposed to be dead. Carrie had thought she was. But it was no good. It would have been better if Essie had been both Snow White and the Wicked Witch. Terrifyingly, blankly innocent, but demanding parts of you, evidence, entrails, the lungs and liver, the whole thing, threatening to eat it, to eat you. *Bring me her heart in this box. Off with her head. Bring it to me.* That's another queen, but still.

They were little kids then. Them.

❧ ❧ ❧

Now, I imagine it. What would happen. What if. What if I just wasn't there, if I were the one to jump off the cliff, or crash the car, or take the poison. Mum and Dad would have to tell Essie. Would she *nip out*? Would she vanish, in a puff of smoke? What would she say?

That's what I'm supposed to do. That's supposed to be me, she would argue. I know what she'd say. And then what. She would have no life to follow. I was supposed to do it for her.

All of this stuff was a long time ago. But we're not really other people. She's still there, always. And I will live with it, myself as she sees me, as she's made me. I've made her, too. I'm the writer: her words. I'm the husband, the escort. I'll live with that, too: my knowledge that I'm supposed to go on into the future, and she might not, if I stop thinking about her. That I will wander that tightrope forever. Listening with apprehension to weather forecasts for days ahead. Partly cloudy this afternoon, chance of showers tomorrow, brisk south wind for the rest of the week. The guilt of my working lungs and liver.

# For My Sins

WHEN I THINK ABOUT IT, IT'S HER. She was in the back of my mind when I started thinking, and making this list, before I realized it:

– Yes, I probably am a bad friend. This is why I don't have many. I am bad at phoning people back. I have had many friends, over the years, but they drift. And I don't mind. Maybe that's worse.

– I have coveted other people's boyfriends. Spouses. I haven't done anything about it, but I've thought things. Two of them were named Darrell. One Darrell had a brother. Darren, I think.

– I once ran over something, a little animal, with the car, and I was too cowardly to go back and look at it. I kept going. I was late for something. The dentist. I'm sure it was dead, though. I could see it squashed on the road, in the rearview mirror and in my mind. It might have been a squirrel. I like squirrels, too. Worse, again.

– As a teenager, I wasn't any worse than most, I suppose. Some social things. Sly, shy insults I knew I was making. Wanting the power to enchant and stab. Vanity, vanity.

I used to babysit a lot, and would let the kids stay up too late, watching bad TV. Talk shows, prime time dramas. They liked it, so maybe that wasn't too bad. I do remember one thing, another thing. I fainted at school. It was a fake fainting. I'd heard someone had done it one year, at lunch hour, in front of the principal's office. People talked about it. She was anorexic. I tried it, in front of my locker after school. I wasn't anorexic. Not many people were there, so it wasn't a huge scene. Just the sudden decision, the thumping surprise. The embarrassment came afterwards, with blood banging in my elbows. But I talked myself into believing it, that I had really fainted. Talking about it, I could see the outer space before my eyes, when I closed them. The world going blue and shadowed. I did feel it, so maybe it wasn't entirely fake.

 – I've been happy when others get acne or scars or wrinkles. I've bought expensive, expensive cream to fix mine. And children are starving throughout the world. Starving, but wrinkle-free.

Was I any better as a child? In some ways. I was obedient, happy. I can remember feeling that way: happy about being obedient. I did throw rocks at a friend once, my mother tells me, although I don't remember it. She was surprised. So was I, to hear that. She likes to bring it up. She said that we were playing nicely in the backyard in the summer, and I stepped out of the wading pool, strolled to the driveway, picked up a rock, considering, and threw it at my friend's head. I hadn't been trying to throw it into the water. You aimed, my mother said, wonderingly.

❧ ❧ ❧

It wasn't Penny, the one I threw rocks at. Or the one at whom I threw rocks. I should put grammar on the list. I don't remember that other girl, or the rock throwing. Penny was my closest friend in elementary school, though. Our mothers had been friends since elementary school, theirs. So what happened was a double wreck. Penny and I were at the same school after her family moved back into town. Our mothers must have met up again, and probably suggested we could play. Same age, just the same. How do child friendships start? Want to play? Okay. Something like that.

We did play. Ladies was a game we played a lot. We had a box of clothes that my mother had bought for us from the thrift store. There was a red silky dress with thin straps, which we both coveted and had to take turns with. It was probably rayon, that whispery slide. Ladies sometimes evolved into Hairdresser, which I was good at. Maybe I should have taken it up as a career. Maybe that's what I'm missing now. I liked doing Penny's hair, the ropy ease of it. She never minded it. She said it didn't hurt, even if I pulled hard when I brushed. Her hair had mass, the colour of dirt. I liked that about it. Nature. Her skin also had a tone to it, a slight frosting of dirt colour, darker than mine. I liked dirt.

Usually, we played inside. She came over after school a few times a week. We were peaceable, non-bored. I was usually the one to think of things. This is how it went:

Me: Do you ever play like you're dead?

She: (Looking at me blankly.)

Me:  Dead like Sleeping Beauty.

She: (Getting it.) Yeah.

We both knew it then, after my prompt. A common vision, mystical cartoon beauty and death, revival. Perfect. I knew she saw it too, in the same flat cartoon colours. Our minds linked in identical genius. The perfect story, the perfect pitch. That disappears, though.

She: Snow White, too.

Me: Let's play it.

We abandoned our glasses of milk. My mother never minded us leaving things around, which was part of why it was better at my house. Also, I had a vast Barbie collection, inherited from my cousin who hated me. They were useful. Most of the shoes were lost, but the gowns covered the Barbies' bare rubbery feet anyway. Little puffs of slick material and rasping net. Wonderful things. We found Ugly Barbie, who was faded and had shorter hair than the others, and dressed her up. A white dress with a hoop skirt. She didn't usually get to wear that one. She didn't usually get to wear anything, nude and facedown at the bottom of the box. The others got dressed too, in their usual ball clothes, toned down a little. You be Ugly, I said, and Penny said okay, and we hitched the doll to Barbie's horse with a ribbon. Penny pulled the horse and Ugly down the living room carpet, very slowly. I was the crowd of other Barbies. I propped some of them up against the coffee table, and they wept as the procession went past. We did it all afternoon. Poor dead Ugly. Why weren't they our size?

The funerals went on longer than most of our other games. The seriousness. I asked for black Barbie clothes for my birthday, only all-black ones, and received some navy ones, although my mother said even those were hard to find in the Barbie jungle. I told her about the game, and she watched us conduct a procession once. You girls are very creative, she said.

But we weren't. It was mostly me, and I had a one-track mind; I knew the corners it would take. Penny got tired of the funerals before I did, so I had to sneak them in sometimes when she was happy about something else. Let's do one, I would say easily, as if it had just occurred to me, and sometimes she would agree. She was usually agreeable, with her round face and eyes, and her dirt hair. It made me think of something else, then, when she was slow-motioning the horse forward. Something I had heard.

Me: You know when you're dead, they put you under the ground.

She: I know that already.

Me: So do I. You get dirt in your hair.

She: No you don't. You're in a coffin. I saw my grandpa's when he was dead.

I hadn't been to any funerals, real ones. Jealousy cramped me. Not all the time, I said. Knowledge descended. I said, The coffin gets rotten after a while, and the dirt gets in.

Oh, she said, in her agreeable way, again. The dirt would never show in her hair, I knew. I knew my own hair was pale and flat, without looking at it. Dirt would cake and rust it.

Me: Let's play funeral, but not with the Barbies. For real. I'll be the dead person, and you can cry.

Okay, Penny said. Her agreeable self. I put on the special dress, the slippery red one, and lay on the living room floor with my hands crossed over my ribs. My heart flapped as I lay there, as Penny cried. You have to be louder, I said. Be really sad. And as she bawled to the ceiling, my hands quivered.

The games bound together. Dead Ladies now, or Dead Lady Funerals. We recycled it in various ways, but on the same theme. It ran through my head during school, and at night, like a slow train. I could hardly sleep. Sometimes Penny would be the dead lady, and I would mourn, although not with much feeling. She was better at that. I would lie with my eyes closed, breathing in tight, quick sips to stop my chest moving. She would cry softly or fully at my direction, and her crying was wonderful. Once my mother came in, thinking Penny was really crying. I didn't tell her what we were doing. Just playing. But excitement panted in my chest.

᪥ ᪥ ᪥

School, though. A galaxy far, far away. It was stranger there, in some ways. Penny and I usually played together at lunch, walking around and around the field, laughing at anything. It wasn't real. Even the air looked different. Too many people. The ceiling in the classroom felt high, with its pencil-studded foaminess, and the lower part of the windows were painted over so we wouldn't be distracted by outside. In the sealed classroom one day, early in the year, just before lunch, a girl surprised me. She came up to me. I don't know where Penny was. I don't remember the girl's first name. Her last name was Tuke, I remember that. And that she had odd, reddish freckles on her face, an evil sprinkling, the devil's mark, as I thought of it. She hadn't been at our school very long. This girl, this Tuke, said, Can I play with you at lunch?

I was surprised, an honest surprise. She had never occurred to me before. And she could talk. I said, Oh. Ask Penny.

Tuke said, She said to ask you.

I said, Ask her again. And when the bell rang, Penny and I plunged to the farthest corner of the field, behind the baseball backstop, where it was quiet and the grass was wet.

Again, I'm telling the truth about the girl; she left my mind completely. Penny came over after school, and things were fine. But the next day, the girl inserted herself again into my view, looking sulky and spotted and asking whether she could play with me. With us. I had no idea what to say, so I said nothing. Mute. I turned, and went to the cloakroom and got my jacket. Penny was there, and relief. We went, talking. Singing, I think, too. We did that sometimes. Penny said the girl had also asked her once again to play. We decided not to talk to her again. It seemed reasonable. She was not real to us. I think it was Penny's idea not to talk to her, which is surprising, maybe. But I really do think so. *Let's not talk to her anymore.* I can hear it, in Penny's voice. Sometimes, at school, she showed that side, more in charge. When the Tuke girl came up to Penny the next day, Penny didn't look at her, and hitched one shoulder higher than the other. I did it too. The Tuke girl cried to the teacher, and real disdain planted itself, then. I suppose I should add all of this to the list. I'd forgotten that girl until now. But we hadn't been trying to be cruel.

– My skin. My vanity, even then. Write it down.

Also, I was prettier than Penny. I was, then. A fact. She did have the hair, its fall of fat brown. But. She was slightly thick elsewhere. The beginnings of thick legs. You can sense these things. I have often foreseen how people will look late in middle age. Sometimes this embarrassed my mother, if I spoke up about it. That lady will get a big bum. Or, That lady has a moustache. She's getting a beard, too. I would see future spread, the growth of things. I could see Penny as a lady, a real one, and I knew she would never be really beautiful. Just normal. I knew I would never be either, but I held out hopes for myself. We were both cute, the usual child-cute, like all children for a while. Except the Tuke girl, maybe. Penny had cuter younger siblings, real babies. How many? They made her house noisy and foreign. It made me feel sorry for her. Not for them.

Penny got tired of the Dead Lady game before I did. It was starting to get warmer outside. It must have been spring. She wanted to play in the yard, but I didn't. She would go on with the game, agreeably, for my benefit, but she wasn't in it. Her crying falsified, metallic. I woke from the dead and sat up from the carpet, my heart set low. But there had to be other things. I could think of things. My mind worked in its usual ways. I felt something drift up out of its well.

I said, You know what. I had a dream about something.

She said, What. She was fiddling with the straps of her thrift-store sundress. I'm going to get changed, she said.

No, just listen, I said. It was about adults, I said. She knew what I meant; that's all I needed to imply. We had edged around this before. I really had had a dream some time before, although I remembered it only vaguely. It came back up. Naked people outside, adults, walking in the street, with their hair and weirdness, just going about their business normally. With shopping bags, and things. I bejeweled it. I said, These people were naked outside. In the street, and in the store, and in the grocery store, and they did it, and then they all got babies, I said. I could see it, as I invented it.

Penny raised her head from the carpet. Its dirt halo was staticking around it. She said, They did?

Yes, I said. Feeling disgust at myself. My nostrils pinching. All of them, I said.

I knew what could happen. I knew how to suggest, to intimate. I went to the corner and dragged out the Barbie box. We had ignored them for quite a while. I dug for the Ken, the only Ken in the horde. He was conveniently naked. I found a naked Barbie as well, and pressed them together to kiss. Her hard breasts prevented true fulfillment. But still. Penny was interested. She took off all the remaining Barbies' clothes. We had seen them naked many times, between clothing changes. And Ugly was naked most of the time, except at funerals. But now we left them all that way. Penny mated them, lying them down together, stiff-armed, and smiling and smiling. I watched, presiding, as if I were an examiner. We had only one Ken, so polygamy was rife. Then I suggested cutting the hair off a spare Barbie. Ugly. She ended up stubbled and hatched-looking, but she was hardly male enough.

&⅋ &⅋ &⅋

It was my idea. Penny took it over, to an extent. I pretended that I was just being agreeable, just like her, when she suggested we play it. I would wait for her suggestion. Just going along with things. All the mating. We dressed them up, just so we could take off their clothes. But I enjoyed it in the pit of my heart. The happy, sick taste. They had dozens of imaginary babies; I didn't have any dolls small enough. They kept at it. It was not boring for a very long time.

– I wasn't such a good child. The kernel was there, very early.

I haven't really forgotten that, although I tell myself I have, if it rolls out of the back of my brain. Ancestral Puritanism kicking out of my genes, with pointy shoes. Disgust, still, although I shake my head, smile. Kids. I say that in my mind. *Kids.*

I don't have any, though. Surprising, perhaps, given those imaginings of populating the earth with Barbie babies. But I don't even like the word kids, really. Baby goats, skull-butting. Now, I work in real estate, so I don't deal with children often. Sometimes people bring them along to view a home. I see a lot of people, but I don't have to deal with them in much depth, with personality. It's fine, and I like it. Worse, as I said. Worse and worse.

One woman from the office asked me out for lunch a few weeks ago. I went. We chatted, and agreed about things, and had salad, and I was surprised at how happy I felt afterwards, for a time. Not quite like myself, though. My real self. I was out of town for a few days afterwards, at regional meetings for the company. When I got back in, she said we should go for lunch again. I said we should. But we didn't. I didn't say anything about days or times, and she was very polite.

I show people around other people's houses. Real estate is a good profession. I'm not myself then, either, but in a good way, when I'm showing. A surprise, my energy. My bright voice. I tell people when the house is right for them. Sometimes you just feel it. That's the truth. When the owners are out, I like waiting in the house for the viewers to arrive. Sweeping the floor around the entrance. Imagining the upstairs floor plan before I go up. I usually know how it will be. Master, ensuite bath, two more beds, maybe another bath, jack-and-jill between the other bedrooms. That's what it's called. Most modern houses are the same, or variations on the same theme.

I know it wasn't long after that lunch that I thought of her, Penny, again, for the first time in years. The house, four bedrooms plus den, is up near where her parents used to live. It's quite new, and very modern, but the owners are selling. People like to move. Penny's house was built before these newer ones, farther from the road. It was set into the hillside, and I remember it looking flattened, somehow. A sandwich. We were usually at my house, which was much closer to school, but on weekends sometimes, we stayed over at hers.

When I thought of the house, I thought of orange. I don't know why. Were the carpets orange? There was an amber glass panel by the front door that made things look wavery, nauseous. Maybe that's it.

A little, scrubby golf course wasn't far away from the house. We would walk up to it, to get away from the younger ones, with their teeth and bawling. We would walk around the grass, picking up golf balls. What did we do with them? I don't know. It wasn't a very well-tended course. It never seemed to have any players, but lots of balls. Perfect. One day, after we wandered the brownish lawns, Penny took off her shoes, and stepped into a little flat lake at the bottom of a slope. We called it a lake, although it was just a water trap. I watched, then went after her. Cold mud. My toes throbbed and sank. We loved it, although my skin feared the brush of fish. I said, Pick some up. The mud. My idea, as usual.

Penny sank her arm into the lake, and her sleeve sagged, dripping. But she had a handful from the bottom. Pure stuff, fundamental. She squelched it in her fingers, then did it again, harder. I watched.

At her house, later, we got in trouble for having dirty clothes, and I had to wear hers. They smelled different. Orange, maybe. I kept sniffing the sleeve.

The next time I was there, we went back to the uninhabited golf course. We went in the lake again, or she did. We waded around for a while, until my fear of fish mouths drove me out. I said, Let's go.

This time, though, Penny returned to the bank, but peeled off her shirt, then her pants, and stepped back into the water in her underwear. Hers had the days of the week on them, always wrong. I noticed when we changed for gym at school, and I noticed now. It's not Tuesday, I said. It wasn't.

She said, So? She didn't care what I meant. The air was white. I stood on the edge. I shoved my wet feet back into clinging socks. Her bare stomach, her popped belly button, a little creature. Mine wasn't like that. I couldn't help looking. Looking and looking, as if I'd never seen her in her underwear. Her brownish skin above the water, her back to me, a plain brown expanse, a new thing.

You're going to get in trouble, I said.

She didn't say anything. She walked farther out. Then she said, There's tons of golf balls in here.

What could I do? I stood by the water and watched her find nests of muddied golf balls, pulling them out and setting them on the bank. Those are mine, she said. I stared. She splashed and streaked mud up her arms.

You're all wet, I said. Alarm was beginning. People are going to see you, I said. And you'll get in trouble, I said, again. My uselessness, my nag. There was nobody there, ever. And she was still splashing, sending up dull spray, all by herself. But this was the source of my alarm; no one must see her.

Let's play something else, I said. Let's go home. My throat was hurting and tight. She wasn't being right. I said, Let's play a real game. Let's play Dead Ladies. You can be dead, I said. This was a sacrifice. You can lie up there, on the grass, I said.

It didn't work. She stayed out in the water, away. My mind was rattling. Her torso, lifting itself above the cold. My shoes on the bank, saddened, emptied. She squatted down, then leapt up. Water flew from her. I yelled, There's a man up there. You're almost naked, I said, gaping and staring. But there was no one. Just us, and the dumb-faced golf balls.

She was totally uninterested in me, my warnings. Then she turned, and said, Boo, and laughed out. She scooped up more water. Mud flecked her.

It was cold. I said, Now you look like that girl. Somebody's going to see you. Then I said the girl's name, although I can't remember it now. The spotted, irritating girl in our class. Tuke the Wretched, Tuke the Miserable.

Penny sent a charge of water at me. It dashed my arm and stomach. Little dirt dots, spreading circles. She laughed again, shrieking. She said, You're her. You're her. I was freckled with the weepy mud. And she kept shrieking the name, the one I forget. And then she just kept shrieking, You, you, which had the sound of a terrible insult.

Here is what I did. I walked away, all the way back to her house, by myself. I told her mother I wanted to go home. I felt my face set in a certain way. The bones.

What had happened? She didn't know me. I thought she had seen me, the actual me, private and gleaming, the inside of a shell. I had showed her things of me. But she hadn't. At all. She didn't know me, or anything. She knew nothing. She was vacant, a monster. And she came over the next week after school, as usual, but I didn't speak. Disgust was all there was. When she took out the Barbie box, I turned and looked out the window. My mother said we should play Candyland, or Monopoly, and she even set up the board for us. Penny said, Okay. Agreeable. But we didn't play. Penny twiddled the pieces and hummed. After she left, my mother said, What's wrong between you and Penny?

I said she was being bad. Just, you know, bad. That's all I said. But I knew the way to say it. The implication. My mother looked sad, or tired. I said I didn't want Penny to come over anymore, and my mother bought it. I wrote a note that said *Dirty Habbit*, which I planned to put in Penny's desk, to show her what I knew, and that I had withdrawn. The malevolent, puritanical doubled *B*. I didn't put in the desk, though. At school, I walked around and around the playground, in a slightly varying oval, by myself.

– It was fine until then. I ruined it, with my pushing. My want. This is love and how it operates.

I do remember it, the golf course, and the neighbourhood, and things that happened. The house up there that I'm showing is enormous. It's surrounded by others like it. I'm not sure that Penny's house is even there now, although I haven't looked very carefully. This house has ensuites for three of the bedrooms, and a very large walk-in master closet. The master ensuite is astonishing. The shower doesn't even need a door or curtain, it's so large. Last time I was waiting for some viewers, I stepped into it. A cave, clean and hollow. I wished I could try it. But not really. The viewers were coming. I looked out the bathroom window and thought of the golf course, now an eruption of condominiums. Maybe the lake is still there.

The house hasn't sold, though. I waited for an hour for those viewers. I'm not exactly certain what's wrong with it. It is blue, which is the least sellable colour. I don't know why. And its door is a darker blue. Blue doors don't work either, according to surveys. These are the kinds of things I know. But the owners have gone to Florida for the winter.

The next time I was up there, checking on the house, I walked into the huge shower again. The pale echo. The viewers turned up eventually, and I showed them all around. The double kitchen pantry is a good feature. And of course the shower. After they left, I dusted a few surfaces. I went upstairs. I took off my shoes, and then my stockings. Some other viewers turned up later. I thought they might ask why the shower was wet, if the owners were away, but they didn't. I'd cleaned it well.

I've been staying late a night or two during the week. The owners asked the agency to look after the house. The neighbourhood is so quiet, but I'm not entirely sure it's safe. The neighbours don't know me. But it's a change, anyway. At night, from the master bedroom, if you look out at an angle, you can see the whole spread pool of the city, and the dark spots where golf courses are. The newer ones. I sit on the edge of the bed and look, and the list forms itself in my mind, sometimes. Penny keeps arising in the background. Matters to do with her.

I tidy the big house, and show a few people around when they come. People do like the ensuite, and the kitchen, but there's always something. Too much space. Not enough storage. Too big a yard to look after. Too close to the other houses. No view. None of them has been to see the night view, though. They just look at the condominiums, the former golf course ones. The house overlooks them from the master bathroom. I was in the shower in the evening, and I forgot to close the blinds. I realized it after I got out and was dry. Caught, for a moment. I stood near the window, peering, and felt embarrassed at myself. A man was standing in his condominium yard below, watering tubs of plants. His back was to me, which was a relief.

But the next day, it was the same. I had a very long shower after the last viewers left. They hadn't liked anything at all, and my voice got tired. When I got out of the white shower, I dropped the towel. The blinds were open. I saw. Then I walked over to the window. I just did. I stood at the window that way, facing forward. I didn't look out, at first. Then I did. The man was there, below, shielding his eyes, looking towards the house, pale as a prawn in the evening light. I'm not sure if he saw me. Yes, he did.

– People don't know. I did start things. I do. I am the same.

Penny left the school after about another year. We weren't friends anymore. Neither were our mothers, because of it. Were her parents getting a divorce, or transferred? They moved, at any rate. I had no reason to go to her old neighbourhood much. It was far away, and I didn't know anyone up there, and children don't get to dictate many things. Not many. Houses got built. It looks different now. And I'm sorry, Penny, I am sorry, but I hate you still.

# If You Think You're Never Wrong

## 1

*The scene:*

THEY WERE BROTHER AND SISTER. They had to share a room on the trip. The stuff of sitcoms and farce, the stuff of plots. In the motel at night, they were orphaned, but in a fantasy sense, forgetting the parents were in the next room, forgetting there were parents at all. They had already forgotten the grandmother.

2

*Some events:*

They were idle on their beds, on the heavily washed motel sheets, with the garage-sale prints of fruit bowls above them. The Sundowner Motel. There was a choice of three motels there, this being one; the others were the Tel-A-Frend Motel and Le Unique Motel. So this one was the least intriguing, although its name did have connotations of alcohol. It had no pretensions to friends, or frends, or uniqueness. It was a blocky building, and it had satellite TV, one of the old, enormous dishes plaintively tilted to the sky, looking for anything it could get.

He was rolling through channels. Spectators at a tractor pull, cheering, then overtime in a hockey game, then some medical show, somebody's chest cracked open. The vast satellite bounty offered up things for his specific viewing pleasure, it seemed. Porn was also on offer, although it seemed to be a pay-per-view setup. The previews, though, were free.

Two women were doing something to each other, not quite pornographically. One of those suggestive scenes they always warn you about first. Suggesting: hey kids, try this. Then the name of the movie appeared: *Quadruplets II*, with more suggestions suggesting how to order the whole film, which would presumably include the missing quadruplets.

3

*Some dialogue:*

Why is it always women? she said.

I don't know, he said, slowly, as if he were genuinely thinking about it. He flipped through more channels. Something burst into flames.

No, seriously. It's degrading, she said, which is what you're supposed to say about it.

Yeah, I know, he said. He narrowed his eyes at the screen, watching the explosion fallout.

Quadruplets. Why would you need four, she said. She pulled her book out of her backpack and slumped against the pillows, but she kept watching, too.

He said, So it's not exactly logical. It's not supposed to be. He was logical. He thought about things, and gave measured answers, and understood features of physics. He changed the channel again. Soon enough, another preview found him and sprang across the screen, with bumping music. Again, the women, the suggestiveness. *Fire and Ice.*

At least it's only two this time, she said. Why do you watch that stuff? She was acting, a little, filling a role, casting him as the slavering brute; he didn't really watch it, did he?

Then he took the bait. I just can't help myself, when you're around, he said. Baby, you're so cold. He looked at her, grinning.

Yeah, well, where there's ice, there's fire, she said.

Let's watch a movie, he said, still grinning. Let's get you fired up.

Those are adult movies. Get it. For mature audiences. Viewer discretion is advised, she said.

He made a great, heavy moaning noise, launching himself facedown onto his bed, as if in mortal struggle with the slavering brute within. She started laughing, and threw her book at him, and he moaned again. Shut up, they're going to hear you, she said, retreating from orphanhood. You'll wake them up.

One more moan, shorter this time, cutting himself off, and he turned the TV back to the medical show. Stitches, and dire intonation from the voice-over, trying to make things even more dramatic. He got quiet, watching.

She said she was going to sleep. She turned over, and she could still hear it, the echo of his sound in the room, under the surgical commentary. *The patient will have to be very careful if he doesn't want to get an enormous infection.*

4
*Events continue:*

Their parents took them to see their aunt and uncle and cousins, which was part of the point of the trip, while the grandmother was visiting. It was okay there. They remembered the general layout of the flat-roofed house from when they were little, which they mentioned, trying for polite conversation. Their cousins were a little younger, both pale and quiet. They sat at the kitchen table and had tuna sandwiches, which she didn't eat because tuna kill dolphins, or tuna fishing does, at least. It was a conscience thing: one of her friends had started a campaign at school, and now she was a little scared to eat tuna. He ate quite a lot. The sandwiches cheered him up because he'd started working out recently, and had become a fan of tuna. He talked about protein intake for a while. He seemed to know quite a lot about it, suddenly. The cousins looked interested. They did look a little anaemic.

In the living room, the parents and the aunt and uncle talked on and on, smiling. The old, disconnected list of remember-that-time, punctuated by yeses. The grandmother sat with a teacup, smiling too, trembling a little, as if she were bursting to jump up from the slipcovered couch, maybe for a jog. But it was only age. Her wobbling head made it look as if she agreed with everything anyone said. The cousins giggled a little from the kitchen, but the grandmother turned and smiled deafly at them, then went back to her teacup surveillance.

The girl said, Poor Grandma. She's getting so old. One of the cousins looked abashed.

He said, though, Maybe she thinks we're quadruplets. And he put his arm around her waist.

You're so suggestive, she said, and one of the cousins said Ew, and then he kissed both the cousins on the cheek, and they laughed into their hands, and turned a little grey, which might have been blushing, for them. The grandmother was watching again, vibrating. He waved, and she waved back. Her fingers didn't open fully, so it was a catching motion.

⁂

They went to look at a river, which involved no tuna, but was supposed to have salmon. She didn't want to look, so she sat in the car. The parents gave her a look that said, *Teenagers*, but they were half-smiling under their rolling eyes; they liked to show they understood teenage ways, as if they had studied the textbook, passed the exam. From the car, she saw him helping the grandmother over the rocks, her high-shouldered upper body leaning towards him.

They were staying two more nights at the Sundowner. He put the TV on again when they were in their room, slumping onto the foot of her bed. You have your own right there, she said. But he wasn't listening. A semi-erotic scene was on the first channel that appeared via the satellite gods: not quite pay-per-view, something in smudgy focus and complicated period dress that took a lot of taking off.

Frankly, my dear, you can't complain about this one, he said, with a large, romantic sigh.

She sighed back at him, louder. Shut up.

He sighed again, half-moaning, fainting off the edge of the bed, making it bounce stiffly.

They're going to hear you, she said. And you'll be the one in trouble.

Maybe I want them to hear me, he said.

We're supposed to be in bed, she said, and then she realized it, what she'd said, and she started laughing so hard that she couldn't stop, and threw her pillow at him, where he lay on the floor, sighing.

※ ※ ※

It was funny. It began to be, in that bright way, edged with hysteria. They didn't want to go and see the wilted sights of their cousins' town, so the parents said they would pick them up later to go back to the relatives' place for dinner. The parents had that happy eye-roll going again, confirming that this was teenage behaviour, predictably awful. So he and she stayed at the motel, and wandered around the building, encased in its breeze-block comfort. He pretended to rush lustfully at a pop machine, and she bent in pain with the laughing, which hadn't stopped since last night. He actually licked the front of the machine, and someone came out of the door just across from there, looking for pop with quarters and hope. They took off back to the room, and laughed for about half an hour, and decided to go and inspect the motel's indoor pool, one of its proclaimed highlights, or probably hi-lites. She told him not to watch her while she got changed, and he rattled the bathroom doorknob, and she gave a little shriek, which echoed surprisingly.

The pool was a tank in a cellarlike cavern below the rooms, with a low ceiling and thin lighting. They went in, uneasy. Well, first, he threw her in. His arms strong, with small, hard muscles in them. Have you been working out? she said, sputtering, and he flexed, and dove in, too.

Then they hit the Jacuzzi. They said it: Let's hit the Jacuzzi. The ceiling dripping down on their heads. Spawnlike foam drifting in clusters. It's not very bubbly, darling, she said, in a bubbly voice.

We should put some shampoo in here, he said.

Do you want to? she said, laughing again, open. All seemed possible, hilariously, luxuriantly so. Like watching a comedy, and being in it, at the same time. Her heart beating loudly with the heat, the jets of the Jacuzzi motor. He closed his eyes, his head back in the moiling water. His chin a little dark, a little prickly. Since when did he need to shave? Thinking about it, she could still feel it on the edge of her arm, from when he'd tossed her into the pool. She splashed him.

Out of nowhere, the Grandmother appeared, making her slow, trembly way over the wet tiles, in a relic of a bathing suit and a swimming cap. Her blue-skinned legs, her dutiful, battle-weary look. Oh my God, maybe you should help her, she said to him. And he stood and reached out to help her down the Jacuzzi steps. The grandmother almost collapsed into the water, and they smiled at her, uneasy again.

They were all quiet. Then he sighed, and it sounded the same as it had last night, and she started smirking, and he did too. Then he put his arm around her, nonchalantly. They both smiled brightly at the grandmother. Her trembling made them want to laugh out loud, in their bright bubble, and he sighed, again, deeper, and squeezed her shoulder, and she had to pretend to have a coughing attack, to cover up the laughing. The grandmother put her head under the swirling water for a moment, and emerged with tarry eyelashes, weepy makeup, eyes open.

5

*I know what you are going to do.*

6

*Bad.*

7

*The other stories:*

Everyone knew the stories. The grandmother was the keeper. There were arguably five major ones, and spinoffs of these. Usually she was the reluctant hero of some kind, the reluctant speaker, forced to tell of her rightness or good deeds.

*The War.*

*The End of the War.*

*Marriage.*

*Early Life.*

*The Dog.*

*The War* is self-explanatory. The poverty, the bravery, the long slog, the getting on with things. *The End of The War* is not what it might seem. There was victory, yes, but more poverty and hardship. The family did receive a box of new clothes from a charity, though the shoes on offer did not fit her. She didn't say further, but the implication was that she continued to do without. An image would hover of the young her, in clownish, newspaper-stuffed boots, or barefoot.

Marriage — not an intimate portrait, although there were generally a few hints. The husband, who is dead now, had an idle, apparently oafish streak. She cooked and cleaned for him daily, and didn't stop him from napping or spending on clothes for himself when all the children needed coats. She did the best she could: a refrain, with a snappy little nod. Normally people who say this have done something wrong. Early Life was an extended variation of this, back in time: sharing the bed with sisters, the only one who would help much around the house. Didn't they help? Oh, no, no. Doing the jam and the canning. Boiling and sterilizing, cutting up fruit. Cherries were a relief because you don't bother stoning those when you can them. If people want to eat cherries, they can deal with the stones themselves. This is the usual end to that story.

*The Dog.* The unusual one. The story tied in to the others, at least partly; it was set during the war, when she was young. The dog's name was Lolly. Oh, what a dog. She didn't know what breed: oh, probably a mongrel. What was so good about that dog? What, she couldn't say. But her eyes would almost swim with tears. Lolly.

So: the opening reluctance. But she would tell easily enough, and in the same phrasings, after a prompting, or a lull in conversation.

We probably became one of her stories after what happened.

## 8
### *More about her:*

She remembered all the dates of family deaths and funerals. She got annoyed at birthdays when they were at inconvenient times, such as too close to Christmas, or at the beginning of the month, so when you turn over the calendar you've already missed it. Mine is on January first. She did send gifts. When she visited that time, she brought socks for us to share. Large white tubular socks, clearly masculine. Maybe she knew something already, about me.

What do I know? What do I know about her? Her hair used to be brown. She walked very fast, and played tennis.

The lip. The thrombosed blue lump in it, just off-centre. When I was little, I thought it was something like a jewel, a bluish, dull pearl, ornamenting her lower face. Something she must have had done on purpose, like the ladies in India with their red-dotted foreheads. And the soft, tissue-paper skin on her upper arms, hanging in empty purses under them. I felt it between my fingers, and said it was nice — nice. And she laughed, I remember.

There was a dog, a large enthusiastic one. She would lavish attention on it while it ate, talking to it in a low-pitched doggy voice, but we weren't allowed to talk to it then, in case it turned on us. But then if the eating went on too long, or the dog started barking in response, she would snap off the voice and turn away coolly, someone else. That dog wasn't Lolly, was it?

I used to call her Grammar. Maybe that was prophetic. Labels, order, rules. And unfathomable twists in rules. *Because I said so, that's why. Because that's the rule.*

I never asked about the lip; I knew that was rude, and when I asked my mother privately, she didn't know what had happened. It was just there.

I liked her, of course. Seeing her when she visited later on, after we moved away from my childhood house, induced a kind of nostalgia, but for what? Maybe for the stereotypical cookie-baking grandma, which she wasn't. Like seeing something in the pitch black along the highway in the middle of the night. Something not really there, but which seems real and physical for that split second.

9

*How it happens:*

Here is how we became the story. Those notes, of course, are at the heart of it.

❧ ❧ ❧

Back to the trip. It wasn't just the Jacuzzi, or the TV, or the noises they'd made in the room at night. The trip had continued. The parents had wanted to do something of teenage benefit on the long drive back home from the cousins'. They'd left the Sundowner and its Down Home Hospitality, and he and she sat in the back of the car with the mum, while the dad drove and the grandmother was in the front passenger seat. They'd been stifling their laughing again, especially after he suddenly did one of his sighing moans; the dad had asked expectantly if he was bored.

Miniature Land: their stop. It was in the middle of nowhere, off a side road, a fortress-like concrete building, perhaps a former warehouse, or prison. No other cars in the parking lot. But they entered, and the parents paid the admission for everyone, and the man behind the desk looked as if he couldn't believe his luck. It was very dark inside, with a carpety smell. The offerings began with a display of miniature fruits and vegetables in a chiller cabinet, with hand-lettered tags. *Smallest ear of corn known.* Next to it was a small glass case of dusty stuffed animals, which appeared once to have been alive. *Chihuahua. Smallest breed of dog known.* The *known* had a cunning anticipation, as if more miniature things still were out there, only waiting to be discovered.

And there were. They carried on into the building, and more miniatures. Model trains that would veer around their tracks, through shiny depopulated towns and mountain passes, if you pressed a button on the case. A scene of war, with hordes of miniature army-green plastic men in identical squatting positions, as if war were akin to an aerobics class. Then a large sign led them into Fairy Tale Alley. It was still very dark there. Forest creatures made of cement loomed miniaturely. A cement Snow White, with seven appropriate dwarves, which had looks of relief on their faces, as if they were finally, finally at home. She liked them; they reminded her of being little. Happy endings.

He thought it was pointless, and was obvious about it, which made the dad nod and smile: *I knew it.* The grandmother wandered around, looking at everything closely, shaking a little. He watched her for a while, and said, Grandma's scared.

Yeah, well. Shut up, she said. Look at Hansel and Gretel. The candy house had a gloss, an appeal, even though the concrete figurines looked as if they'd had a bad reaction to it, holding their stomachs and squinting. The witch was peering out of the window at those two.

He poked her, and said, Guess who?

Don't be so mean, she said.

She's watching. And you knew exactly who I meant, anyway, he said. So who's mean?

Those poor children. She wants to eat them, she said.

Mmm, he said. He took her finger and pretended to bite the end of it. She laughed, trying to keep it silent, pulling her hand away. Then he pressed up against her and put his hand flat and low on her back. It's okay. I'll take care of you, he said, into her ear, suggestively.

The buzzy hilarity rising. She was laughing out loud now, and started trying to say, viewer discretion. But the grandmother was standing just behind them, trembling, and they got quiet. The strange feeling in her fingertip, as if his teeth were still about to touch it.

There were other things in Miniature Land, but who can say now what they were? They drove home, and it was late when they arrived, so they went to bed. Her room was quiet, TV-free. Her body seemed to be waiting for something to happen. Eventually, she got to sleep. In the morning, there were two notes pushed under her bedroom door. The first one said, *I know what you are going to do.* And the second one said, *Bad.*

## 10
### *The ending:*

Did she add it to the repertoire? Did she go on to tell that story about us, about what she knew, about our badness? She never told it to us. But it burst that bubble, that laugh riot we'd enclosed ourselves in, forsaking all others, laughing at everything non-us. Those notes. I was so disconcerted, I nearly passed out. At first, the sibling's automatic lament: *he started it.* But then it changed. She'd seen right through me, she saw something in me. She knew what I was going to do. I didn't.

She never said anything. She was still smiling, trembly, closer than ever before to cookie-baking, cookie-cutter sweetness for the rest of that visit. I stared at those notes over and over until my eyes burned. The tremble in the handwriting. But it wasn't from sorrow. It was just matter-of-fact, just a recording of what was happening, like a boring diary. The *Bad* seemed an afterthought. It must have been written second; I can see her writing it. The dutiful hero of the story taking on her role again, as if training a dog. I was no Lolly. Was she right? I began to see myself luridly, full of lurid potential, sliding down an incestuous slope into the pit.

And her: I thought I'd got her well enough. I knew all the stories. I could practically tell them myself: the war, the cherries. I never thought about her. She loves me; she's my grandmother, for God's sake. That complacency. That love I assumed wasn't false, just gone. There, then gone, as if someone is alive, then dead, or passing under lights, then back into the shade.

And they see, too, those quiet spectator types we pass. The narrators. *I know what you are going to do.*

11

*Then what:*

I wanted to transform the ending, to show her. I kept to myself, and started to see him, my brother, entirely differently, as someone foreign. I had a hazy memory of how I hated him when he was born, which I resurrected. I also remembered how I used to have dreams about the baby-him falling through the ice on the pond in the winter, which weren't bad dreams. But then, as we grew up, we were very close, until that trip. It was different afterwards. I can feel the hair rising on my head when I think about it. I did it, too. That flash of transformative vision. How easily we can make things change.

# THE OLD FAMILIAR

*Farm.*
*Front room and I am inside to the left of the door. Anaglypta.*
*A ceiling fan overhead. Large.*

WELL, IT WAS HIS HANDWRITING. Frank was reading over the page, which was a small scrap, in rumply script. He had written this. Yes he had. He thought of it now, what had been going on when he'd written it. He'd been thinking about things, seeing them, very hard-edged, photographic. What it was, was the house. Home. It's mine, he had thought. The memory popped, bright and clear, pleasing him. The web that had been knotted up in his guts loosening. Yes, that is what it had been, home. When he closed his eyes, he could see himself as an atom pinging off the universe's hard insides, then landing right there in the old place. The living room, when he was a boy, with all its old hard furniture and its rag rug, smoothed wood floor. Raised, patterned wallpaper, as if for the blind. Its thick smell. *Anaglypta.* The word had come happily to him, like a good dog. Beautiful. They had saved up for that paper. They'd sold off some of the land, but kept the house. He was still oscillating slightly, from the impact of finding it again. There, he could see, and was safe. 1471 Bankhead Avenue. Easy. His eyes weren't so bad yet, though they'd been floundering for a few years. The air was cool on his eyeballs. Even when he did close them, he could feel the room's height. The cathedral amplitude. The wallpaper rising. *The house where I was born.*

He remembered this, now, but there, he didn't have to remember anything. Anything he wanted to, he could think, or not think, and that was a relief. He could take a good look around. The rooms were big, bigger, like wrapped-up gifts, but he was already inside, and knew what was coming. Being inside the wrapping. Being the gift itself.

He sat, now, and read over his scrap again. He had written slowly. His knee hurt him there at the kitchen table. The same old pain, but out of place with what he'd been thinking. He could identify it, this pain. It went with the kitchen, the new place, the plastic finish on the table. When he had been thinking, earlier, though, his knee and hip hadn't been annoying him. He was different. But it wasn't as if he'd been young again, dreaming of that. Who would want to be? He'd felt better than that. The biggest, oldest thing in the world.

*A ceiling fan overhead. Large.*

This was vague, for a moment. Carefully written, though. Important. Was this in the old house? Yes, later. For the summers. Hotter, when he was young. He always said so. His mother had wanted the fan. Its slow, glossy swoop balanced on the air. The blades like wings over water, making shadows beneath. Swoop, swoop. The perfect rhythm. It dragged just behind a good waltz tempo. Counting, one two three.

The heaviness of the one, the first swoop. He thought of it. Prickling tears at the thought that it was there to keep time for him. This is what it must mean. Everything had slowed down, and this was a way to understand it. The fan was slow, but imperturbable. And he was getting sentimental.

He'd never been one for symbols and visions and all that jumbo, but they kept coming. This is why he had started writing things down, to think about, or laugh about, later. Sometimes they turned out to mean things, or relate to other things, if he thought long enough. A good thing about now was that he could watch the workings of his brain as if from a little way outside, as if it were his own pet. Sitting there, he found another scrap of paper in his pocket. The paper said, *Gwen. Standing up.*

This was separate. Yes, he had also seen a picture, or something like a picture, or like a painting, when he'd been thinking. It showed his wife. Gwen, years ago. In her early forties or so. She was in a pose. Whose was it? That woman's, Marilyn Monroe's. That name was easy, too. Standing over an air vent, with her dress parachuting into the air around her. Her mouth open, her hair excited, her hands pressed to her thighs. Looking somewhere off to the side, not at him. He noticed the heels, so high that they knocked her ankles inwards. Gwen had thickish ankles. He loved them. They had always made him think of her Russian peasant ancestors, slogging across fields in boots, passing on the thick ankle genes she would need. Gwen. What was she saying, in the picture, with her open lips? Was she talking to him? He felt the leap of desire low in his chest. Was she wearing a garter belt under there, like they used to? Like they should. He would have asked her. He liked to shock her, in that way, about bed, and relations. He remembered her expression in the picture, and wondered if she'd only been pretending to be shocked, all their married life. She looked as if she knew everything about everything. Old lust thickened in his veins, thick soup. So he wasn't changing, really, even in these visions and little hiero-glyphic notes. There was some kind of certainty to things. He had drawn a little stick figure of her in the pose, to remind himself.

But the fan, in that room, in his mind, like spinning wings. It was the old place, the real home. He could see the walls of the old place, practically right through the good anaglypta, to their cavities and insulation. There had been another picture there, on one of the walls. Pencil strokes. A sketch. It was a rainbow, or something like it, in black and white. He looked from the darker bands to the lighter ones at the bottom, the fall into white.

*❧ ❧ ❧*

When the doctor had first said the word to him, Alzheimer's, Frank had thought, Aha. As if he had caught it. *Ahalzheimer's* was how he said it to himself, as a reminder. Sometimes he said it this way to friends, a joke. But they only saw it as a symptom, and smiled, and shrugged, because that's the way things go. It had been creeping along for some years, and now was beginning to make lace of his brain's surface, needling holes into it. Early stages, still. Gwen didn't like it, either, his joking. She had seen it all coming. He had been writing notes to himself for a long time, practical ones, so he wouldn't slip and forget to do things. Once or twice, or more, he had found himself somewhere out of the house, or in a store, with no idea how he got there, or how to go home. No notes then. Home was always an imperative, in that first panicky state. Gwen said he had walked away from buying something at a store counter, announcing he was going home. This is when she had taken him to the doctor. The doctor also talked about fugue states, which was another joke. Fogue states, more like. Frank would say this. Fogue states for a fogey. He would laugh, and sometimes Gwennie would too. For a long time after that first diagnosis, nothing much had been wrong if he stayed around the place. Just little things. He'd be listening to records and find that he couldn't sing along in the middle of a line. The tune would pass straight out of him. He lost the singing he'd always been half-proud of. Oh well, that wasn't so bad. He didn't mind forgetting where things like the keys had been put. It didn't bother him. He still felt at home in the house, in his skull. He still knew the moles on his forearm. *Those are mine.*

Now, it was progressing. He was given to writing these more fanciful notes, which sometimes rang bells later, but not always. Gwen was better. She left him notes everywhere, sensible ones, asking him to do things if she went out, or reminding him where things were. They were becoming little encyclopedias. Funny. He had one in front of him on the table: *Franklin. Water the flowerbeds. The roses (pink flowers at the back of the house along the fence) need lots. Don't give the marigolds (orange and yellow little ones in pots on patio) too much. Just one watering can (the small green one on the patio). Put the sprinkler on the back grass. The tap is near the back door. Leave it two hours. I put your alarm clock on the kitchen counter beside the sink.*

She never signed the notes, or wrote *Don't Forget* across the top, which she used to do, at first. Frank liked them. They made him feel like a visitor, a house-sitter. Nice, thinking of yourself as a guest, sometimes. He'd always liked gardening, he knew that. Gwen did too, pruning rosebushes and such. She wore flowery gardening gloves. He loved the gloves, and all of her. A few times he'd asked her to wear them to bed. The smell of the soil was on them. This made him feel as if they were in a field together, outside.

Outside used to be better. But he did like their house, too, living inside it. Familiar, but newish to him almost every morning, now. He enjoyed walking around it, seeing what stood out. The TV always the same, and the paisley biology of the couch and armchairs. The kitchen complex but friendly. Cans and jars. *Pickled Beets. Homestyle Chicken Cacciatore. Ready to Serve.* He liked to read. He still knew where most of the dishes and utensils went when he washed up. In the basement, a few times, when he found himself down there, his brain went to static. Tools and paint, yes, fine. But an old tin sign saying *Molson* baffled him. It had a Fahrenheit thermometer in it. He had no idea where it had come from, although it had the same dust on it as everything else. But it jammed the machinery, stopped the pattern. He didn't know whether the temperature was right, either. He left it where it was, and found the stairs up. He didn't ask Gwen about it. He didn't think about it anymore.

They had lived in the same house since they'd gotten married. It had just been built then, a new postwar street. A small front porch, and big windows split into quadrants looking out onto the road. Not too far from town, from where he got a job in the office at the fruit cannery. Enough to feel you were out of the way. The roof and trim were dark green, still were, which gave the place a cottagey look. He had made a wooden sign for beside the door, with *The Bledsoes* scorched into it, identifying them. Had they ever rearranged the furniture since they'd moved in? Maybe not. Just adding a few things. Two bedrooms, one bathroom. Their double bed spread its hips wide across their room. He'd banged into it, this morning, or yesterday, and had been very surprised. He'd never done that before. He knew the furniture, the floors, the walls. Could things have moved? Aha. Aha.

*❧ ❧ ❧*

The tub was still the same. His usual fit. He was in the bath now. Because it was darkening outside, and he had been out there, in the garden, long enough, so it was all right. Yes.

He had told Gwen that he was going up for a tub, which is what he always did. She was watching something on a video. The TV looked at him with its amiable eye, full of people. Gwen said, Do you want some help? Her voice had a tiny, wary catch. Not wanting him to want help.

But Frank didn't want it anyway, the help, or the question. I think I can still manage the old carcass, he said loudly, over the sound.

Well, all right, Gwen said. She wasn't looking at him. The people on the screen were singing, holding out their arms as if to catch bundles. All their heads tilted to one side, synchronized. You had to wonder how they got it just right like that.

Frank had gone on upstairs, counting the steps. His knee creaked. The number should match with the stair sounds. He heard the rhythm. The stairs, his joints. He got them all. He passed. He liked these little tests, when they went right. He was still himself, just about. He looked forward to feeling the cold wings of the bath curled around his shoulders. With the door closed, he turned on the hot tap and got undressed. Slippers, then shirt, then pants, then socks, then underwear. He sat on the edge of the toilet seat and waited for the bath to fill. You know, the bathroom wallpaper was pretty. He noticed it. Shells and waves. Then he wished he hadn't. It wasn't new, was it? He picked up a bottle from the countertop, and read its label. Labels were full of interest now. *A luxurious foam bath to take you away from your daily cares.* Woodfern, it said. Was it right? Well, the bottle said it was for the bath. He read it again. Sure. He drizzled in some of the greenish blue. The smell. Someone's idea of a chemical forest. All dirt removed. Not like the garden, he knew. Smell was still working. The foam rose, and he added some cold water.

*I know how. I know how.* His foot touched the bubbles. Then the heat of the water covered his foot and leg, and he folded himself in. He lay back and closed his eyes, grinding the base of his skull over the bath edge. Then comfortable. The water covering him, the little crisp sounds of the foam. Its scent sharp. This he was used to, but not here. It was from somewhere else. Well, it was Gwen's smell, wasn't it? Sure. She smelled like it sometimes. Her nightie did. He sighed. The heat began to nurse his hip and knee, and he noticed his body relaxing itself automatically. He sighed again, loudly. What he always did in the tub was sing, but he couldn't think of anything to sing. No music or lyrics would come into his head. None at all. All he could hear was the sound of his feet going up the stairs, playing over and over. The stairs' particular creakings. Probably he'd only be bothering Gwennie anyway, with her TV. That's what she was doing. Enough singing.

There must always be something to think about. What was he trying to think of? A book. The name of a book. What was the last book he had read, if he had ever read? He felt his mind quivering, trying. Then he noticed it. The bubbles had stopped. No brittle popping noises. There was no sound at all. Was it all right? Was he deaf?

What were things supposed to sound like? He splashed a little with one hand. No water noise. Well, he could see fine.

Things where they should be. Towels, thin white soap, shower head, a bottle with something written on it, *Woodfern*, its aimless cap beside it. He had slipped under water. Drowned. But no. There was the water's plain, his body beneath it. Knees camping above, head above.

A weight on him, though. Not heavy, but there. The foam was not light. It was as if a body were lying just above his own, as if the foam were a mattress for it. He beneath. He felt the shifting of legs, the light push of an elbow, as the body turned. It was asleep, and he was still under it. It rubbed its head back and forth twice. His face was the pillow. The weight breathed in, a sleeping pattern. Deep inside his ears he heard it. He thought he did, though his ears seemed switched off. It was hearing, yes. A kind of voice. This was how he recognized it, after a moment. It was high and soft, maybe female. It said something. It sounded kind, remote. He felt pity, and wanted to speak back. He could, although he remembered to feel foolish, outside himself. Funny, how shame stays. The wish to look right.

Then it all stopped, the breath and the sound. He coughed. And he did hear the cough. It echoed in the bathroom, and the weight evaporated from him. The bubbles dissolving now, a few sad pods left floating. He called, Gwennie. The name was automatic. But it wasn't her. From downstairs, the sound of a movie burst in. Gwennie was watching it. He was a silly old coot. You can hear everything in this house, he thought. The walls are built so thin.

❧ ❧ ❧

He was alone, but it was only for a while. It was all right. It was later, days or weeks. He hadn't written notes about the bath, and it had left him. He was thinking of Gwen, and where she had gone. He thought it over and over. To get a few things. Back soon.

He did still like being in the house on his own. He was outside, but not far, just on the patio, in a plastic deckchair. He looked at the yard. The day was pretty warm. June, July, September. There were Gwen's flowers in the beds around the grass, and in pots. Crocus. Roses. Daisies. Dalmatians. Roses. No. He had many names, but what were they? The flowers looked almost beaten, but not quite. Had he watered them that morning, or yesterday? What was he supposed to be doing? His mind flapped softly. Thought flattening out into a nice hum. If he hadn't been able to see his dirty outdoor shoes on the ends of his legs, he might not have known he was there, himself. He felt suspended between layers. Long-legged, between two glass slides, preserved and looked at. He dreamed vaguely of glory.

The house was right there behind him, he knew that. He tried walking himself through the rooms, for practice, in his head. Hallway. Stairs. TV. Living room. There, it felt higher, better. Ah. The light thin and clear. The books he saw were bound in grayish blonde. He moved like a sidewinder. Natural. The top shelf had two books. He was closer to the bottom, which was nearly level with the floor. This was it. His favourites. He saw the bottom shelf, crouching down. He puffed a thin skin of dust from the tops of the books there. Little clouds, skittering away on journeys. The fan stirring the air. He touched the books, and pulled one out, although it almost didn't come. He had to wriggle it. He was lying on the wooden floor. The walls looked very high, with their papery topography. The cat came and rubbed against his face, and someone was saying something to him from out in the kitchen, but he knew what the book was. *World Book. XYZ.* A slimmer one, the last one. It was his, in his house. He was small in it. The right house, where he should have been all along.

❦ ❦ ❦

Gwen here, with bags. It was her voice talking. The patio, outside. He was there, on the patio. He hadn't been asleep, he said. She was there, with bags. He looked for a note, but he didn't have anything in his pockets. The odd feeling of being reminded, as if he'd come out of a movie theatre and it was still day outside. Oh, yes.

Gwen looked downy at her edges. She said, How are you doing? Her voice clucking, indulgent.

Frank sat up. His mind milled. He said, Well. What's in the bags? Shopping, eh?

Gwen said, Oh, just a few things.

Frank said, Shopping. You girls. You'd ruin us poor fellows with your ways. Now he felt awake. He was quick, getting it right.

She said, Oh, you. She laughed, happy, and said, It's so nice out. It's supposed to be hot again this afternoon. The poor roses, she said. Did you water them?

Water, he said. Well, sure, he said. He had a little list of appropriate phrases for when he wasn't quite certain. *Well, sure* was one of them. *Well, you don't say. Is that right. Sure, sure.* He hadn't written these down yet.

She looked in his direction, but slightly to the left of his face. He felt her tightening. Well. Would you like some coffee? she said.

Water, he said. Then he said, Coffee. Sure. He closed his eyes. Something still floated. We should get a fan, he said.

He went inside. Coffee. Coffee. And cake. Was there cake? Yes, he knew where it was, down the hall, in the kitchen.

Its usual tin, with the cake cocooned in waxy paper. A little present, every time. Gwen was already in the kitchen, with shopping bags, putting things away. He turned and passed her. He was going upstairs, because. Because he wanted his slippers. His feet in their socks knew the way. The safe carpet runner. He was at the bottom step. Gwen called, Where are you going?

Coffee. Coffee. He stopped. He said, Well, a fan would cool things down in here.

There was a gap. Gwen said, What would?

Frank was still at the bottom of the stairs. He laughed, and said, A fan, of course.

She said, Oh. You said something else. He was on his way up. One, two. Then he heard her say, What are you talking about, Franklin?

Still, he kept moving up the stairs. He was at the top, on the landing. It was warmer. Safe. He had lived here a pretty long time, now, he knew that. His feet had probably worn a quarter-inch off the stairs over the years. When he was a boy, their old house, the house, had steep steps rising. He'd fallen a few times. The crack of wood on his tailbone. That hurts, you know. But that was another house. He was home here, now. In the bedroom, he opened the closet door. What was he looking for. A precarious enjoyment, still, of seeing what would make him slip. Give him the slip. Slippers and shoes did it often. He had to laugh at that. Where were the slippers now? He was in his socks. The bones in his feet were forgetful, or wanted freedom. He had gone up a shoe size in the last year. At this age. There was a new shoebox in the closet, the higher number stamped on it. Not his size. At this age.

Someone had just left the room. Or come in. He turned, and looked at the bed. The bed was breathing. The flowery cover was moving up and down shallowly, gently. Sad little sounds. It even coughed once. Frank's feet were cold. It, on the bed, was not right. Sick. He watched the bed breathing as the sun moved on from the window. The bed breathed. Its springs propelling its lungs. It kept going. Then he knew.

It had been there a while, he saw now. He could see outlines sharply. Colour and depth. It was a figure, an old bent person, gasping. Thousands of wings beat just under Frank's skin. He looked. The figure, the person, was trying to sit up, and coughing with effort. Finally it stopped. It raised its head, with terrible slowness. Effort. A woman. Her profile, her head turned and dropping. Well, she wasn't so old. She was quite young. She kept at her work, pushing herself up. Gwen, he thought. She had a little of Gwen's look, or not. One of his sisters, maybe, or his mother. When they were young. She was someone he knew. He knew that much. Her dress was open, a little. She stopped. She wasn't coughing, and began to look a bit healthier, more herself. But her eyes seemed to be sewing themselves shut. She was smiling at him. Still unwell, though she looked all right. She seemed uncertain of why she was there. She shrugged, without her eyes, and lay back again, and he knew what she was. She was someone he knew, from the past. He did know this. Yes, it was his mother, as a younger woman, when he was quite small, maybe. She was only ever healthy and strong. Such a worker. That's how he always saw her. Fast, scrubbing, ironing hands. Strong big legs. But she had been very sick, suddenly, before she died, an old woman, at home. He hadn't seen her much then, after he and Gwen had moved out of town, to be closer to her folks. He didn't remember her sick. Though the seed of it had been there all along. The future.

He was there, interested, watching the bed to see what would happen. The Alzheimer's meant that he was no longer surprised about things, not entirely surprised, not really. Or afraid. Just a little sentimental, again. What would come? His eyes slipped off the bed, down to his feet. Socks. Slippers. Then, when he looked up, the bedclothes were smooth. Gwen always made it her way, so perfect. Gwen's bed. The room quiet, with pictures on the walls, and a smell of Gwen. He had seen what happens. He had his paper in his pocket, so he wrote something down, squeezing it from him.

He went back down the stairs, holding the wooden banister hard. The familiar, smooth path leading him. A vase sitting on the table on the landing quivered. He knew its rattle, he knew his own weight, for now. At the bottom, he took a breath and fixed a little smile. Shoulders set. He slid on his socks down the hall to the kitchen. Gwen, Gwennie was there. He said her name. It took a moment, a very brief moment, to find it. The smell circled him. It was coffee. Her back was to him, a little stooped. She was slicing a cake, but she heard him. She didn't look. She said, Do you want some cake? Now, she added.

Oh. Cake. I always do, he said. Sure.

She put a yellow slice on a rose-speckled plate. They'd had those for years. Those were my mother's, he said. He remembered them, in this house, and in the other house. They had been in a dresser there, in the dining room, lined up, showing off. Their age. He was happy, seeing the one on the counter, still there.

Yes, Gwen said. Now go on and sit at the table.

He looked at it. Waiting. His heart skittered for the right moment. Gwen poured. The dark liquid arc. Coffee. He stared. Gwennie, he said.

She said, Here. Don't forget your cake, now.

Gwen, he tried. She half-turned towards him. Her eyes on the sugar bowl. Lovey, is what he decided to say. Lovey, he said. Do you have any cigarettes?

She stared at him. What was it? It was wrong. She didn't smoke. He hadn't smoked for months, or weeks, or years, since the doctor had told him to stop. No, he said. I know. I mean. I mean, he said. Nothing plausible came. He said, I just want a smoke. One won't hurt. He tried to look pathetic.

Now Gwen looked at him. He felt her sharpness. Could you get me some? Please, he said. I. I can't remember the way to the store. This was not true, not exactly, not entirely, but he knew it would win.

She stopped seeing him then. Why didn't you tell me before I went out? she said. Her lips shrank.

Ah, come on, please, he said. I just feel like a smoke with my coffee. Come on, what do you say, he said. Old times' sake, he said. He tried to look like a harmless old man. Capricious. He even shuffled his feet, a little, in their socks.

Gwen said, The doctor told you. Then she stopped, and picked up her purse from the countertop. All right, she said, brightly. If that's what you want. She brushed past him. I'll be back in fifteen minutes. Do you need me to write that down?

No, no, he said. I'm not going anywhere.

All right, she said. The door bumped shut. The turn of the lock. Again, he couldn't think of her right name, for a moment.

Gwen. Gwen. For a few minutes, he sat, reciting internally. Cigarette sticks danced in his head, for a second or two, then left him. What was it he had to do? He had his little piece of paper. It said, *Upstairs*.

He went up the steps to the landing. Which room? He turned left, which went into the bathroom. Yes, this must be right. He knew what to do in here. Purpose. There were ways back, and forward. He turned on the water. This is what he did there. He knew. Clothes off, in order. He bounced up and down on his toes, bare now, as he waited for it.

When it was full enough, he splashed in. Not enough cold. His skin twitched. He ignored it, and began to relax. He closed his eyes. Could he feel anything on him, or near him? A soft, sleeping blanket of weight. No. It was gone, the thought of that, of what had been in the bath. He could hear the tick of the pipes, the shiftings of the house. Just the house talking. But not right. In the old house, the right house, they'd had a tin bath for years, before the bathroom was put in. The sloping metal sides of it, in front of the kitchen stove. His head peering out of the top. Singing about birds, and girls, and their hair. Somebody else's water, always.

Now, he breathed deeply, and could hear his breaths. He focused. The trick, the joke of it all. The backwards motion. The not knowing, but knowing that you don't know, and will know less.

A bottle of bubble bath on the tub's edge. He picked it up. Its chemical smell. He took a sip, experimentally. Thick. Tasting of forest. It burned and soaped its way down his throat. Then he tried a sip more, tipping back his head, feeling the strength of porcelain behind it. He raised his knees, sliding into the water. He put the bottle on the bath's edge. Now. Now what? He opened his mouth, and made a singing sound, with no real language. Waiting for something. Not knowing it, exactly, but what he wanted was that weight, again, the breath and roll, to show him the way he could go, while he still might know to follow.

## ACKNOWLEDGEMENTS

I'm grateful for the support of the Faculty of Arts at Okanagan College and the Banff Centre for the Arts. I'm also thankful for the collegiality and friendship of the Department of English at Okanagan College, a strong group of thinkers and writers who make working life a pleasure. Craig McLuckie, Department Chair, has been unstintingly helpful, as has my colleague and friend Mary Ellen Holland. John Lent is an assiduous and insightful editor with whom I've been honoured to work. My family is also an inspiring support. I'm especially grateful to my husband, Mike Hawley, my parents, Peter and Jocelyn Bunyan, and my siblings, Carolyn, Laura, and Jon Bunyan, for their willingness to read and comment on drafts, and to my late grandfather, Arthur Burtch, for the title.

Author photograph by Mike Hawley

ALIX HAWLEY studied English Literature and Creative Writing at Oxford University, the University of East Anglia, and the University of British Columbia. She is especially interested in nineteenth-century writing and children's literature. She is a fourth-generation resident of Kelowna, British Columbia, where she lives with her husband, Mike, and teaches at Okanagan College. *The Old Familiar* is her first collection.